Strange Stars and Stranger Songs

Christina Dickinson

Published by Christina Dickinson, 2020.

This is a work of fiction. Similarities to real people, places, or events are entirely coincidental.

STRANGE STARS AND STRANGER SONGS

First edition. September 19, 2020.

Copyright © 2020 Christina Dickinson.

ISBN: 978-1952009044

Written by Christina Dickinson.

To NSP, TWRP, Tenacious D, Weird Al, and any other
artist that ever made me smile.

To Terence, for being the best weirdo I could've ever chosen
to spend my life with.

Prologue

MEL ABRAMS SANK INTO the green room couch. His costume helmet, normally light enough that he forgot he was wearing it, felt like it was slowly crushing his head. Fumbling with the padded chin strap, Mel removed the protective shielding between his privacy and his fame.

On stage, he was Lancel♡t, with the "o" shaped like a heart. With Frimmydukes and Lady Bug, they formed the Magical Space Skeleton Army. The lore of the band pointed out that they were not an army, and they were obviously not skeletons, but in order to strike fear into the many orifices of the Dread Pirate Planet Jenkins, the marketing department of their homeworld had exaggerated a bit. It also stated that they had forgotten where they were from, so until they remembered and could head back home, they figured they would play music while they were on this strange planet that was awkwardly full of water.

In reality, Mel had been friends with Betham and Jessie Dallas since high school, where they had tried their luck with an Oingo Boingo cover band and not been overly successful. They had learned the instruments, they sounded alright, but the stars had never aligned back then. Maybe it was that they had been in a small town, in the middle of Illinois, or maybe it was that they were high school students and their talent needed to age a bit. They had all moved to different states for college (though Mel had only gone as far as Indiana), only remaining in touch via social media. Mel had dropped out of college after two semesters of floundering grades and lack of interest. He'd never been the best student, and it just didn't seem worth it to rack up the student loans with no clear vision of where he'd end up. Rather than go home, he got a job in the Cheesecake Haven in Indianapolis and acquired a roommate. He thought that life was going to be pretty uneventful, outside of maybe going to Gygax Con every year, until the day that Betham had shown up on his doorstep, Jessie in tow, and announced that they were going to try again.

This time, the stars were right. That was where Mel had gotten the confidence to ask out the pretty blonde girl with the shy smile when she came in for a slice of plain cheesecake for the third time in a week. That was why he was sitting in a green room with a heart that felt like a windshield in a hailstorm.

He should have been basking in the afterglow of one of the best concerts of his career, but even with the screams of fans still reverberating through his bones, the only thing he could think about was the empty apartment that would be waiting when he got back home. Stephanie was moving out, even as he sang the song that he wrote for her to a sold-out house. She wasn't going to be won over by the fact that her song was the most requested, especially since she hadn't much cared for the song's subject matter from the offset. In retrospect, Mel had to admit that "Then She Puked On Me" didn't exactly spell romance.

"Great job tonight, man," Betham Dallas pulled off his own mask, which was just a luchador souvenir from a trip to Mexico some years before. It was going to need to be replaced soon, as the fabric was beginning to fray. Normally, Betham wore a hat as well, but it had been thrown out into the crowd during the high point of a keytar solo.

Jessie Dallas, Betham's sister, sat down next to Mel and offered him a water bottle. "Show some sympathy, ass. He's obviously not thinking about the show," she snapped at Betham. Her costume's headpiece was more involved than either of her bandmates' face coverings, so Mel found himself looking into her bug-eye faceted goggles as she turned to face him, "Did you try calling her?"

"Between sets. She's blocked my number," Mel said.

"Holy shit, dude," Betham perched on his stool. It traveled with them, like a piece of stage equipment. Betham had been sitting on it when he decided that they were going to form a novelty band, and Betham being Betham had attributed their success to the stool.

"Yeah," Mel sighed. "I didn't realize that it was that bad, but I guess it was."

"What was?" Jessie asked. "You said that you didn't do anything."

Moments of his relationship with Stephanie flashed through his head: their initial meeting when he had still been working as a waiter; followed by their awkward first date where he had taken her to the Bodies exhibit, unaware that she was squeamish at the sight of medical journals, let alone horror movies; and then the three years of shared habitation.

During their first year together, as unlikely as it had seemed, Betham's idea had gained traction on the internet, and the Magical Space Skeleton Army grew a devoted fan base. Stephanie had been supportive at the beginning, when Mel had realized that between the band's music video views, funding site patrons, and album sales, he had reached a point where he could devote himself to his music full time. He left his job at Cheesecake Haven and took Stephanie out to celebrate.

Somewhere in the second year, things seemed to change. The Magical Space Skeleton Army had its first live concert, and Mel had assumed that Stephanie would come to the show. Betham and Jessie had helped him arrange things so that it was on even on Stephanie's day off, even though Monday wasn't usually the best night for a concert. Stephanie had smiled when he asked about it, but then, on the night of the show, she said she didn't feel up to going. Mel had left, somewhat disappointed. He returned with a take-away container of soup and a stuffed bear. When plans were starting to form around the second concert, Stephanie didn't smile as much.

By the third year, it was clear that Stephanie and the Magical Space Skeleton Army were not compatible. She refused to come to concerts, calling his music and his fans juvenile and worse. She claimed that Mel didn't spend enough time with her anymore, and she wasn't even sure he really knew who she was. Worse, she accused him of cheating on her during their first tour. It didn't seem to matter that he hadn't, because no matter how he tried to reassure her, it only cemented her belief.

"Maybe I just wasn't there enough," Mel said. "Maybe she was right, and I didn't really know who she was. I thought I did, but I definitely didn't see this coming."

"I'm sorry, dude," Betham popped up off the stool and started pacing. "I gotta say, though, maybe it's better that you can't talk to her right now."

"But... I loved her!" Mel protested. "Doesn't that mean something?"

"Did you mean to use the past tense?" Jessie asked, her voice pitched low. It was a soothing, reasonable tone. It was a tone that she didn't use very often unless she really wanted the person to listen.

Mel wanted to deny it, but as much as he was hurting, there was that tiny place inside of him that was relieved that Stephanie had ended it. Even though he had resigned himself to an ordinary life after college, he was no longer content to go back to that place. The Magical Space Skeleton Army was more important to him than Stephanie, and maybe she had been quicker to realize that. Or maybe he had grown to care for her less because she had tried to force him to choose between her and his passion. Whatever the reason, their love had ended before their relationship had.

He wasn't going to come to grips with that overnight. Fortunately, they had four more cities, and five more shows, to blunt the edge of his heartache.

Chapter One

LEAH KOZIOL HOVERED her mouse over the replay button. *I really shouldn't,* she thought. *I should be working. It's one thing to have it playing in the background, but I've been watching this video for nearly an hour.*

She glanced at the clock in the corner of her screen. *Over an hour,* she mentally amended.

Leah was new to the Magical Space Skeleton Army fandom, which had dubbed themselves "D'weasels" after a song in the discography entitled "Dweeb Weasels from Space." The song slowly edited the word dweeb from the chorus until the "d" was all that was left. It was an entertaining song, but Leah was currently fixated on one of their first videos. "Then She Puked On Me" had been on repeat most of the morning, as Leah tried to focus on her email.

With a sigh, she pressed the button and allowed the Magical Space Skeleton Army to take over the monitor once more.

Frimmydukes wore an older mask in this video, more like a luchador's than his current one. They were both metallic blue with white squares around the mouth and eyes, though the eye squares on his new mask were tilted more, and had white fluffy eyebrows sticking out of the seam. His new mask also had ear holes, which allowed him to wear ear tips like an elf or Vulcan, and the back of it was the same fluffy white as his new eyebrows. In an odd way, the mask was now reminiscent of Doc Brown. The rest of his outfit was basically the same, minus the bowler hat. Frimmydukes had a blue unitard that he wore under a pair of harem pants and black sequined vest. He alternated between the keytar and the bass, sometimes during the same song.

Lady Bug's costume had steadily improved over time, even though it was the best to start with. Her early headpiece with the faceted goggles, which was in use in this video, had changed to a mask with frosted faceted eyes and mandibles that swept along her cheekbones. In the early days, her spots had been part of a cape that draped over her shoulders and she wore a black corset and shorts over a red bodysuit. Now her cape had been replaced with sculpted, ethereal red and black wings and the corset and shorts were accentuated with red piping and lace, while the red bodysuit was now a shade darker and was speckled with black sequins. It was very elaborate, but since Lady Bug was the drummer, perhaps it made sense. She did seem less likely to rip her wings than someone that spent most of a concert running around the stage.

Lancel♡t hadn't changed his costume at all since the band had started. In keeping with his name, he had a medieval helmet (though it was more viking than knight). It exposed his mouth and chin, probably to make singing easier, but he'd filled the eye gaps with dark, reflective material and it was held in place with a padded chin strap that made it hard to interpret his jawline. He had a grey body suit that he covered with a red tunic emblazened with a golden heart on the chest. Bright yellow sweatbands on his wrists and ankles, and red shoes completed the ensemble. He was lead singer and guitarist.

The video followed the plot of the song, wherein each member of the band goes on a date and gets puked on, followed by a wedding which also leads to getting puked on, and then they have babies with heads identical to the band members that puke on their parents. It should have been grotesque, but rather than actual liquid, the video used animated rainbows and edible glitter to simulate the up-chucked substances. It was campy and fun. It made Leah smile. Most days. At the moment, even though she'd watched it for over an hour, it wasn't quite giving her the lift she had hoped.

It wasn't the video. The Magical Space Skeleton Army was taking a bit of the edge off, but it couldn't fix the problem. That was an entirely different issue.

There were only so many jobs that a person could do from home, and of those, Leah had chosen to be a travel agent. She often enjoyed her work, and the fact that she was helping people enjoy their free time was a big bonus. Sure, there were occasionally people that called to complain. You got that with any job. For the most part, people contacted Leah to be pleased, and were well satisfied with her service. Leah got paid, and everyone was happy.

Except Leah wasn't really happy. She had been, in the early days. Back when she had first started booking people's getaways, cruises, and safaris, she knew that it was just a matter of time before she would be booking her own vacations, too. The problem was that this morning she had booked a couple to go to Spain on their honeymoon, and she had yet to leave the country. There was only a week and a day before she would turn thirty; it made her feel like she'd wasted her twenties. Leah had the perfect work-from-anywhere job, but she hadn't gone anywhere.

With a sigh, Leah fiddled with her wedding ring. The problem was that Alan didn't really like to travel. Before they'd gotten the house, Alan would take time off from work or school, and they'd go on drives across state lines or down to Galveston. Even those trips had more or less dried up in the last few years.

"Enough," Leah said. She left up the window that still held a frame of glittery spew and shut down her computer monitor. It was about time that she took a day off, anyway. If she left the house now, she could make it to Alan's office for lunch. It was time for them to have a serious talk about some things.

"SO WHAT DID YOU WANT to talk about?" Alan said. Between his dark eyes, black hair, and extremely tan features, most people assumed that Alan was Hispanic or Native American. Living in Texas all his life, he'd learned enough Spanish to be conversational, but people were often shocked to find out his family was Polish. It was nearly as shocking to these people when they saw him stand next to his much paler, much taller, twin brother. He had a sharp nose, well curved lips, and an infectious smile. The third shock to people was generally that Leah was his wife.

With an average height, more hips than chest, and wardrobe that hadn't changed since college, Leah was far from the arm candy that most people envisioned when Alan said he was married. Her hazel eyes were her best feature, and she knew how to watch a make-up tutorial when the situation called for it. She also owned a flattening iron for her bushy, naturally red hair. Normally, she was just a rushed ponytail and lip gloss kind of girl. Assuming she remembered the lip gloss.

When Leah had texted Alan from the parking lot, he'd come out to greet her with a smile and a kiss. A rush of hot summer air was quickly subdued by the A/C in Leah's blue Chevy Cruze. (She'd picked it because the color had reminded her of the T.A.R.D.I.S. When a police box decal had come her way, Leah had been only too pleased to put it on her back window.) The humidity had to be at least 80% out there, but that wasn't unusual for Houston, even though it was an hour and a half drive from their house to the Gulf

They'd debated where to go eat for a few minutes, but ultimately ended up at the same Peppers on the corner that they usually did. Alan only had an hour for lunch, and there wasn't a lot near his office, aside from other office buildings. It wasn't long before they were seated with drinks and a plate of Southwestern Eggrolls nestled between them.

"How'd you know I wanted to talk about something?"

"Please, love," Alan reached forward to give her hand a squeeze. "Give me some credit. I'd like to think I've learned a little bit about you by now."

Leah looked into Alan's soft brown eyes. He was being sweeter than usual, and it made her feel a little uneasy. What did he think this lunch was about? "I wanted to know if you could get some time off, and maybe we could go somewhere," she told him.

"Time off?" he repeated. The soft, dreamy look on his face was melting away. Whatever he'd been expecting, it apparently hadn't involved a vacation. "To go somewhere?"

"It's not like we never talked about going somewhere before," she reminded him. "Back when we first started dating, we talked about going to Ireland or Japan for a month."

"You want to leave town for a whole month?" Alan asked. "I'm not sure I can take that much time right now. I just switched teams, and you know how that goes."

Leah shook her head, "I'm not asking for a whole month. Just a week? We can go to Britain, Australia, New Zealand, Tahiti, Mexico... I know I can find us a good deal. Even an all-inclusive island resort somewhere would be nice. I'm going to be thirty next Saturday. We could call it my birthday wish."

Alan picked up one of the rolls and bit into it. He wasn't looking at Leah at all at the moment. "You know," he seemed to be speaking to the eggroll, "we used to talk about other things, too. We were going to run a coffee shop where people could run their roleplaying games. We talked about making a Let's Play channel. We talked about having kids. I figured this was also one of those daydreams that we just talked about."

"Kids... You thought I was pregnant," Leah said, suddenly comprehending what he thought this conversation would be about. Frustration and anger surged within her. "Alan..."

"Don't, okay. I know. I know it's stupid that I went there..."

"No!" Leah said, aware that her voice had raised, and not really caring. "You don't get to throw a hissy fit because I wanted a vacation for my freaking birthday, and you thought I was having a fucking kid! You... You were there, in that doctor's office, with me!"

"I know, I know... Calm down, please... You know I still love you," Alan reached for her hand again, but Leah yanked them away from him.

With the inevitable timing of a server, theirs chose that moment to approach the table with a smile and a tray. "Who had the burger?"

Seething in her seat, Leah glared at the oblivious employee until he backed away enough for her to get by. "Good luck finding an Uber," she snapped at Alan, who was still looking bewildered. They'd fought before, but never in public, and she'd never been angry enough to drive off and leave him.

"AND THEN HE HAD THE gall to say, 'You know I still love you,' like that's even supposed to be a question," Leah sighed into the phone. She could still feel the angry tear streaks burned into her cheeks. They felt like they had been tattooed into her flesh.

"I'm sorry, hun, I really am," the voice on the other end of the phone said. "But how surprised are you? Really? I mean, you said he's been having trouble dealing with it."

"So am I," Leah felt her jaw tighten. "That doesn't give him license to act like it's somehow my fault."

Not for the first time, Leah really wished her best friend wasn't also Alan's brother. It made venting like this dangerous, should she tell Troy something that he really felt Alan should be aware of, but she had to talk to somebody, and Troy had actually answered his phone.

"Do you want me to talk to him about this?" Troy asked, almost like he had been reading her thoughts.

"No," Leah said. She was sitting in the parking lot of a drive thru taco shop, not sure where she wanted to go next. "What I want is for life to make sense, again. Things have gotten so far off course recently."

Eight years had passed since Troy had invited Leah to come to his house to try out a new sci-fi roleplay that he'd found at their local game shop. She'd come to Houston to attend college, not knowing a soul, and nervous that she'd never make any friends. Troy had worked in a sandwich place at the time. He started watching for her to come in when his shifts coincided with her classes. Despite her shyness, Troy had learned about her hobbies and interests through their conversations at the counter. She met his then-boyfriend, now ex-boyfriend, Anthony, and several other friends when they would pass through the restaurant to visit Troy. The invitation to his house included Anthony, two others, and his brother, Alan. Where Troy was slim, Alan was burly. Both of them were taller than Leah, but she didn't have to tilt back so much with Alan. He was 5'11", while Troy was 6'2". They were fraternal twins, and Troy wasn't subtle when it came to introducing Leah to his straight, single brother.

During the course of the game, Alan had apologized for his brother's obvious attempts to match make. Leah had reassured him that she wouldn't hold him to anything that Troy promised her, except for one thing. Alan had asked, and she had answered, "No disintegrations." He'd asked her out for coffee.

"That's the thing about life," Troy said. "It hasn't really got a course. It's more like the ocean. Sure, there are currents, but there's no telling if they're with you or against you on any given day. People who plan things out are always going to be off course because they're not going with the flow."

"Troy, when have you even just gone with the flow? You're the one that practically pushed me into your brother," Leah couldn't help but grin.

"So I stole some kid's fortune cookie to give you advice," Troy's tone conveyed the shrug he was almost certainly giving the phone. "Here's something that's genuinely from me to you; that band you're currently so enamoured with, the Magic Skull Raiders or whatever..."

"Magical Space Skeleton Army," Leah said.

"Yes, exactly what I said," Troy agreed. "They are going to be in town soon. Check your email. I sent you the link."

Excitement swelled within Leah. It washed out most of the weariness that the day had accumulated. It wasn't a trip, but it was something that she could look forward to with equal enthusiasm. "Oh my god, are you serious? Please, tell me you're serious. You cannot joke about this right now. I need this too much for it to be a joke, Troy."

"Dramatic much? Yes, I'm serious," he laughed. "Now, go home, and let your husband know you're alive, please. He's been texting me non-stop since the last time you declined his call. Apparently, he took an Uber home instead of back to work, and he's convinced that you drove straight into the ocean."

A feeling of foreboding wormed its way back into Leah's excitement. She didn't look forward to revisiting the fight with Alan. Still, it wasn't like they could pretend that today hadn't happened, either. After exchanging goodbyes with Troy, Leah started her car and began her drive back toward the house. It would be better to have it out in person after leaving Alan behind like that.

Chapter Two

MEL STARED AT THE BLANK open document on his computer screen and tapped absently on the backspace. It was impossible to delete anything because he hadn't successfully written anything. He ran a hand through his wavy, chestnut hair and then rubbed his jaw with the same fingers. The words were just not coming. Betham and Jessie had presented their songs for the new album two days ago. It wasn't like Mel to get blocked, but he couldn't seem to make his cursor move at all.

Enter.

Enter.

Enter.

There, he thought. *It moved.*

With a sigh, he deleted the only progress he'd made all afternoon. Most of the songs penned by the Magical Space Skeleton Army were collaborative efforts between Betham, Jessie and himself. Jessie was the one that had suggested that maybe they could divide and conquer on the new album. She had some ideas that she wanted to surprise them with, and thought it was a good chance for the three of them to flex their creativity. Betham had jumped on board with the idea as soon as Jessie had put it on the table, leaving Mel with his brief thoughts of protest unvoiced. It wasn't that he didn't like the creative freedom, but it had been ages since he was left alone with a blank page. The last song he had written on his own had been "Then She Puked On Me" something like five years ago.

Maybe I'm overthinking this, Mel considered. All he needed to do was start with a few killer titles, and the lyrics would follow. That was the way they worked best when they were creating together, after all.

"Dweeb Weasels From Space" had only been a joke that Betham kept suggesting in the late hours of the morning during their planning session for the second album.

With that thought in mind, he opened a second tab and began typing out anything that seemed like it could be a title that popped into his head.

Don't Worry. The Space War is Over.
Don't Worry. The Space Butler is Dead.
Don't Want to Go in the UFO.
If It Were Me, I Wouldn't Be A Gorilla, Dad.
Funky Tooth Decay.
No. No. No. Nonononono. Maybe.
Listen to the Thing in the Dark.
Member of the Regency: Stan.
Battleground: Arkham.
It's All Fun Until the Werewolf is Real.
You're Standing on my Waffle.

Mel leaned back and contemplated his list. It wasn't very long, but a few of the ideas had some potential. This was a far cry from his earlier progress anyway. If he could fill the entire page by lunch, he'd start the selection process after a break to refuel and rest. A knock on his front door chased the next half-formed title out of his fingers before they could transfer it to the page.

He checked the peephole and let a partially drenched Betham into his front room. "When did it start raining?" Mel asked.

"Maybe half a second ago," Betham grimaced. He squeezed his blonde hair through his fingers and let the water drip onto the hardwood floors. "I only went from my car to your breezeway, and, bam! The heavens burst forth, bro."

"Let me get you a towel," Mel said. "And maybe then we can get into why you're here?"

"No worries, dude. I'm cool," Betham slung a messenger bag off one shoulder and sat down at his usual spot next to the dining table that they usually used for brainstorming. It was the only original chair that the table still had, the rest having been slowly exchanged for computer chairs. Betham didn't mind having a stationary chair, as he usually ended up jumping up and pacing for most of a brainstorming session.

For someone raised in the Midwest, Betham had always had a bit of a surfer vibe. When it had come time to pick a college, no one had really been surprised when he moved out to California. He'd been majoring in filmmaking when he showed up on Mel's doorstep all those years ago. Mel had asked several times what had happened, and why Betham had suddenly left California. Betham had always just smiled, given a "Don't worry about it, bro," and moved on. It took most people by surprise that Betham, with his blue eyes, blonde hair and super-Bro speech, was a walking player's manual when it came to all things RPG related. There were few manuals out there that he didn't own. Fewer still that he hadn't read. To round things out, he was ridiculously athletic. He'd been varsity goalie on their high school soccer team as a freshman.

If it hadn't been for Jessie, Mel doubted he'd have been on Betham's radar during high school. They had met during a lunch period where he'd been planning out a dungeon on graph paper. Jessie had recognized what he was up to instantly and asked who was in his group. Mel had explained that he hadn't found one, as he'd changed school districts over the summer and didn't really know anyone yet. Jessie had announced that she would fix that, ran off, and came back with Betham in tow.

Mel was initially disappointed that the cute, mocha skinned girl was that eager to bring her boyfriend into things, but things were cleared up in a hurry. Jessie was not going to date him, as she was not really a fan of relationships, and Mel reeked of commitment. Also, this buff, blonde dude was her brother.

Jessie was a year younger than Betham and Mel, and her biological father was Betham's adoptive father. When people met the siblings, they generally did a mental tango, trying to assess how a black girl and a blonde surfer dude were biologically related. When they met Brock Dallas, a black man with muscles that could've been on loan from Dwayne Johnson, they no longer wondered about Jessie and usually didn't dare ask about Betham.

The truth was that Kelly Dallas, their mother, had been enamored with a man when she was about nineteen. He'd been less enamored with her. After Kelly told him she was pregnant, that man had evaporated into the night. Brock had met Kelly during her second trimester. They'd dated for only two months before he proposed. Brock loved both of his kids, and really enjoyed giving people the over-protective father lean.

Mel shook his wandering thoughts back to the present, where Betham was still dripping on his floor. With a sigh, Mel went into the kitchen and grabbed a hand towel and two sodas. "What made you decide to stop by?" Mel asked, as he handed one of the sodas to his friend and bandmate.

The hand towel got tossed on the floor and nudged into place with a foot, even as Mel popped the tab on the remaining soda.

"Oh! That's right! You didn't answer my texts, so I asked Jess, and she said we should just show up, seeing as you were probably home and still working on your songs," Betham said. "She was right, as per yoush."

Checking his pockets, Mel realized that his phone was not on his person. "What were you texting about?"

"Mostly to see if you were home," Betham took a swig from his soda can before beginning to set up his laptop. "Jessie should be here in a minute. She said she was going to grab some food for everyone before she got here."

"Are we ditching the making songs on our own thing?" Mel could feel some of the tension draining from his frame. He didn't realize how much he really wanted the support of the band until this moment.

"No, dude. This is more of a working-alone-together thing. Besides, Jess and I had something we wanted to talk to you about," Betham said. He hit the power button and a glow immediately tumbled over his features. The screen that came on showed Mel that Betham had made roughly three songs' worth of progress.

"About the band?" Mel asked. A brief jolt of fear ran through him. Did they want him out? He'd been the lead vocalist for most of the Magical Space Skeleton Army's run, but that didn't mean he was irreplaceable. Both Betham and Jessie had taken vocal training, and it wasn't like there weren't other singers out there. The chance to audition for a successful band, even if they kept the name out of it...

No, Mel slowed himself down. *Betham wouldn't be this laidback about something like that. Besides, the paperwork says that we're all equal partners in the company. Without some sort of gross negligence on my part,* Mel couldn't help darting his eyes toward his own laptop that was set up on the opposite end of the table, *it wouldn't be that.* He hadn't written a song by himself since "Then She Puked On Me." Was that considered negligent?

"Not exactly," Betham hedged. "Better wait for Jess, though. She's got more to say than I."

Mel went back to his computer and they both started tapping on keyboards in silence for a few minutes. The rain was now audibly drumming against Mel's balcony, making an odd sort of counter to the rhythm of their typing. Inspired, Mel hit the recording button on his microphone. He wasn't sure that even the strongest mic would pick up something so soft, but it was worth a shot.

That was when Jessie knocked. Her muffled voice came from around the door frame, "Hey guys, it's me... I brought burritos."

Shutting off the recorder, Mel got up to open the door.

Jessie had shaken off the worst of the damp outside before she'd even knocked. She hadn't bothered with makeup today, but she still managed to look like the most together person in the room. It was just Jessie's way, to make life look effortless. No matter what life threw at her, Jessie was somehow above it. When Betham had convinced her to take up this weird band idea, she had been going to school in Boston. Though she'd been undecided as far as major, Mel knew she'd have made people stand up and take notice no matter where she ended up. Lady Bug was generally regarded as the fan favorite, and Mel couldn't begrudge Jessie the admiration.

"I got your usuals," Jessie said, extending the burrito bag to Mel as she removed her shoes and placed them on the rubber mat near the door. "Carnitas, sour cream, pico, no beans for Betham. Beef and chicken, guac, sour cream, medium salsa, pinto beans, extra cheese for Mel. How you've gained no weight since high school is beyond me."

"Beats me," Mel shrugged. "I'm not about to complain, though."

Betham jumped out of his seat and grabbed the thinnest of the massive foil bundles and held it up like it was a baby lion cub being presented to its kingdom. "Praise be the mighty burrito gods, and their blessing of my sister, the burrito messenger, who has brought forth such bounty!"

"Is that from one of the songs you're working on?" Jessie asked.

"No," Betham plopped back into his chair.

"May I have it?" Mel and Jessie asked in unison.

With a long chug on his soda, Betham drained the last of his can and put it back on the table with a solid metallic thunk. "Tell you what. Whomever so blesses me with my next can, may be the prophet of the burrito gods," Betham grinned.

Mel exchanged a look with Jessie. His was an invitation to compete, while hers was more good-natured exasperation. "I thought I was already a blessing from these burrito gods. I bought you food."

Since Jessie was going for the argument angle, Mel decided to go ahead and make for the kitchen. There was more than one way to win a race, and Mel was going to make Jessie work for it. If things got heated, and the argument started to get serious, he'd just concede. It was better for the band to be unified, especially with another leg of their tour coming up. *That's right,* the thought pounced on him. *We're in the middle of a tour. They wouldn't choose now to replace me. Where did that even come from?*

"Mel supplied us both with most excellent spaghettis not three days ago," Betham countered. "As the current instrument of the gods, I'm only trying to judge with a fair hand."

"I concede," Jessie said before Mel could. "We're going to have to trim my list down anyway. I did four extra. Not all of them are winners, but I figure they'll make excellent content for our patrons."

The sounds of a chair being pulled out and sat in told Mel that Jessie wasn't planning on coming into the kitchen at all. "Soda, water, lemonade?" he asked.

"You've got lemonade?" Jessie sounded surprised.

"You've got lemonade," he said. "You left it here on Thursday, when we decided to write our own songs for the next album."

"Oh, yeah... Definitely lemonade," Jessie said. Rustling plastic and maraca-like sounds followed. It sounded as though she'd gone for a bowl today. Unlike the guys, she didn't really have a favorite burrito. Whatever she felt like on any given day was bound to change.

As Mel brought in the drinks, the mood shifted. Betham had warned him that they wanted to talk to him, but Mel had let his guard down when he convinced himself the impending conversation wasn't about kicking him out of the band. It couldn't be, or why would they have given him the burrito gods? The odd mood continued as he sat down and pulled the bag toward him. Chewing and the smell of grilled meats occupied the table. Crinkling the foil back, Mel took a large bite of tortilla, beef, beans, rice, and cheese. It seemed the spread of his burrito's ingredients was quite uneven, much like the atmosphere in his apartment. "Okay, I give up. What's going on?"

Jessie placed her fork in her bowl, propped her chin in her hands, and gazed at Mel for a long moment. Uncertain of what she was looking for, Mel waited. Betham continued to happily eat his burrito.

"How long has it been since Stephanie left?" Jessie asked.

How long... Mel tried to think back. "I don't know. Maybe two years?"

"It's been four years, dude," Betham said. He popped up out of his chair and went into the kitchen, returning with a roll of paper towels. "Maybe a few months, too."

"Okay, so four years, then," Mel said. He didn't bother to ask why Betham knew how long ago he'd been with Stephanie. Betham was weirdly accurate with dates and calendars, despite never writing anything down in a planner or even an app. "Why does it matter?"

Jessie sighed. "It matters because you haven't had a serious relationship since. And like I told you back in high school, you reek of commitment. It matters because she took your voice."

Reflexively, Mel patted his throat, as though he thought Jessie had somehow meant Stephanie had literally robbed him of his vocal chords. "Took my voice?"

"When we started this band, who wrote most of our songs?" Jessie asked.

"Well, I did most of the lyrics, but Betham always did the..."

"Yeah, I found tunes and Jessie found the beat," Betham grinned. "Solid from the get-go."

"And then Stephanie," Jessie continued, as though the question had been rhetorical to start with. "You wrote one of our best songs ever before she left, and then you kinda dried up. We kept thinking, if we gave you some time, maybe you'd come back to yourself. Now, it's been four years."

"But I always contribute to the process," Mel protested.

"Yes, you do. This isn't about us feeling like you don't pull your weight or anything like that," Jessie said. "This is about us wanting to see our best friend reach his full potential. If we can help you come back from wherever it is you got pushed, we're not just going to make it as the Magical Space Skeleton Army, we're going to shine. Betham and I, we can write lyrics because you taught us to write lyrics."

"Dude, you're like the music DM. Jess and I just roll our lyrical dice and hope to impress you. We're an awesome team because we're all awesome. It's like, somehow, Steph made you afraid to embrace that," Betham said.

Mel stared at his lunch, no longer entirely certain that he wanted it. He felt like he'd been gut-punched by someone he thought had been leaning in for a hug. "I'm not sure where this is coming from," he said. "I mean, yeah, I know I don't write like I used to, but I'm well over Stephanie. I wouldn't take her back if she showed up on my doorstep in nothing but a raincoat."

"Glad to hear it," Jessie said. "She was completely wrong for you. A Yoko if I ever saw one."

"So you don't want me to track her down," Mel clarified.

"No, but maybe it's time for you to get back out there," Jessie said. "Find someone new."

"I'm going to find a new girlfriend, and somehow, I'll magically be able to write again," the skepticism within Mel's voice sounded a little sour, even to him.

"How much have you gotten down on your current songs?" Jessie asked.

The sudden shift caught Mel flat-footed. He looked from Jessie to his computer screen that had a lot of titles and not much else.

Nothing else. A series of titles and not one single lyric. He thought back to the days before Stephanie had left. Words had come easily back then, almost as though they had existed on a different plane and he'd merely been the conduit through which they flowed. If he hadn't noticed the change, why would he have gained this recent fear of replacement? Some part of him recognized that this conversation was coming, while a deeper part of him insisted it was long overdue.

"Okay," he said. "You may have a point. Do you have a solution?"

With a grin that told him he may have made a mistake, Jessie handed him a flyer.

Chapter Three

"HELLO? ALAN?" LEAH called as she came in through the front door.

Their house had three entryways: back door, garage door and, of course, the front door. The back door led to the backyard, which was barely enough yard to qualify for the title. The garage was similarly unimpressive. It was only large enough for one car, and also functioned as the laundry room. Alan's car being the newer of the two, he parked in the garage. *Though*, Leah thought, *he's probably left it at the office if he took an Uber from the Peppers. I didn't even think to check.*

Glancing into their combination kitchen and dining room didn't reveal Alan at his usual perch at the bar. Most days when he got home, he would set his laptop up and check his social media feeds on his phone while the laptop was tapped into one of their streaming services. When they had moved in, Leah had loved the open feel of the kitchen flowing into the dining room, but now it irritated her that she could see the dirty dishes from the table every time they cooked. She had never really cared for the overly white cabinets, but she still liked the cement countertops. They'd been dyed burgundy and had been the selling point for her vote on this house.

Moving farther into the house, Leah tried again, "Alan? Troy said you were here."

A very muffled, "In here," reached her this time.

Leah walked through the living room feeling oddly like a guest in her own space. An old love seat, two shelves of DVDs that were slowly being upgraded, a recliner that no one ever sat in, and a TV that was attached to three or four gaming systems... This was where Leah spent a good deal of her time in the evenings. She was currently playing through some old classics on an original Super Nintendo that Troy had given her last year for her birthday.

"Where?" she asked, even though she already knew.

"In here!" the bathroom door said.

Just where I wanted to have this out, Leah grimaced. "I'll be in the office when you're done."

"Wait," Alan said. He sounded urgent enough to give her pause. Was he really going to apologize from the toilet? "Could you hand me a new roll?"

Ah, Leah rolled her eyes at her own expectations. *Of course.*

She went to the hall closet where they kept linens, towels and toilet paper. Even as she wrestled a new roll out of its plastic, she had another thought. "Why didn't you go to the one in our room?"

"It was out of paper!"

This conversation was not improving her mood. Leah wrestled a second roll of paper from its plastic prison and stuffed it under her arm. She opened the door and averted her eyes as she extended the first cylinder of precious papers to her ignobly throned husband. Once they'd been yanked from her grip, she deposited the second roll in their other bathroom. It was tempting to flop onto their king sized bed and just doze for a bit. There was that sense that if she could go to sleep and wake up, things would be different. Today would start from the beginning, and she'd surprise Alan at work, they'd go to lunch, he'd be on board from the start, and she wouldn't drive off feeling somehow cheaper. A bargain-bin wife.

Leah shook her head and stiffened her back. There was no reason she should feel like this was her fault. Alan was the one that got mad and sulky because of something that was beyond her control. She'd told him to meet her in the office, so she was going to wait in the office. It would give her something to do while he spent half an hour on the toilet, playing whatever was on his iPhone today.

When she switched on the screen and saw the Magical Space Skeleton Army paused in mid-sprinkle spew, Leah remembered Troy's news. Other thoughts were put on pause as she rushed to open her email and click on the link.

Pictures of Lancel♡t, Lady Bug, and Frimmydukes jumped onto the screen, followed by the usual tagline of "Coming soon to a city near you!" The ticket links were farther down the page. Leah clicked on the Houston tab, and drummed her fingers as she waited for the new screen to load. *How long ago did they announced the tour?* the question popped into Leah's head a split-second before the page slammed into place.

Sold Out.

"What?! No, no no no... C'mon! Please!" Leah hit the refresh.

Sold Out.

Refresh.

Sold Out.

Refresh!

Sold Out, Leah.

Refresh!

Seriously? This is getting ridiculous.

Leaning against her high-backed, mesh computer chair, Leah let out a disappointed sigh. She could always check the scalping sites, but she hated to encourage them. Also, that would probably mean one hell of a markup on even the cheapest sections.

"Hey," Alan's voice came from the doorway. He sounded despondent, maybe even a little contrite. Or perhaps, Leah just really wanted to hear it that way. She wasn't going to pretend she could read his mind.

"Hey," she said.

"So..."

"So," Leah echoed. A spark of refreshed anger threatened to swell in her lungs. She pushed it down, but not entirely away. If Alan was fishing for her to apologize first, he was going to have a very long wait.

"May I come in?" Alan asked.

It was technically their office, but since Leah actually worked from home, it had slowly become more her space. Still, he didn't have to ask, so Leah appreciated that he did. "Have a seat."

Alan sat on the edge of his chair and scooted it forward so that his knees were touching hers. Leah found herself focusing on the way her jeans looked next to his work slacks. Normally, it didn't bother her that she was so casual next to his business wardrobe. After their fight, it just seemed...wrong, somehow. Out of balance.

"Look..." Alan said. He took one of her hands and swallowed. "I know I... I didn't mean... I love you. I do. It's just been... Hard. You know?"

"It hasn't exactly been easy on my end of it, either," Leah grasped at Alan's hand. She felt like she was trying to keep herself above water, or maybe she was trying to pull him out of the water. One or both of them were floundering, but maybe that one point of contact could save her, him, them. Perhaps their clasped hands were the only thing that was keeping their marriage afloat. An ice that burned hotter than the fires of her rage suddenly gripped her spine. When they'd received the news that Leah was infertile, she'd been thrown into a state of shock. Alan was the one she'd counted on to keep her grounded, but instead, he'd become distant. She'd leaned on Troy, who had been a real pro at keeping her spirits up and telling her to just give Alan time to process.

Then they'd gone to lunch and everything exploded.

She'd been angry at Alan before, but it was different this time. Fear was starting to push the anger down, a fear of the rift that was growing between them. Leah found herself hugging Alan with all she was worth, seeking comfort from his physical grip to combat his emotional distance. Hugging somehow led to desperate, passionate kisses, and someone's shoe flying off. A shoe led to a shirt, and frantic fumbling with a belt. Pants disappeared between one breath and the next. A whole half hour blurred into half-formed images of arms and legs. The impressions of fingers trailing over skin and lingering in secret, forbidden places seared forth from the haze. One moment of pure bliss, where all Leah could see seemed to go white and dazzling, signaled the end of their frantic love-making.

Alan curled up next to Leah and started to snore softly, despite it being the middle of the afternoon. She watched his chest move as he breathed and felt her heart sink. It had felt good to let all of their worries melt away for that half hour, but they hadn't really solved anything. The ice around her spine hadn't so much as chipped.

IT WAS SATURDAY, BUT Alan went into his office anyway, saying that he'd left some stuff undone after the lunch incident. He also wanted to get his car. Leah had offered to drive him in, but he'd told her it wasn't necessary. His ride was already on the way.

"Are you going to be home for lunch?" Leah asked. She was barefoot, still wearing pajama bottoms and a spaghetti strapped sleep shirt, while Alan was once more in a button-down dress shirt and slacks. He looked professional, and distant.

"It depends on how much I get done," he said. "Why don't you make plans with Troy? Or Nessa?"

"Sure," Leah said. "I'll see what they're up to."

With a quick kiss on the cheek, Alan rushed across their front lawn and jumped into the car that was waiting for him at the end of the drive. "Not even an 'I love you,'" Leah said aloud.

As much as she wanted to call Troy, she felt weird complaining to him again after the fiasco from the day before. Nessa was a much better bet, and Leah was wearily amused that Alan was the one that suggested contacting her. Nessa Fierro was technically a client of Leah's. She'd booked several flights through the small agency, and everything had been professional contact until they ran into each other at a convention. That was when Leah discovered that Nessa was actually a cosplayer that she'd been following on Instagram for over a year. They'd spoken on the phone often enough that Nessa had done a double take when Leah had asked for a picture. "Oh my god, Leah?! Leah Koziol?"

The tiles on the kitchen floor radiated air-conditioned air back at Leah's feet as she reached into the glasses cabinet and pulled down her favorite cup. She filled it with ice and then poured herself some orange juice. She knew it was weird. Every single server at every breakfast restaurant she'd ever been to had made the same face when Leah asked for ice with her orange juice. Still, she liked the way it diluted the sweetness. Leah padded her way into the living room and turned on the tv and her current game. Even after clearing a level, it was obvious she could only distract herself so much.

Nessa had never really taken to Alan, even though she and Leah had become fast friends. The lack of feeling was pretty mutual on Alan's part. Nessa was on the small list of friends that Leah had confided in when she and Alan had come back from the doctor, and she had told Leah to call her whenever she needed to talk. *Well*, Leah thought. *I could definitely use a talk.*

Grabbing her phone, Leah sent off a quick text.

Within a few seconds, it emitted a high-pitched, "Yoshi!"

Leah had forgotten that she'd changed the text tone.

It seemed that she now had plans for lunch though. She decided it was probably time to go get dressed. After the next boss fight.

LEAH PULLED UP IN FRONT of the building and grabbed her purse out of the front seat. It was a purse that Nessa had made for her, designed to look like Vash the Stampede's red coat. Leah never failed to get the random Trigun fan stopping her and asking (demanding) where she'd managed to find it. Of course, she usually saved it for conventions and the occasions she was out with its designer, which meant that it was being displayed to its target audience.

As usual, Nessa had chosen some obscure hole in the wall, where she likely knew the owner, manager, and manager's third cousin. Nessa had a gift with people. She seemed to have friends everywhere. It astonished Leah how easily Nessa seemed to keep up with everyone. This restaurant was called "Escape from Philly Burger." The problem with Nessa knowing the people who ran some of these hole-in-the-wall places was that it sometimes made it hard to be honest about how much Leah enjoyed her food. She really hoped this would be better than the last place.

The decor was largely '80s themed with a cartoonish painted mural of Snake Plissken holding a burger and shooting the Liberty Bell amid a broken cityscape. The face was so distorted that it almost looked as much like Bill Clinton as it did Kurt Russell. Posters from other classic '80s movies were framed on the opposite wall. Despite that, the booths were relatively modern, and the layout looked like a place where they took orders at the counter and gave out little plastic numbers. Leah felt a bit of tension ease out of her shoulders. This was her kind of place, as long as the fries weren't too greasy.

"Leah!" Nessa stood up from somewhere near the back, waving.

Hesitating for only a moment, Leah made her way through the labyrinth of tables and chairs. Some of them were even occupied, which was already different from their last lunch. More unusual, Nessa was alone at their table.

"Don't we have to order at the counter?" Leah asked once she got to the booth.

Nessa shook her head, and her long, black hair gently echoed the movement. She looked enough like a young Marissa Tomei that people occasionally mis-tagged some of her pics on Google. Some of Nessa's best cosplays took advantage of her dark hair and delicate features: Inara from *Firefly*, Sango from *Inuyasha*, Asami Sato from *Avatar: The Legend of Korra*, and Violet Parr from *The Incredibles*. That was far from her full catalogue, many of the others involved wigs or prosthetics, but they ranked among Leah's favorites.

"We don't have to go up there," Nessa said. "Ray will be out here in just a few. He already knows what I want, but they're waiting on you to put the order in."

"Okay," Leah slid into her side of the booth and Nessa handed her a menu. "So more like a Steak n' Shake than a Five Guys?"

"Something like that," Nessa said. "I'll wait until you order to ask, 'What's up?'"

Leah noticed the menu in her hands was actually a take-out menu. Not so much a place that waited on tables, but another one of those places where they were receiving Nessa-level treatment. Swallowing a comment, Leah turned her attention to the menu items as opposed to the menu itself. She'd learned over the past few years that Nessa didn't demand special treatment, but people tended to go out of their way just to make Nessa smile. Nessa usually returned the favor. It wasn't that she went totally overboard, but she genuinely seemed to notice everyone in that special way that she had.

Sure enough, when Ray showed up for Leah's order, he was polite and professional with Leah and genuine with Nessa. It was like they'd known each other for years.

As Ray left, Leah couldn't help asking, "How long have you known Ray?"

"We met at my supermarket last week," Nessa said, the edges of her lips twitching in the beginnings of a grin. "He helped me choose some steaks."

Leah's eyebrows crinkled together as she tried to form the question that felt lurking somewhere inside.

"No, we're not romantic," Nessa said, the smile hovering at the edges of her lips burst forth. "Ray's involved with two other girls at the moment: his wife and daughter. You know I hate competition."

"Oh," Leah knew Nessa was teasing. She'd never date a married anybody, or even flirt with a married anybody. Still, Leah found it hard to joke about marriages at the moment.

Nessa took one look at Leah's face, and dropped her teasing manner. Concern replaced her happiness and she reached across the table and grasped Leah's wrist, offering what comfort she could even as Leah's resolve to pretend everything was okay melted. "Something happened," Nessa said, not making it a question.

Leah nodded and tears huddled near the edges of her vision. She tried to wipe them away before they could make a true break for freedom. It was never her intention to become the weepy friend. When Leah thought about what kind of friend she wanted to be, she usually saw herself as the fun friend or the sweet one. She would even settle for the shy and unassuming friend (that was probably closest to the truth anyway). No one wanted to be the weepy friend. Still, Nessa was here and willing to listen, so Leah told her about the aborted lunch attempt at Peppers, the not-quite apology, and the weird tension when Alan had left that morning.

"I haven't even tried to bring up traveling again," Leah sighed. "Hell, I tried to get tickets to the Magical Space Skeleton Army yesterday, and they were sold out! Not that that really has anything to do with Alan... but it was just one more thing during the shitstorm, you know?"

"Have you and Alan considered seeking outside help? Counseling or a marriage workshop?" Nessa asked softly.

"Footloose?" Ray interjected, holding two baskets.

"That's me," Nessa said, allowing a brief grin to flash up at the restaurant owner.

He placed a large bacon burger and bacon cheese fries in front of Nessa. There was a side of ranch teetering at the edge of the basket, threatening to douse the table. "And that would mean you get the Terminator with cheese," Ray said, placing the other basket in front of Leah.

Even though she was still upset, Leah took a deep whiff of her burger. It smelled as spicy as she had hoped; jalapenos, triple pepper sauce, chipotle mayo and cheddar cheese. The fries also had jalapenos and cheese. This was not a restaurant that would help her watch her waistline, but it was great comfort food. The tears she'd held back earlier were already starting to fade as Leah's attention was turned toward lunch. *Please, be fading*, Leah requested, picking up her burger.

For a few moments, the only sounds at the table were chewing and sipping as Leah tried to remember where the conversation had last drifted. Nessa seemed to be waiting for her to say something. "Oh, counseling..." Leah said, recalling her friend's question. "No. The doctor advised it, but on our way home from the office, Alan said he wouldn't do it. Something about it never working for his mom and dad."

Their table went quiet again. Leah could see that Nessa was processing something, but there were no clues visible on her friend's face.

"I was going to save these until next week when I could give them to you on your actual birthday, but I think you need them now," Nessa said. She used a napkin to wipe off her fingers before she dug into her purse. A large envelope with Leah's name written in pen got shoved across the table, as Nessa smiled her biggest smile. "Happy birthday!"

Feeling oddly unsettled, Leah took the envelope and turned it over. It was unsealed, which was a blessing because her hands had started to tremble. The tears that she had managed to turn back were beginning to well up once more, but not in quite the same manner. There was a bit of excitement mixed into the emotional stew that bubbled within her. Two VIP tickets to the Magical Space Skeleton Army.

"Oh my god," Leah said.

Nessa's smile brightened.

"Oh my god," Leah repeated.

"I know, right?"

"Oh my god! Nessa!" Leah jumped up and ran across to the other side of the booth. Nessa got to her feet so that Leah could hug her. "You're amazing! How did you...? When...?"

As they were sliding back into the booth, Nessa grabbed one of her fries and took a rather smug bite. "Okay, so I have a friend that works for the venue. I told her to keep an eye out for certain bands for me, mostly so I can do things like this for some of my friends and family. Nothing shady... I don't get pre-tickets or anything, but she gave me a call the instant they went on sale. I figured, even if you got them, you'd probably only go for the cheapest option. Don't make that face at me, you know it's true."

Blinking, Leah shook her head and stowed the tickets in her purse. She pulled out her phone and put the concert on her calendar. It was only a week and a half away!

Chapter Four

MEL RAKED HIS FINGERS through his recently shortened brown hair. He was nervous; he could feel it in every inch of his wiry frame. His gray eyes were probably using semaphore signals to plead passersby for rescue.

"Why are we doing this, again?" he asked. Jessie stood next to him as they looked at the front of a sports bar across town from his apartment. It was on the small side, but comfortable. It had that well-nestled look that a bar only acquires after its second or third decade of continuous patronage. There was a sign in one window advertising karaoke on Thursday that looked as though it had been posted for five years, and a fresh sign next to it that read: Speed Dating Event this Wednesday! Free first round for participants!

"You're doing this because you need to get back out there. I'm doing this for a free mojito," Jessie said. She looked amazing, wearing a yellow top with a ruffle along the shoulder-baring sleeves and a high-waisted black skirt. Her makeup was all gold and brown tones that made her look like she had cat eyes, and her dark hair was pulled into a braided bun. "Don't grumble. I gave you a choice; it was this or Tinder."

Mel scrunched his face up at the reminder. He'd been against the idea of dating apps before Jessie even mentioned it. Online dating matchups were all well and good, but the idea of choosing someone off of a selfie or two... It didn't appeal to him. Maybe it had something to do with being in his thirties, but he thought it was more likely that it was just the romantic in him. Although, that same romantic in him had insisted on jeans and a loose button-down shirt over one of his favorite t-shirts, rather than the suit he had for weddings that

Jessie had wanted him to wear. Now that they were here, he wasn't sure he should have listened to his inner romantic on either count. With Tinder, he could've signed up and then deleted the app after a week or two. "Are you sure you want to go in there with me?"

Jessie laughed and grabbed Mel by the arm to lead him into the door. "Mel, I go to these all the time. It's fun. I like meeting people and sometimes I really click with someone, you know? If it helps, I'll end up being one of your dates at some point. We can both take an extra five-minute breather."

A blast of cool air gusted past them and into the humid, August sunshine. It would have been more welcome if the recent rain hadn't brought the beginnings of fall with it. Mel felt a bit of a shudder run through his body. At least, he tried to convince himself it was because of the cold. His nerves weren't really letting him believe it.

"How does this even work?" he asked.

Jessie's eyes were searching the bar for something or someone, but she turned her attention to Mel and seemed to soften. It wasn't until that moment that Mel recognized the set of her jaw as being determined. She had been waiting for more of an argument, but his genuine confusion had reassured her somehow. "Come on, we'll take a seat and I'll talk you through it. We're almost half an hour early."

A server came by checked their IDs and scanned their credit cards to start a tab for each of them, and then Jessie began to walk Mel through the process. "First, we have to find the host. They'll take down a few particulars: Name, phone number, email, that sort of thing. We'll receive a scorecard, which is kinda like those middle school notes that people used to get. Remember? 'Do you like me? Yes/No,' and you had to circle one."

"I never got one of those," Mel said. He hoped that the waitress would come back so he could order a drink. He felt like his nerves were about to vibrate right out of his body.

"I can see that about you," Jessie said. "Middle schoolers aren't really savvy enough to notice adorkable. It's kind of a look that people grow into."

"Wait..." Mel's nerves practically did a double take with him. Even as blunt as Jessie tended to be, he'd never heard her comment on his looks one way or the other before. He'd always assumed that she didn't find him worth commenting on. "I'm 'adorkable?' Really?"

With a small grin, Jessie said, "Don't let it go to your head. But yes, I'd definitely say you've got that geeky/nerdy charm thing down. People just don't usually look past Betham and me to see it."

"Oh," Mel's momentary distraction began to flicker out. "But..."

"Once the dates start, we'll get five minutes with each of the other participants. The theory is that during that five minutes we'll have an idea as to whether or not we want to spend more time with the person across from us. At the end of five minutes, the host will ring a bell and either the men or women will rotate. As they rotate, that's when people usually circle yes or no. If we say yes and they say yes, then the host or hostess will email us with contact info. That's it," Jessie explained. "Easy."

"Right. Easy," Mel echoed. Jessie got up and hauled him to his feet, pulling him over to the bar where a plump blonde woman held a leather notebook.

"Hi! Are you here for the speed dating? I'm afraid we don't take couples..." the blonde woman looked at Jessie and then Mel, as though she were trying to see the threads of attachment that could possibly bind them together.

"Good to know," Jessie smiled. "This is my friend, Mel Abrams, and I'm Jessie Dallas. We are here for the speed dating as a matter of fact. Poor Mel got dumped a few years ago, and I'm hoping this will help bring him out of his dating slump."

"Jessie!" Mel said, his eyes going wide. "You don't have to tell everyone!"

"I'm not telling everyone. I'm telling Claire, who just wants to make sure that everyone here is here to make a real try of it. Right, Claire?" Jessie's smile didn't waver.

Claire's eyes darted from Jessie to Mel and back again. Whatever she saw convinced her that Jessie was being genuine. The host pushed her notebook toward them. "If you'll just fill out the next available line, I can get you set up with a name tag. We'll start in about twenty minutes, so if you'd like to get your drinks," Claire gave Mel a significant raise of one eyebrow, "that can really help take the edge off."

As Mel was smoothing his nametag down, Jessie slapped hers onto her chest. A new thought sprung into Mel's head and made the rest of his worries seem to clack about like billiard balls in his brain. "Wait, Jess, what if someone asks me what I do for a living?"

"Tell them you work for our band," Jessie shrugged. She leaned across the bar and made eyes at the bartender, who gave her an appreciative smile back. "A mojito over here, please. My friend would like a Coke with vanilla vodka."

"But... We... How...?" Mel wasn't even sure how to phrase the question without giving their identities away. He had a sudden fear that the whole world actually knew who was under the masks of the Magical Space Skeleton Army. They would never be able to get groceries or eat at restaurants unmolested. They'd have to wear disguises to amusement parks and conventions or risk getting swarmed. A vanilla vodka and Coke, on the rocks, appeared in his hand and he gripped it without really noticing it was there.

"Like how I'm the social media coordinator," Jessie said, her voice low enough that even Mel could barely hear her. "You could say you're our manager, or sound engineer or something. How many people actually know our stage crew by sight? Just make sure you sound important enough to earn money, but not like you're in a position to give an introduction. Why do you think Betham and I haven't had strings of lovers flooding through your apartment?"

"Because you guys actually like me," Mel muttered. He took an absent-minded sip from his drink, forgetting about the vodka until it hit his tongue, then scorched its way down his throat. With a sputtering cough, he set the glass down on the bar and closed his eyes. Jessie clapped him on the back twice; a friendly pat, rather than trying to help him swallow.

They had plenty of time to drink in the atmosphere of the bar while they waited for the dates to begin. Much like the outside, this place looked settled. Neon signs, sports memorabilia, and old license plates decorated the walls. Though they were clear of dust, all of the decor had that long-established look. An antiquated jukebox had been watching people laugh and drink for years, likely since the bar had opened. Grandkids of the original patrons were probably taking selfies in front of the same bright pink baseball statue near the bathrooms that earlier generations had snapped polaroids with. Yellow and white neon gleamed off of the well-worn wood of the bar. There were televisions mounted around a center dais, pointing at all of the booths on the outer ring. Inside the dais, it looked like it was set up for the dating event. Tables on the dais, unlike the outer booths, were draped with dark blue cloth and had numbered placards shooting above their salt and pepper caddies. The dais met with the far wall, and the back tables had a solid booth instead of chairs. It was the kind of place that big chains tried to emulate, but never succeeded in duplicating.

More people were approaching Claire as 7:00 drew nearer, which was the official starting time. Mel couldn't help but notice that his casual attire was a little out of place, but it seemed Jessie's flair was on the opposite end of the spectrum. He went through his entire first drink before Claire stood up and clapped on a tiny desk bell ten or twelve times until all talking in the room died out.

"Okay, so I see a few familiar faces here, today, but most of you are new! Welcome! Also, a full house today, which is wonderful! I'm going to touch on the basics, but we all want to get started so I'm not going to spend too long on this. We're going to let the ladies find their tables, and then I'll tell each of you guys which number to go to. No talking until everyone is seated. I'll ding the bell to begin. The next time the bell dings, I want the men to switch seats. Number one goes to two," Claire pointed from the first table to the second, and then continued to point at each of the tables in the circuit, "up to twenty. At twenty, you go to number one! All clear? Great! Good luck!"

Jessie walked away from Mel without so much as a wink. He watched her make herself at home at table six. There was a certain bitter taste in his mouth that hadn't been there earlier, though that could've been the aftereffects of the vodka. Now that she wasn't at his side, Mel was tempted to make a run for it. How was making his stomach tie itself into knots going to help him write songs? Though, now that he thought about it, they were a comedy band with their largest hit being about vomit. Stomach problems might just be the answer.

When Mel came even with Claire, she glanced at his name tag and down at her notebook. "Ah, yes. Mel... I think I'll have you sit across from Gwen. That's table one, dear."

Mel's feet started across the floor of their own accord, carrying him toward the farthest table in the room. The woman sitting there, Gwen, was not exactly striking, but she had a quirky cuteness to her features. Her face was very round, framed by shoulder length, curly brown hair. Her freckles looked like they had been applied to her face like grated parmesan on a pizza. *Maybe this won't be so bad*, Mel thought as he returned the friendly smile that Gwen was giving him.

When the bell sounded, Mel opened his mouth to introduce himself, but Gwen was already talking.

"OMG, right? Can you believe how lame this is? It's like, I can't believe people actually do this," Gwen said. "Are you like, seriously looking for someone or did you get dragged here by your stupid friend too?"

"Um... I guess?" Mel said. Redness was creeping up his cheeks as Gwen pelted him with stones of embarrassment, and he signaled for a waitress. He really felt that another Coke was an order, with or without a shot of something stronger. He glanced back at Gwen. Probably with.

The waitress came and went. Gwen didn't seem to notice, even when asked directly if she wanted anything. She just pulled her phone out of her bag and placed it on the table, face down.

"It's like, I came here just because she wanted to try it out, and then at the last minute, after I already signed up, she like, fucking bails! What's up with that?" Gwen continued.

"Right," Mel said, just for the sake of saying something.

"So I'm going to be stuck here all fucking night, chatting with a bunch of losers, no offense, because I'm like, too nice to leave. Whatevs. It's not like I don't have better shit to do! I could be at home right now, getting it on with some hot guy! Netflix and chill, right? I mean, don't get your hopes up. I'm not offering." The longer Gwen talked, the more Mel felt like time was lengthening around his table. He'd found himself in a black hole, where time and light were as stuck as he was, with no hope of escape. "It's like, I'm always doing this stuff for my friends and they have no concept of gratitude! I'm like, the giver of my group, you know? There's no fucking way that they would've come here for me. Do you mind if I text someone?"

Gwen was actually looking at him, as though his answer mattered. Mel shook his head. A fresh glass appeared on the table next to Mel and he thanked their server.

"Are you seriously flirting with her right now? OMG, you're totally on a date with me right now! Why are you looking at her!" Gwen rolled her eyes and began to text someone. "I'm telling all my friends what a total dickbag my first date is. Happy, now?"

"I..."

"Just, don't even. I can't even," Gwen sat back in her seat and focused on her phone.

As soon as the bell rang, Mel marked the "No" next to Gwen at table one. He had a feeling he was in for a very long night.

TWENTY MINUTES LATER, Mel sat back with a grateful sigh at the chair in front of Jessie.

"Cheese stick?" she offered.

Mel took one and bit into it, not caring that his previous date gave him a contemptuous glance as the cheese stretched from his lips to roughly the centerpiece. Her name was Julianna and she'd told him that she hated all forms of cheese, and that he should forego any cheese-based appetizers for the rest of the night if he wanted the slightest chance of impressing her. Before Julianna had been Mina who liked the outdoors but hated animals, and before Mina had been Kristen who had broken up with her fiance only two days before, having decided it was time to find a new soul mate. Not to mention Gwen, whom he still considered the worst date of the evening, thus far.

"Things are going well, I take it?" Jessie was obviously fighting to keep a straight face.

"Thanks ever so much for this," Mel said. "I will find a way to repay you, I promise."

"Bring it," Jessie laughed. "Seriously, though. Things may get better before the night is out." She dunked a cheese stick into the cup of ranch and managed to bite it clean through.

"I never much cared for this part of dating, honestly," Mel admitted. He rolled the other half of his cheese stick in between his fingers before checking his thumb for grease. It was mostly clean, if a few crumbs still clung on. "The searching bit? I honestly always thought that if a connection was meant to be, it would just happen. We'd meet in a bookstore, looking through the same section, or she'd be at a con, dressed as one of my favorite characters..."

"She'd ask to be seated in your section three days in a row, asking for plain cheesecake?" Jessie asked. "Love is not a game for the passive player, my friend."

Popping the rest of his cheese stick in his mouth, Mel avoided Jessie's gaze. It was the first time he'd really thought about his relationship with Stephanie as a passive thing; however, now that Jessie had put it out there, it was hard not to see. "You think I should try harder."

Jessie leaned forward, "I've never wavered on my stance that Stephanie was wrong for you, but it was your relationship. How hard did you fight for her? You were upset that she was leaving, but you didn't even ask to delay the concert. You never cancelled an engagement or booked a special suite at a hotel for her. She couldn't cope with sharing you with the band, but from her point of view, maybe you never invited her to."

Mel remained silent, just absorbing this entirely new point of view. He hadn't tried to include Stephanie in his world. She'd been resistant to participate, so he'd let her be. The worse things got, the less he'd tried to talk to her. He hadn't done anything but let her get more and more distant, until one day, she left. He, Mel, had let her leave. One phone call, after she'd already blocked his number; that had been the extent of his chase, and they'd been together for three years.

It was worth some thought.

"So, any of your rejects that you think I might be into?" Jessie asked after a long pause.

"Kristen, table two. She's looking for a new soul mate," Mel suggested, giving Jessie a half smile to show that he understood she was trying to lighten the mood.

"Hmm...soul mate?" Jessie wrinkled her nose. "You know I'm not a creature of commitment."

"She broke up with her fiance two days ago."

Jessie gave a sassy head bob that ran into her shoulders, "Well, that may be worth looking into."

Naturally, she had timed it for Mel's next sip. The next thing he knew, he was snorting vodka and Coke through his nose instead of swallowing it. It burned, but he couldn't stop laughing. That set Jessie off. They nearly missed the dinging of Claire's little bell.

"MY NAME IS NATASHA," the woman at table seven greeted Mel.

"I'm Mel," he said, offering his hand. She didn't take it but sat watching him expectantly.

Natasha had big brown eyes and deep golden hair. She was extremely thin, but it seemed natural rather than unhealthy. Her blue button up shirt looked more like it was for a job interview than a date. Mel wanted to adhere to Jessie's advice and make an effort, but Natasha wasn't giving him a lot to work with.

"What do you do for a living, Natasha?"

"I marry," Natasha said. "I've married three times. Every single one of my husbands left me. I don't want to be alone, so I made up my face, and I came here. No one ever asks for my info, though." Natasha's face started to turn red, and then purple as tears seemingly came from nowhere. "The more I try the worse I feel! Why doesn't anyone want me? Am I unattractive? Do I smell?"

Mel wasn't at all certain what to do. He signaled the waitress and asked for napkins.

His date started to wail. "That's it, isn't it? I smell like diapers and cinnamon! No one wants a woman that smells like me!"

"I'm sure that's not it. I can't smell you at all from over here. I'm sure you smell just fine," Mel tried to make his voice as soothing as possible. A small part of his mind clung to the oddity of worrying about the scent of cinnamon in conjunction with the smell of feces. It was just one more thing in a night of extremely weird human interactions, but it threatened to crack open a safe of manic laughter. He didn't want to be the man that laughed at the crying woman.

"Really?" Natasha sniffed. "You can't smell me?" She was making little hiccuping gulps, now. When the waitress dropped off a stack of napkins, Natasha took one and began dabbing her eyes. "Would... Would you like to smell me? Just to make sure?"

"Um..." Mel gripped the table with his hands to prevent himself from running away. He was pretty sure this was not what Jessie had in mind when she was encouraging him to make an effort. "I don't think that would be appropriate..."

Painted red lips spiked downward as the little resolve left on Natasha's face melted into a shower of salty sobs. Other couples were gawking at Mel and Natasha from their tables, as though wondering what exactly Mel had said to make his date so upset. A few of the men unfortunate enough to have already visited table seven gave Mel understanding nods.

Claire came over and made soothing hush sounds at Natasha, "Come on, Natasha. You're doing really well today. You made it through six whole dates this time! Do you want to go powder your nose, freshen up a bit... Or are you done today?"

"I want... to go... home..." Natasha gulped in tiny gasps taken between sobs. Mascara was creating little smokey rivers down her slim cheeks. She glared at Mel, as though he were the source of all of her grief, beforing pushing away from the table to follow Claire down to the bar. The two women spoke to the bartender, and a large glass of something colorful was presented to Natasha while Claire made a call.

The other couples turned back to their dates in progress while Mel sat in stunned silence. He heard Gwen's voice rise from her corner of the dating arena, "...knew he was an absolute bag of dicks..."

Seven down, he thought as he polished off his third drink of the night.

Chapter Five

LEANING CLOSE ENOUGH to the makeup mirror on the counter that there wasn't much visible past her eyeball, Leah waved her mascara wand as close to her eyelashes as she dared. She managed to dab a line of black on the mirror instead. The mirror had been a gift from Alan's mother a few Christmases ago, "to encourage someone to make more of an effort," or so said the card. Leah considered the splotch on the mirror for a moment, before pushing the wand back into its mysterious, inky home.

"You know what, good enough," she told her reflection.

It was her thirtieth birthday. The Big Three-Oh.

She'd expected to feel different. Somehow, thirty was going to have some sort of magical girl transformation and she, Leah Koziol, would suddenly look and feel like she had her life together. True, she had a real, grown up job. It didn't pay as well as Alan's job did, but roughly forty thousand a year wasn't bad. It was enough to pay off her college loans (granted, a certificate for a travel agent wasn't exactly a doctorate), and had been enough to pay a lot of Alan's expenses before he'd graduated. Her job had kept them afloat in most of the bad times, and now that Alan was making entry level computer engineer money, they had a house. Not the nicest house, maybe, but it was theirs.

In a few years, we could... Leah couldn't imagine a satisfying end to that sentence. In a few years, they could what? Move to a larger house? Go on a mind-altering vacation? She still hadn't managed to talk Alan into going somewhere for a week this year, or even booking something for next year. The half-formed thought echoed in her mind, *In a few years, we could...*

Visions of memories began to slide between her thoughts. The more Leah remembered, the more she felt like she wanted to cry.

After her first semester, she had realized she wanted out of school as fast as possible.Leah had been living in a dorm room, but she'd started keeping a toothbrush at the rental house that Alan and Troy had shared with two other roommates. Alan's plans had included a degree in computer engineering, and he'd been looking to move to Austin or Seattle after graduation. He'd spoken often of getting into game design after college. During those conversations, Leah had determined that her best course was to find something that she could do from anywhere. It seemed quite likely that she and Alan were going to be together for a very long time, and she'd wanted to do what she could to help him pursue his dreams. Even so, she had taken two more semesters of general coursework before she had happened upon the idea of becoming a travel agent. It had appealed to her adventurous side, it had gotten her out of school before her younger sister even started college, and it had had the versatility to go with Alan when he was ready to move.

Only, moving day had never really happened. After Leah had graduated, she'd been hired by a local travel agency thanks to one of Troy's connections. As soon as she had found a job, Alan had suggested moving in together. He had been working part time as a cashier at a grocery store at the time. Those had been some of their best years. She'd immediately loved being a travel agent. When Alan would get home before her and wasn't swamped with homework, he'd greet her with an already set up board game or hand her a controller so they could play Portal 2 or Halo together. When the weekend came, they'd thrown an overnight bag into the car and driven until they'd gotten low on gas, and then they'd spent one or two nights in a hotel. They had gotten engaged and married during the spring break of Alan's senior year. They'd driven to Austin and spent their honeymoon in a chain motel. They had eaten snow cones across the street from some video game development offices, while they'd talked about their plans for the future.

After that, Alan had lost his job. He'd had a professor that didn't like him and he'd had to repeat a class, which had broken their already-strained budget. Troy had moved in with them to help soften the financial burden, but Alan became very prickly toward his brother instead of grateful. Alan and Troy had ended up fighting, Troy had moved back out, and Alan had ended up having to ask his mother for help.

She'd agreed. With conditions.

Debbie Koziol didn't like her daughter-in-law. She was not happy with Alan for having married Leah, and she'd never been happy with Troy for introducing them. Debbie had seen Alan's love of video games and gaming as a serious character flaw. The only way that she'd been willing to help was if Alan agreed to get a job at, as she'd put it, a *real* company.

Leah had argued against it, telling Alan that they could find a smaller, cheaper apartment. She'd offered to ask for more hours or take a second job. There had been other options. Despite the fact that Leah knew her family wouldn't have been able to do much, she'd even talked to her dad about money.

Leah's parents understood. After all, Leah had been named for Princess Leia, but when the nurse had assumed a more common spelling, they'd not bothered to change it. Her little sister, Ellen, was named for Ellen Ripley of the Aliens franchise. Yes, they understood, but they couldn't help.

During that year, Alan had grown a little more fiercely competitive. Gaming against him had been much less fun, and much less frequent. They'd stopped going anywhere on weekends. When Alan had graduated, they'd had another hurdle. He had had trouble finding a job. He'd finally gotten something, but it was far less something than they'd hoped. Alan had spent the next two years at a Starbucks.

Things had gotten better again as far as his competitive edge. Troy was given an apology and had become a regular visitor once more. During his third year at Starbucks, Alan had been offered a promotion. He had quit before his shift was even over.

Unlike the previous time that Alan had been unemployed, Leah had been making enough money to make ends meet. Things had been tight, but it was enough. They'd fought, often. Alan hadn't even discussed whether quitting had been an option, he'd just done it. He'd found an IT job with a small security company, and he'd stayed with them for about a year and a half.

Then Debbie had told them that if Alan didn't find a job that she approved of, she was going to demand repayment. In less than a year, he'd found a computer engineering job at his current office. He'd stopped playing video games that weren't on his phone.

Stop it, Leah tossed her head back and blinked until she was certain she could manage not to cry. *It's your birthday. Cake. Friends. Presents. Fun. That's what today is about.*

Her make-up was minimalist, but she had managed a touch of eyeliner and a bit of blush. It would do. Leah grabbed her favorite pair of army green capris out of the dresser. She'd found them a few years ago at an Old Navy, and they'd achieved that level of worn-in that meant they were probably two sizes larger than the tag indicated. The day that they died on her, she would probably cry. At random, she pulled a t-shirt off a hanger on her side of the closet. It was a sepia-toned shirt with bold brown lettering that read, "Always be yourself, unless you can be Kaylee." Kaylee was underlined with a wrench.

Alan was sitting at his perch, leaning the barstool he was on back onto only two legs. The rich aroma of his favorite coffee blend permeated the air. He was watching some sort of B movie extremely half-heartedly while he jabbed at his phone with his thumbs.

On the leading edge of her early memory storm, the smell of coffee reminded Leah vividly of the happy window of time that they had shared while Alan had been a barista. Floating into the kitchen on a wispy cloud of contentment, she poured herself a mug out of the coffee maker and added her usual amount of sugar and milk. Leah started to smile and tell Alan good morning, when she noticed that he was wearing slacks and a button-down shirt. Again.

"Alan?" she tried to put all of her questions into that one syllable. She made herself walk toward him, though her legs suddenly felt a bit like lead. Her coffee cup sat forgotten on the counter, but going back for it would have taken more energy than she currently possessed.

Immediately, Alan let his bar stool settle onto its front legs, though he didn't bother to look up from his phone. "I know, hun. I'm sorry. It's just a habit, you know?"

"Actually, I was asking about..." Leah reached forward and pinched the smooth, slightly crisp shirt that clutched her husband in a choke hold. "Are you going to the office today?"

His eyes drifted to her fingers. He met her gaze with a reassuring grin, setting his phone on the bar with a thunk. Tapping the spacebar to pause his movie, he turned on his stool, took both of her hands in his. Alan practically beamed at her as he said, "No, Leah-bee, I'm not going to work. Turns out my jeans are all in the wash, and I wanted to be decent when I took you out for your birthday breakfast. Strawberry pancakes?"

"Yes!" Leah agreed hard enough that she bounced off of the floor. The movement reminded her of two things. "Oh! But first, shoes... And coffee..."

She turned around quickly enough that she slammed her shoulder into the bar and nearly fell over the trash can. Her shoulder screamed at her. Massaging the sore spot helped, but there was a dull throb that didn't quite fade, promising to become a bruise later. With a few reassurances tossed in Alan's direction, Leah was ready to bring a little brightness back into her day.

AFTER BREAKFAST, ALAN allowed himself to be towed back to the house and changed into newly washed jeans. Leah found her favorite of Alan's shirts and tossed it on the bed while he was still hiking up his pants. She left the room to start a new load of laundry since the dryer was free. When she came back, she caught Alan pulling the shirt away from his ribs and frowning at it as though it had farted and he was trying to locate its butt.

"Something wrong?" she asked.

"No, nothing," Alan said, still looking a bit unhappy. "I just don't think I actually like this shirt very much."

"Is it too tight? Too loose?"

"Not the fit," Alan shrugged. "It's fine."

It was a black t-shirt with a cutesy version of Cthulhu wearing an apron and chef's hat, holding a tray of steaming cookie skulls. A few years prior, it had been Alan's go-to con shirt. That had been before he stopped going to cons with Leah, but he'd kept the shirt. She'd always kind of assumed that he was keeping it for when he decided to start accompanying her, again. "I... We could find you a different one," Leah offered.

"It's fine. Really," Alan said. "Aren't we supposed to be at Troy's by noon?"

Leah nodded, "Right. Noon."

"OH MY GOD! LEAH! HAPPY birthday! How long has it been!" Anthony, Troy's ex-boyfriend-but-still-good-friend, answered Troy's door on the second knock. "And Alan, of course! So good to see the two of you!"

"Anthony!" Leah reached out for one of the best hugs in the universe. The scent of him invaded her nose as she was pressed into his doughy center; he smelled of fabric softener and blackberry tea. Anthony was the type of person that didn't give a half-hearted hug. He just wrapped his large arms around a person as though they were his favorite human on the planet, and nothing was more important than letting them know that via squeezing. She had cried when he moved out of town, and though they exchanged the occasional text or tweet, Anthony wasn't the best at keeping in touch. "I didn't even know you were in town!"

"You think I'd miss your birthday, sweetie? No, I flew in this morning, and Mr. Illium picked me up. I'm here for a whole week! We'd best be seeing each other for some Wood for Sheep. I want my rematch!" Anthony led them through the foyer and into Troy's living room. His vividly blue eyes twinkled behind his wire rimmed glasses and his ginger beard was well-trimmed, lending his plump face more definition than it held naturally. Even though he was wearing cargo shorts and a plain white t-shirt, Anthony looked like he'd be much more comfortable in a sweater vest and tweed jacket (which to be fair, was what he wore in all of his professional photos).

"When do classes start?" Alan asked. He didn't look surprised to see Anthony, nor did he offer a hug. Leah wondered if the lack of enthusiasm on her husband's part had to do with prior knowledge or a lack of caring. Much like he was with Nessa, Alan had never seemed overly fond of Anthony.

"Too soon, and that's the truth," Anthony's smile didn't dim in the slightest. "This is my last week of freedom before the little freshmen arrive with their starry-eyed dreams and wait for me to tell them that the university is really Hogwarts and I'm a wizard that will send them on a magical journey through learning. It'll be about a week after that that they realize they're actually on a dungeon crawl with a sadistic DM that enjoys making them cry."

Leah laughed.

Anthony continued to guide them from the living room into the den. They had to pass the staircase that led to Troy's office/library. The entire second story was one big great room, nearly the length of the entire first floor. When Troy had first moved in, he'd told Leah that he'd envisioned it as the game room where they could hold their weekly sessions, but things hadn't panned out. They'd had to cancel once, then twice, and by the seventeenth cancelation, Troy had decided to reimagine the space.

It wasn't entirely due to Alan and Leah's schedule, even though Leah felt guilty that they had stopped even checking to see if Troy was available. Originally, Anthony had been a big part of their group, and then he'd gotten hired as a professor at a university in Indiana. Troy had cancelled for almost two months when he'd had a super, mega, ultra-romance with some guy that none of them ever met and apparently never would because it was just a fling that had flung. Nessa had been invited, but it was a night that she already had weekly plans.

In the den, Troy had a print of the TableTop parody of the Last Supper, with the practically faceless Wil Wheaton spreading his arms over the gaming table. On the same wall, framed film posters including Back to the Future, The Last Starfighter, Labyrinth, and the original Tim Burton directed Batman were spaced between small shelves full of gaming manuals. Troy had an entire collection of framed movie posters in the walk-in closet off of his second floor and rotated them when the mood struck. The center of the room was taken up with an old poker table, freshly felted with the graphic of a large d20 showing a dagger on its face.

Compared to the completely normal living room, and the classic dining room around the corner, Leah always felt like this was the room she'd most like to steal. It was pretty close to what she envisioned at the ultimate gaming room, and she loved that Troy had told her not to make any plans for her birthday because they were spending it at the table. This room spoke to her on a level that was almost spiritual. If it had stayed in the large upstairs space, she could only imagine that Troy and Alan would've had trouble prying her fingers off the door frame when it was time to leave.

The doorbell rang again. "Ah, that must be this Nessa person I've heard so much about," Anthony said, grinning at his own joke. In one of those strange twists of fate, he'd known Nessa before she and Leah had accidently met. "You two get comfy, back in a jiff."

Alan gave an odd little grunt and wandered toward the kitchen which was visible from the corner of the den. The dining room was on the other side of the kitchen, and was also accessible through the living room. Troy's bedrooms were down a short hall behind the dining room. His house could easily swallow the house that Alan and Leah owned, but then, Troy had been able to save for much longer and had made some really good investments over the years. Troy's monetary success was part of what had led to Alan's irritation when the three of them had lived together, even though his brother had only moved in as a favor in the first place. With two people Alan didn't much care for, and the party being at his brother's house, Leah was starting to worry about how well her husband was going to behave during her big bash. She quelled a flash of irritation. Alan hadn't said anything yet, and he was probably just getting a ginger ale.

This is your day. Relax. Enjoy it, Leah chided herself.

"Happy Birthday!" Nessa rushed into the room and gave Leah a big hug. She had her long black hair swept up into a wavy ponytail and she was wearing an olive green cami under an old, torn up, gray pirate shirt with a red jolly roger that would've bared her midriff and hung off of one shoulder. Her shorts were a darker shade of green than the cami and stopped a few inches below her knees. They had red scroll embroidery along the seams that picked up the red of the crossed cutlasses and skull. "So," Nessa turned back to Anthony as he walked into the den behind her, "We're all at Troy's house. Where is Troy?"

That was when the sound of a garage door announced Troy's arrival. "I believe that would be him now," Anthony smiled. "He was out procuring sustenance for our festivities."

The garage door began its mechanical groan in the opposite direction, car doors opened and slammed, an interior door squelched its welcome to the master of the house, and then footsteps from behind the stairs. "I'm late! I'm late! But I come bearing pizza, margarita mix, and cheesecake!"

"I say we forgive him," Nessa said.

"Need help?" Alan asked. He set his soda can down on the edge of the gaming table, ignoring the built-in drink holder as he sauntered out into the living room to meet his brother. Leah shifted his ginger ale into the proper spot before it could tip over and soak the felt.

Alan and Troy both came back carrying a few pizza boxes apiece. They had to go back to the car, with Anthony in tow, to finish unloading.

"Things going any better today?" Nessa asked in a soft, not-meant-to-carry, voice.

Leah glanced at the door, checking to see how much time she really had to answer. It sounded like the guys were talking about the twins' mother. She knew that Alan still hadn't told his mother about their fertility results. Given the argument at the Peppers, Leah wondered if that decision had been fueled by denial. It took an effort to bring her brain back into her current conversation. "I... thought so, this morning, but then we had this weird moment when he put on his shirt..."

"Not a sexy moment, I take it," Nessa frowned.

"No..." Leah's time was up. The guys brought in two tubs of margarita mix, three cheesecakes, a large wrapped box, and single foil helium balloon. "Holy shit. Troy, how many people did you think you were feeding?"

Troy grinned at her and handed her the foil balloon, while holding a chocolate cheesecake in the other hand. "Twenty-seven? But seriously, we're gonna need the fuel. I have rigged up one hell of a dungeon crawl for you, birthday girl!"

IT WAS ALMOST 4:00 when Alan's character, a dwarven ranger, fell in battle against the old man that was trying to give them advice.

"How in the hell did the old man in the center of the fricken maze kill me?!" Alan demanded.

"Why do you think an old man is living in the center of something called the Forbidden Maze," Troy responded, his face a mask of DM calm. "It's not because he's a kindly old monk that wanted a life of peace. Why did you attack him?"

"He insulted my character!"

"Babe, he called you stalwart," Leah said, placing her hand on Alan's arm in what she hoped was a soothing gesture. "That's not an insult."

Alan shoved away from the table and crossed his arms, "Maybe it is to my people. Maybe language drift occurred, and now dwarves use stalwart as a synonym for fat. Point is, it's totally stupid that I'm dead right now. Somebody rez me."

Nessa, playing the party healer, examined her spells and shook her head. "No can do. I already used it when Anthony got hit by that goblin golem," she looked from Alan to Troy. "Which, by the way, is still one of the most horrifying things I've encountered in one of these games. Why was there a golem made of smashed-up goblins?"

Troy just shrugged.

"Maybe it's time for a break, anyway," Anthony suggested. He had been holding his character sheet up, looking for a spell that would help them convince the old man to help them, before their ranger had committed suicide via NPC. He hadn't stopped looking for the spell when Alan had fallen, but now that the party was distracted, he'd apparently decided to distract the party. "We're celebrating a birthday, and we've yet to do presents or cheesecake."

Leah didn't entirely like the idea of leaving the table now, even though she had no qualms with the thought of cake or presents. It just seemed unlikely that Alan would want to stay and let her keep playing when he no longer had a character.

Then again, if he's going to be mopey the rest of the night, I could just get a ride home from Nessa. There's no reason that I should let Alan's moodiness ruin my birthday. Even as she thought it, a wave of relief eased a growing tension in her shoulders. *There's no reason I should let Alan's moodiness ruin my fun.* Another wave of tension seemed to ebb. She pushed the realization into a mental filing cabinet to be mulled over later. For now, it was enough to have decided that she was going to game until Troy kicked her out or Nessa got tired.

"Leah already has my gift," Nessa said, sharing a grin with the birthday girl.

"What did you give her?" Alan asked. He was still scowling at the table in general, but Leah thought she detected a slightly sharper edge to his petulance.

"She gave me tickets to the Magical Space Skeleton Army concert on Wednesday!" Leah said. She didn't even try to dial down her excitement. As fresh as the realization was that Alan's resentment shouldn't dampen her evening, she couldn't let him spoil this.

His face started to twist into a sneer, but before he could say anything damning, Troy shot up from his seat and ran over to where his large wrapped box watched them from the dining table. "Not that it's a competition, because I already know I can't beat that, but wait until you see what I got you!"

"Oh, wow! So it is present time," Leah smiled as the sparkling box was thrust into her lap.

"Let me go get mine! Wait, wait, wait..." Anthony's voice got quieter as he half-ran, half-shuffled his way out of the room toward the bedrooms. He could barely be heard by the time he shouted, "I shall return!"

Alan seemed to have a bit of an inner conflict before he shifted in his seat and pulled a folded envelope from his rear pants pocket. He ran his hands over it a few times to try and straighten the wrinkles it had acquired over the course of a day spent pressed against his backside. "I think this may actually be the winner, should this be a competition," he managed to shift his lips into something more friendly than they had been only moments before. Even so, it would be overly generous to call it a smile. "Save mine for last, babe."

Anthony came back in holding a very small box with a very big smile. "It's not much, considering that I am the real gift, but I couldn't come empty handed!" He placed the little box on top of Troy's much larger one.

"You are an amazing present," Leah said. Looking around the table, meeting the eyes of each of her friends and sharing a harder, more hesitant look with her husband, she felt the tears start to threaten a fortress breach at the edges of her vision. "I love you, guys."

"No crying," Troy ordered. "You don't even know what we got you yet. Hint: it's not a puppy."

Leah nodded, and picked Anthony's box off the top of the pile in her lap. It wasn't wrapped, but there was a ribbon that she had to work to untie. Even though she pulled the bow out, it got tangled and wouldn't come undone. She ignored Troy's offer to get scissors and worked the ribbon around a corner until she could slide the entire box free.

Opening it revealed a sew-on patch of a cute Cthulhu sunning on a beach. One of his moustache tentacles held a tropical blue drink with a pink umbrella and a pineapple slice and he was wearing bright yellow shades. As soon as Leah's eyes were on it, she started thinking of all the places she could put it. Part of her wanted to contact the artist and see about using it as her business logo.

"That's amazing! Thank you, Anthony! Where'd you find it?"

Anthony looked a bit smug as he replied, "Gygax Con. I saw it in the dealers' room, and it just seemed to scream at me that it needed you to own it."

She showed it to the rest of the table, where it was met with nods of approval. "Very Leah," Nessa agreed.

Next was Troy's, and Leah showed the silvery, glittery paper no mercy. Troy liked to see how much he could deter people from opening their gifts by finding the paper that would shed the most on his hands while wrapping. The first time that he'd used this tactic on Leah, she'd impressed him with her lack of concern. So, naturally, he'd continued to test her limits.

Troy's gift pushed thoughts of glitter out of her head. It was a hoodie with bloody red handprint; Leah recognized the Skyrim symbol for the Dark Brotherhood immediately. "Oh my god! Troy! This... I've been wanting this for..."

"Yeah, it's been on your wishlist since forever. I figured it was high time someone bought it for you," Troy got up and came around the table to wrap his sister-in-law in a bear hug. Leah still held the hoodie against her chest so that it was like they were hugging the garment as much as each other.

The moment had come to open Alan's envelope. Despite an inner voice telling her not to expect too much, there was something else inside her that triggered a warm wave of anticipation. The scent of freshly printed paper burst forth as she used one finger to tear into the envelope like a letter opener. Maybe, just maybe, Alan had done the unthinkable (for him) and decided to surprise her with the re-quested week's vacation. Flashes of Paris, Hawaii, London and Tokyo frolicked between her eyes and the paper she was unfolding. They all vanished as she translated the words she was reading into actual co-herent thought.

"A night in Galveston?"

"At the Moody Gardens," Alan pointed at the paper. "It's over the weekend, so I won't need to take any time off, and we haven't gone to Galveston in a few years. We'll go tour the oil rig. You always wanted to do that, right?"

Leah wasn't sure she trusted her own voice. Alan had booked a single night in a city they could drive to in an afternoon for her thir-tieth birthday. According to the date on the booking, he'd done so that very morning. Like rubbing salt into the wound, the Orbitz lo-go in the corner told her he hadn't paid any attention whatsoever to conversations they'd had in the past about her job. He didn't have to book through her if he didn't want to ruin the surprise, but to book through an online vendor just stung.

With a single sheet of paper, the person that was supposed to love her most had just told her that he didn't have the slightest clue who she was.

Chapter Six

HELMETS AND MASKS WERE in place, but the rest of their costumes were in the green room during sound checks. Simon, the *actual* sound guy, was performing his pre-show checks, while the lighting crew flashed various bulbs in the band's faces. Mel sang a few bars of "Weird Science," which was the traditional sound check song for the Magical Space Skeleton Army. It was the first song they'd learned to play together back when they'd just been a bunch of high school students goofing around with an Oingo Boingo cover band. Betham and Jessie were adjusting their instruments and performing tuning checks of their own.

Frankie (short for Francesca) Patton, both Tour Manager and Betham's long term girlfriend, stood in the wings. She was older than Betham and Mel by about ten years, while her daughter had just turned twenty in May.

Izzy was surprisingly cool with her potential stepfather only being twelve years older than her. She called Betham her stepdad already, and would sometimes refer to Mel as her uncle. Frankie liked to tell people she'd accidently named her daughter Izzy, because the nurse had misunderstood when she'd told her the baby looked dizzy.

A sharp ringtone cut through the noise of the stage and Frankie pulled her phone free from her denim pocket. Her long blonde ponytail bobbed as she spoke to whomever was on the other end. "Hun, we're doing setup. It's hard to hear you right now," she fluttered her hand toward Betham, who immediately started a riff on his bass. Frankie maintained that it was easier to cut through the bullshit of a business conversation if the person on the other end thought they were interrupting something. "When? Look, I've gotta check with the calendar, but I'll call you back in five!"

Betham dropped his guitar back into its resting position and Frankie jogged onto the stage. The overhead lights caught the rhinestones and studs on her AC/DC tank top. "Guys, they want you for a con in San Antonio in January. Are you interested?"

"AXES?" Mel asked.

"May have been," Frankie said. "I can clarify when I call them back in a bit."

Even with their helmets on, Betham and Mel exchanged looks of excitement. They'd always wanted to get invited to play one of the larger conventions. They'd gotten invited to a handful of smaller cons all across the country and attended those they could.

In his peripheral vision, Mel could see that Jessie was practically vibrating in anticipation. Jessie's favorite part of any convention was the cosplay. She had put together an extremely good Valkyrie after Thor: Ragnarok had premiered and people had begun commenting on her likeness to Tessa Thompson. She also had a costume for X-Men's Rogue based on the 90s cartoon, but she complained that the wig was too hot for summer conventions. "If it's AXES, we are definitely in," Mel said.

"And if it's not?"

There was a longer pause this time. Smaller conventions often popped up around the larger ones, trying to catch some of the overflow as con-goers flooded into a city. Mel recalled one time before they'd hired Frankie, when the three of them had fallen into a trap of a contract stating that they weren't allowed to attend the larger convention as guests because the smaller location had hired them first. Jessie was still handling the occasional email from disappointed fans from that weekend.

"Still a yes," Jessie said, "but make sure we have the option of attending both if we get contacted later."

Frankie didn't spring into action until she had nods of consent from Betham and Mel, too. She'd worked with a few bands before signing on with the Magical Space Skeleton Army, and she knew well how easily the road could wear a band down. Despite being Betham's paramour, she was careful never to take sides or accept the first answer on any question. When Betham was in costume, she didn't even act like they were together. Mel once asked about that, and Frankie had said, "I'm with Betham, not Frimmydukes."

In a professional sense, that was an excellent answer, but it made Mel uneasy. Perhaps it was his own experience with Stephanie, where she had been unwilling to be a part of his life as Lancel♡t, but he wanted someone who was willing to be with him no matter which face he was wearing. Not that he'd pull her out on stage and reveal her identity to the world, but he had a sudden visceral longing for someone who would kiss him as she helped him put on Lancel♡t gear. Mel wanted someone who would suggest lyrics that made no sense because she was half asleep when she felt him getting into bed at 4:00 a.m. after he'd been writing all night. He wanted someone that he could share a knowing smile with in an autograph line because she was sneaking in a magical moment of sanity during the craziness of a signing.

Jessie had been right. He was a creature of commitment. It crashed over him like a soundwave. Mel had no idea who this mythical woman might be, but he was ready to find her.

STEAM MACHINES HAD been running since the opening band had instructed the crowd to give a big cheer to let the Magical Space Skeleton Army know that they were out there. Soft blue lights from overhead gave the mists an ethereal, ocean-like quality, one that Mel generally appreciated much better in videos than in person. His Lancel♡t helmet didn't allow him to see as well as he would've liked. Still, he could see well enough to jog out to his microphone and strike a pose. Betham was running out from the opposite side, striking his own pose on his stage marker.

"Hello, Houston!" Mel shouted into the mic. Between the crowd, the lights and the phantom energy of the two opening acts, his Lancel♡t suit was already moist with sweat. "I am the Knight Commander, Lancel♡t!" He paused to give the crowd's initial cheer a chance to fall.

"I have with me the ever alert, ever vigilant, ever bashful, ever graceful, ever... hairy," Mel exchanged a mock-uncomfortable glance with Betham, as though they hadn't said this in every city they'd visited so far. "Frimmydukes!"

Again, Mel waited for the crowd to have their say. It was an excellent showing in Houston. The theater was packed. Their cheers were like a physical force, and Mel was glad he'd invested in a good pair of in-ear monitors. "And, of course, Frimmydukes and I would be remiss in our duties if we were to neglect introductions to the ambassador of our lovely, er, maybe lovely? Our allegedly lovely homeworld, that we cannot recall but miss dearly," as Mel spoke, he dropped to one knee, and frantically motioned for Betham to do the same. With the helmet on, he couldn't always see if Betham was following the script or not, so he hoped he wasn't just flailing wildly for no reason. "Ladyyyyyy Bug!"

The back curtain was flung open, revealing Jessie and her full wingspan. She stepped in front of her drum kit and spoke into her own mic, "Ever the gentlemen, good Lancel♡t, and brave Frimmydukes. It has, indeed, been long since we've seen our probably beloved homeworld, but it is hard to miss it when we have such a lovely group of beings gathered to listen to us today."

"As you say, Lady," Mel said. "This is probably the best audience we've ever had. What say you, Frimmydukes?"

Betham gave a thumbs up. The crowd rippled almost as much as the waves of mist that surrounded Mel's feet.

"I think we should give this lovely audience what they came for," Jessie said.

"Free beer?" Mel asked.

Betham gave a thumbs up, and someone exceptionally loud screamed, "Hell yeah!"

"No," Jessie said. "I was thinking more along the lines of 'Dweeb Weasels from Space.'"

Through the ear monitors, Mel could hear the crowd beginning a chant of *D'weasels! D'weasels! D'weasels!*

At this point, Betham let loose with the opening chords, leaving Jessie and Mel to ready themselves in a hurry before the drums and vocals joined in. Mel felt the bits of his brain that partitioned off Lancel♡t from his normal life melting as he became the performer he was inside. When he let loose on stage, he felt a calling that had eluded him during other jobs. *This*, he thought. *This is what I was made for.*

THEY WERE NEARLY HALFWAY through the second set, and Mel could feel it. He was singing off of their newest album, a song entitled, "All Hail the Defenders of Mars!" This crowd was his crowd, and this night was his night. Something chemical, something spiritual, something ineffable; he was cocooned in the warmth of belonging in this place, in this time. He couldn't explain it and he wasn't sure he wanted to try. On a wave of adrenaline, Mel tore his mic off the stand and ran off the stage. It wasn't like he couldn't keep up with the others while he was on the move. Taking the steps two at a time, he jogged out into the hall and circled around to the back doors. Two bouncers fell into step beside him, though he almost didn't notice that they'd followed. He needed to be a part of this crowd.

Like high tide, the people around him swelled to fill the space. Faces and hands stretched toward him, blurred by his helmet. "Sing it with me!" he yelled into the mic.

"All hail!"

"THE DEFENDERS OF MARS!"

"All hail!"

"LIEUTENANT ADMIRAL LARS!"

"All hail!"

"THE DEFENDERS OF MARS!"

"Where would those martians be?"

"WITHOUT THE DEFENDERS OF MARS!"

Mel ran his fingers over people's palms like he was testing the water, doling out the occasional high-five or fist bump. Then it happened. Someone, he wasn't sure who, touched the palm of his hand and it was like a bolt of lightning reverberating from the tips of his fingers, threading through his grey matter, lancing all the way to his toes. Intoxicating aftershocks seemed to caress his lips and more personal regions. The performer in him kept him afloat through the end of the song, but his desire was to find that person. Surely, with a spark like that, there was someone else in the room who was feeling every bit as dazed as he did. The desire to yank off his helmet and start looking was so strong that he made himself move back toward the doors. He lingered there, peering through his visor as much as he could until the last note of "All Hail the Defenders of Mars!" and then he hauled ass back toward the stage.

His heart was climbing its way up into his throat. As elated as he had felt earlier, somehow that feeling was now magnified. All of the uncertainty and fears that rose inside of Mel as he thought about the impossibility of the situation were put on hold. For the rest of the show, he had someone to sing to, even if he didn't know their face.

Chapter Seven

WHEN LANCEL♡T LEFT the stage, no one was certain where he was going. Moments later when he came bursting through the door next to the VIP booth that Leah and Nessa were seated in, Leah couldn't believe her luck. Nessa started snapping pictures on her phone, while Leah debated for a moment on what to do. It wasn't until Nessa gave her a gentle shove and mouthed, "Go! Go!" that Leah hopped out of the booth and landed just close enough to the singer that she could join the mass of people that might possibly have a chance to brush hands with the man.

She was not prepared for the surge of emotion that one touch held. Only the press of bodies around her prevented her from dropping to the floor.

Leah was suddenly glad that Alan had refused to come with her. Her hand, and other bits, still tingled with the aftershock of that chemical rush. She'd never sparked like that with anyone before. With Alan, in the early days, they'd definitely shared an attraction, and it wasn't like they didn't have any heat. This had been different, though.

Stop it, Leah, she told herself. *You're just a little starstruck. You're a married woman.*

But for how much longer? a smaller voice asked.

That was her second shock of the evening. She wasn't sure how to respond to the smaller voice. It had been clear that she and Alan had been going through a rough patch, but was she really facing the end of her marriage?

Nessa helped her back into their booth, and Leah was exceedingly glad that they had the sitting room. When they'd first been seated, she'd been a little bummed that they were so far from the stage. Her knees wobbled on her way back up the steps. "You okay?"

It was almost too much. Leah shut her eyes and tried to block everything out, from the spark to her conflicted feelings about her husband. This concert was supposed to be her amazing birthday treat. She was supposed to be having a blast, not on the verge of an emotional breakdown.

Lancel♡t's voice cut through the haze of tears that were starting to form. As he had done many times in the past, without even knowing it, he broke through the heartache and made her laugh as he started singing "Then She Puked on Me." There was a thread of something in his voice that hadn't been there before, but Leah couldn't quite place it.

It's like a vocal hug, she thought, a bubble of giddiness rising from somewhere.

Her thoughts turned back to the spark that she and Lancel♡t had shared. Even if it was all in her head, even if it was just for tonight, she was going to imagine that she was here to cheer on a different kind of man. She would be here for him; supporting, loving, proud.

Chapter Eight

AS MEL STUMBLED HIS way back into the green room after the encore, he released a high-pitched giggle. He felt drunk, or possibly high? It was hard to pin down. *Definitely loopy*, he grinned to himself.

"That was unreal," Jessie said. She was walking more quickly than normal, her wings drifting behind her like sails. It wasn't until that moment that Mel realized his mood had infected his bandmates. "We've got to play Houston again."

"Definitely stellar," Betham's Frimmydukes mask was still on, which made his goofy grin all the goofier.

Mel was content to let his bandmates think that his glow was the same one that they were currently experiencing; it had, after all, been a fantastic show. He'd put everything he had into those final songs, hoping against hope that somehow that one person in the entire crowd would know it was for them. He took his helmet off and placed it on the side table immediately past the door of the green room. He'd have to remember to pick it up again when they left for the dressing rooms.

It was a pretty average green room for a pretty average venue. An old, but mostly clean, sofa, with framed and signed photos of some famous previous performers lined one wall, while the opposite wall had a television. In between the sofa and the tv, there was a wooden coffee table that looked like it had probably come from Ikea. Several more chairs of varying comfort levels were scattered throughout the room. It was obvious that not all occupants of this room were prone to sitting together.

All three of them went straight for the tray of sandwiches that was situated on the coffee table. The sandwiches were chunks of a larger sub, which meant the only real variety came from whether someone decided to add mayonnaise, mustard, or ketchup from one of the little packets that were scattered over one half of the table. Water bottles and paper plates were on the other half. After acquiring a plate, Mel hunted down one of each packet type and began to dribble them over the bread while humming something to himself.

"Dude, are you humming 'Haven't Met You Yet'?" Betham asked, in the middle of doctoring his own sandwich.

Jessie paused, the bit of onion that she'd been pulling out of her own food still dangling from her fingers. She began humming the same song that had absently escaped from Mel's own preoccupied mouth. "Oh my god," she said. "You totally were!"

Mel blushed, but didn't respond. He just placed the top back on his sandwich and shoved it toward his mouth.

Betham removed his mask and leaned forward, "Something happened out there, didn't it? While you were crowd surfing?"

"I didn't crowd surf," Mel said between chews. He could feel his cheeks getting redder. He wasn't entirely sure why he felt as embarrassed as he did. It was probably the fact that he'd been caught humming Michael Bublé immediately following a concert where he'd been singing his own band's songs. *And the closest we've ever come to a love song is one that I wrote for an ex-girlfriend*, Mel thought, as he helped himself to one of the water bottles.

"Crowd swimming, then," Betham said, no less cheerfully. "You came back galvanized, bro. I thought it was just a connection with the masses, but dude... Dude!" Biting into his own sandwich, Betham just beamed at Mel like he'd never been happier for him. Mel found himself smiling back, the momentary embarrassment fading in the light of Betham's approval.

Jessie's food was all but forgotten on the coffee table as she leaned forward in her chair. "So? Spill it, Abrams. What happened out there?"

So Mel told them about the sudden compulsion to be a part of the crowd, the run through the back halls, and the moment that still resonated within his very core. "But there were so many faces, I'm not even sure I saw the person that I touched. How am I even supposed to start looking for her?"

"How do you know it's a woman?" Jessie asked.

Mel opened his mouth, but no words came to him. Jessie's own sexuality was constantly shifting, and on any given day, she was in the mood for something different. *Much like her burrito preferences,* the thought popped into Mel's head unbidden, and nearly made him laugh. He realized he was still feeling a little giddy. "Honestly, I don't know. I've never been drawn to a man that way before, so I assume woman. I've got to start narrowing it down somehow, right?"

"Do you think she's still out there?" Betham asked. "Sometimes people stay back, hoping that the band will visit the merch booth or something."

"I don't know," Mel said. "It's not like I have some sort of radar. Besides, if I do find her while I'm in my Lancel♡t gear, what am I going to say? 'Hello, random fan from most probably Texas! I think we sparked on the concert floor! Come date with me in Indiana! Here is my real name and phone number!" As soon as the words were out of his mouth, Mel wished he could retract them. The reality of finding this one person at a concert over a thousand miles from his home seemed impossible. He no longer felt like humming.

That was when Jessie picked her sandwich back up and began eating with a faraway look in her eyes. "Maybe not that," she said after swallowing her first bite. "This is no good. I'm going to go check with Frankie and see if we can find some post-concert pancakes. Then we can really think."

Dropping her food back onto the plate, she pushed herself up and was nearly out the door by the time Betham and Mel followed suit. Post-concert pancakes were always better than a pile of questionable meat products with some wilting vegetation between bread slices that were an odd combination of plywood and sponge. Despite what many catering venues seemed to believe, subs were better served within an hour of preparation.

Chapter Nine

AFTER THE CONCERT HAD ended, Leah couldn't get out of the auditorium fast enough. While a large number of people headed toward the merch booths and bar, Leah practically dragged Nessa out the door and toward the parking garage where they'd left her car. Even though it had just been a private daydream, and no one knew she'd spent the last few songs of the concert pretending to be involved with a man that wasn't her husband, she felt guilty and embarrassed.

"What's gotten into you?" Nessa asked.

"Nothing," Leah said too quickly. "I... Nothing."

"Leah...?"

Leah dropped her keys as she pulled them out of her pocket. She swore as she nearly fell over trying to grab them off the ground.

Nessa calmly knelt in front of Leah and plucked the keys from her shaking grip. "Leah, come on. I can't let you go home like this. If I do, your husband's just going to say something that wrecks what's left of your evening. There's a Pancake Hut only eleven minutes away. Let's go do some late-night breakfast, huh?"

With a nod, Leah let Nessa bustle her into the passenger side of her own car. They left the radio off on the way to the restaurant, and the silence seemed to help. Nessa allowed the silence to remain unbroken for almost half of the drive. "So, what happened when you touched Lancel♡t?"

Leah only just stopped herself from giving a guilty jump, reminding herself that Nessa was one of the most observant people she knew. Of course she'd noticed that was when Leah's mood had altered. She released a long sigh, and slumped her shoulders, "I was mentally cheating on Alan with Lancel♡t during the last bit of the concert."

"Is that why you're so jumpy?" Nessa was not laughing, but there was a note of glee still evident in her voice. "Leah, you're not a saint! No one who loves you is going to think less of you for daydreaming about being with someone who sings like that."

"It's not just that," Leah said. "We... We had a spark. It was one of those full body lightning bolt types of things."

"Aaaah," Nessa's eyes widened as she took the exit and turned them off of the streets and into the parking lot. "Okay, so that is a bit less daydream, and a bit more physical. But, seriously Leah, your wedding vows aren't going to suddenly turn off your chemical responses. Have you actually ever cheated on Alan?"

"No!" Leah said, both offended and hurt by the question.

"I didn't think so," Nessa said. "I also don't think whatever you experienced tonight makes you a bad person."

They allowed the conversation to lapse as they got out of the car and walked into the overly enthusiastic LED lighting that coated the interior of the Pancake Hut. Several other tables held people that were wearing Magical Space Skeleton Army merch from both this and previous tours. As quickly as Leah had tried to flee the scene, it seemed they were still slower than some. The woman that approached them at the host stand guided them to a separate section, newly opened for the overflow of guests.

"I think," Leah started, but her throat threatened to close up over the words. Still, she was here with Nessa, in the middle of a Pancake Hut that was miles from home and it was the middle of the night. Leah's laminated menu sat untouched in front of her, while Nessa's face was hidden behind her own. If there was ever a good time to be honest with someone, this was probably it. "I think my marriage is about to collapse."

Nessa's menu came down, but the face that it revealed was not at all shocked. If anything, it was sympathetic and solemn.

"It is collapsing, isn't it? Alan and I are about to implode, and I don't know what to do about it," Leah blinked rapidly as the tears started.

She looked away as the waiter came up and asked what they wanted to drink.

"I'll just have water, and she'll have orange juice with ice, thanks," Nessa said.

"With ice?"

"Yes," Nessa assured him. "Orange juice with ice."

Leah gave Nessa a wet smile. "You'd think they would've heard weirder requests."

"You'd think," Nessa got up and scooted into the booth next to Leah, giving her a comforting hug. "Look, no one outside of you and Alan can say when you're over. When was the last time you two talked about your relationship? Like, really talked?"

Skipping past the disaster that was their lunch at Peppers, Leah tried to remember the last real conversation about their relationship she'd had with Alan. She let Nessa hold her, like her mom or sister might if they had been present. Though Ellen wouldn't have let it go this long without at least one, "I told you so." After a while, she pulled away and Nessa returned to her side of the booth.

"It was before the fertility clinic stuff," Leah said. "We were talking about what we'd do with the house to get it ready for kids after they told us everything was fine."

Nessa frowned as she asked, "No plans for if everything wasn't?"

"Alan thought it would be too negative. I think he really believed, well, maybe *we* really believed that if we went in thinking everything would be okay, it really would be," Leah said. "It wasn't, and now, it's really hard to talk about without yelling."

The waiter deposited their drinks and took their orders, disappearing once more through the doorway that led to the other side of the plexiglass wall.

For a moment, Leah watched the waiter bobbing through the other tables, filled with much happier people. She watched a blonde girl use a fork to mime a bomb falling from the sky and exploding upon impact with her plate while the other people at the table laughed. At another, an obvious couple leaned over their table, grinning at each other with that brilliant aura of new love tunnel vision. She took out her phone and tapped on the lock screen. It was her favorite photo ever taken of her and Alan; two days before he had proposed, they were standing together in front of a DeLorean—its door open to reveal its flux capacitor. It was her favorite because Alan had been leaning into her, kissing her cheek, and the picture had caught her mid-laugh. They both looked extremely happy. Sitting in a Pancake Hut, crying to a friend she'd met after the picture had been taken, really brought home to her how long ago those days had occurred.

"So tell me, this thing with Lancel♡t... How long have you been attracted to men in helmets?" Nessa asked. "Is it all men in helmets, or just the ones that sing about saving Mars with a bucket of fried chicken?"

Leah turned her phone back off and stuffed it in her pocket. She was aware that Nessa was giving her an out to move on in the conversation, and she was more than willing to take it. "To be fair, it is a bucket of chicken the size of Phobos."

Chapter Ten

THE NEAREST PANCAKE Hut was only a quick car ride out from the concert venue, and Frankie had decided to go with them now that Betham was Betham again. "We've actually got a day or two of leeway before we have to move on to San Antonio. I figured you guys would want to poke around Texas a little bit. We've got time for pancakes and sleeping in tomorrow."

Frankie was driving, which was only fair since the car had been rented in her name. She didn't mind letting band members drive normally, but she had told them multiple times in the past that she believed concerts were harder on the brain than drugs or alcohol. Even if she hadn't decided to come along, she wouldn't have let them drive after a concert. Riding shotgun, Betham started messing with the car stereo, connecting it to his phone's music. Most of his list included the same bands that Frankie had t-shirts for, which was part of how they'd connected; largely composed of classic rock and metal, with oddities like Oingo Boingo, They Might Be Giants, Tenacious D, and Ninja Sex Party thrown into the mix.

Jessie and Mel sat in the backseat. Mel was reliving the feeling that had fueled him through the end of the concert and hoping that it wasn't going to end as one of those once-in-a-lifetime moments. The more he thought about it, the more impossible it seemed. He hadn't the slightest idea on how to find someone that he'd met in the unlikeliest of circumstances. Looking at Jessie, though, his hopes refused to depart. Her mind was working on the problem, and she wasn't one to be underestimated.

Once they arrived at the restaurant, they were seated in a removed section. There was only one other occupied booth which belonged to two women that were eating pancakes and bacon; one of them was gorgeous with a curtain of wavy black hair, and the other was a super cute redhead. Mel was more drawn toward the super cute redhead, but tonight wasn't about flirting with random women at Pancake Hut. They had to make a plan to find his Spark.

The waiter took drink orders, stopped by the other table to check on the women, asking if he could get the redhead another orange juice with ice. Mel couldn't help but peek back over at the other table after that. The woman with the red hair seemed so sad that his earlier elation felt a little obscene. Her hair was swept away from her face in a sloppy ponytail. Fly away wisps stuck out at odd angles, reminding him a bit of a cat one of his friends had owned when he was younger. Mr. Anderson (named for Neo in the Matrix) had had very pronounced eyebrow whiskers, and occasionally sprouted them from farther back on his head. Her nose had an upturned tip and a dusting of freckles. The dark-haired woman said something, and large hazel eyes swung toward him as Mel suddenly realized he'd passed the time limit for glancing by a few seconds. He looked away in a hurry and hoped he wasn't blushing too hard.

"Mel, did you hear what I just said?" Jessie asked.

"What? No, sorry, I..." Mel fought the urge to look and see if the redhead was still watching him. "I was a bit distracted."

"It might be easier if you just went over and asked her out, rather than having us try to work out your little... problem," Jessie said, sounding amused.

"Not your night for easy romances, bro," Betham said. He was seated on the inside, across from his sister and next to Frankie. Mel hadn't seen him look away from his menu since they sat down, but somehow, Betham still managed to observe, "She's married."

"What?" Mel looked back over and saw the glint of a ring on the significant finger. Even though he was there to focus on someone else, he felt disappointed.

The waiter came back and set down a round of waters, took orders and deposited a check at the women's table. "Okay, so, planning?" Mel forced his mind back to the reason they'd escaped the venue in search of pancakes. They were going to have to go back later and do final sweeps, but Frankie's lieutenant was a very thorough guy, and all of their roadies were veterans from the last tour with the Magical Space Skeleton Army. It was unlikely that anything, including Betham's stool, would get overlooked.

"Planning," Jessie nodded. "We had a full house tonight; that's twenty-four hundred people. You were in the crowd for maybe a minute? How many people do you think got close enough to touch you?"

This time when Mel glanced at the other table, it was to make sure they didn't seem to be eavesdropping. They seemed to be deeply involved in a debate over who was going to pick up the check, so the risk of being heard was minimal. He opened his mouth to respond, but Frankie interrupted.

"Wait. What're we planning?"

"We're going to help Mel find his true love," Betham said. "They met tonight, but he's got no clue who she is, or even where to start looking. It's all a bit Shakespeare, right?"

"He met his true love? Tonight? When? You guys were kinda busy from what I could see," Frankie looked as perplexed as it was possible to get. They were going to have to tell her the whole thing from the beginning. Luckily, the redhead and her dark-haired friend were getting up to leave. That would make it easier to talk freely.

"I didn't meet anyone. Not really... I... I had... one of those..." Mel winced at the way this was coming out. Frankie's no-nonsense attitude and the age difference between her and his friends sometimes intimidated Mel in a way that never seemed to trouble Jessie and Betham. Likely, they were used to Brock Dallas, and thus no one else in the world would ever be intimidating by comparison. Mel's father was about the same height as Mel, with even less muscle mass; Patrick Abrams wasn't even intimidating to the fourth graders that he taught. Mel's mother was rarely intimidating, though the times that Mel had seen her lose her temper stood out in his mind as the stuff of nightmares. Sloane Abrams was a loving mother and supportive wife. She worked as an optician in an optometrist's office. As much as Mel loved his parents, they hadn't really given him much help with self assertion.

"He had one of those sparks that zing like a lightning bolt," Jessie said. Mel nodded and offered her a grateful smile.

"Ah," Frankie said. She sipped her water and pursed her lips thoughtfully. "One of those. And so the three of you are here to figure out how to woo this faceless damsel?"

"Not woo," Betham said. "Find. He's on his own for the actual romance of the thing, but if we can set my bro off on the course to find his lady love, we'll all be cheering for his success, no?"

"What if this faceless stranger didn't feel anything? What if you guys figure out a way to contact this person and find out they are like that redhead you were eyeing earlier? Already attached or not interested? Is this one spark worth putting in the effort of your entire group? What if you do find this person, hit it off, and she wants you to leave the band?" Frankie asked. "I know I'm coming off as a bitch for even asking, but have you guys really thought this through? If you never find this person, are you going to blame your bandmates for a lack of trying?"

No one responded immediately to the onslaught of questions. While Mel's first instinct was to deny that there was any likelihood of failure, and no possibility of splitting up the band, he also knew that Frankie had been in the business a lot longer than anyone else he knew. Her last band had broken up due to some sort of falling out, though she'd never gone into the details with Mel. Betham likely knew the whole story, but he didn't share a lot of what Frankie told him in private.

While they were still sitting in silent contemplation of Frankie's questions, their plates of pancakes, French toast, eggs, hash browns and Betham's burger arrived. "Honestly, I don't think I'd blame them for this not working any more than I blame Jessie for that abysmal night we spent speed dating," Mel said, picking up the maple syrup and pouring over his French toast. "If not for Betham, I'd still be serving at Cheesecake Haven, waiting for my life to go somewhere. Jessie pointed out to me recently that I'm too passive, and I'm just beginning to work that out. I need to take this chance, and I know it's going to take a lot of work. If they are willing to help me, I'm grateful, beyond grateful, to have such good... not good, great... friends. Should we actually manage this, find this impossible person, and then find out that it's not going to work out because she's involved or that first spark was a fluke... Well, at least I'll have actually tried. I won't have left it to fate and missed out on discovering the end of the story. I will know that I made an effort."

"Jeez..." Frankie's fork dropped from her fingers and she blinked a few times as she looked from Mel to Betham and back again. "It's no wonder you wanted him for your front man, babe. My panties nearly dropped after that."

Mel felt his cheeks reddening and he shoved a forkful of syrupy sweet French toast into his mouth to give himself something else to focus on. It was his bashfulness that had brought on the idea to follow in the footsteps of bands like KISS and the Blue Man Group and perform in costumes that hid their true identities. It was kind of fun, having a secret identity, honestly. If he'd received superpowers at the same time, it would've been all of his childhood daydreams come true.

"And it's not like Betham and I can really complain, since we recently ambushed Mel and told him to start dating again," Jessie said.

When Frankie looked like she was going to interject, Jessie hurried to continue, "So now that we've cleared that hurdle, we need to get started on the next part. How many people do you reckon were close enough to touch you? One hundred?"

Recalling the sea of blurred faces and hands wasn't difficult. Trying to remember how many had actually been able to reach him through the barrier that the bouncers had created was harder. "Maybe? Probably somewhere between fifty and one-fifty."

"Those doors that you popped out of; those are right in between the main floor and the VIP section," Frankie offered. "I'm not sure how much that helps, but if the person you're looking for was in the VIP seats, you could likely put up some sort of give away for anyone with proof of VIP tickets. Then you'd get some addresses and names."

"Good thought," Jessie said. "Betham?"

"On it," Betham whipped out his phone and began typing. "Vippers prize for addies."

"Maybe we could say I was another fan that dropped something in that area, and ask if anyone's seen a watch or wallet?" Mel suggested. "We may get a few people on our social feeds that admit to being in that area."

Betham tapped that out with his thumbs, and then continued tapping for far longer. "Social media concert tags, #Lancel♡tonthefloor, #ReceivingLancel♡tsColors, #Lancel♡tHighFive."

"The tags are an excellent idea, B," Jessie grinned. "I can work something official out on that tonight before I turn in. We may get a pretty good scope of the crowd if someone was standing in the right place."

As they continued to brainstorm into the early hours of the morning, Mel started to feel like things weren't as hopeless as he'd originally assumed. *Nothing like amazing friends and French toast to make the impossible seem achievable*, he smiled to himself as he finally flung himself into bed that night.

Normally, nights on the road held a soft pang of loneliness for him, but not tonight. Tonight, he was drifting off on a cloud of happy anticipation.

THE NEXT MORNING, MEL was checking his phone for messages. He didn't normally pay much attention to his social accounts, but he did occasionally use them to look in on the Magical Space Skeleton Army and the D'weasels. True to her word, Jessie had put a call out to the D'weasels asking them for their pics of the concert, including the hashtags #HoustonDweasels, #MagicalSpaceSkeletonArmyinHouston, or #Lancel♡tinDweaseltown.

Mel understood the need to keep things discreet, but he wished the call to action was a bit more compelling. *Then, again, maybe it is enough*, he thought. *If I went to a Weird Al concert and he had a post asking for any of my pics, I'm sure I'd respond. Not that we're anywhere close to Weird Al in terms of talent or anything.*

A few text messages came in letting Mel know he was on his own for the day. Betham and Frankie were driving down to Galveston to spend the day together on the beach, while Jessie had met someone that she wanted to spend her own special time with. The pang of loneliness that hadn't made itself present the night before threaded its way into Mel's chest and nestled in, becoming like sandbags in his lungs.

Another message caught his eye in the scroll of personal messages that were also slightly impersonal. A friend from college, Ray Neumann, had apparently moved out of Philadelphia and opened a burger place in Houston. Ray and Mel had met during their freshman year in a short-lived roleplaying club which had never really found its feet, but a few of the members had continued to hang out for the next few years; they'd held 80s movie marathons and fighting game tournaments on weekends rather than going to the regular keggers and parties. Ray had moved to Philly for a job, gotten married and had a kid. They hadn't really gotten to hang out in years, but still, Mel thought it'd be nice to stop in and see the new business.

He checked both Uber and Lyft; the Lyft driver had a better rating and came in at a cheaper estimate. Mel confirmed his choice, grabbed his stuff (checking to make sure his keycard was in his wallet), and headed down to the lobby. As late as they'd stayed up the night before, his day was starting at about 11:00. Not his latest start ever, but it was a shame on what looked to be an amazing day outside.

Exchanging absent-minded pleasantries with the driver, Mel watched the city slide by through the windows. The shopping center that held Escape from Philly Burger looked a lot like every other shopping center in Urban America. It was a little early for the lunch rush, it seemed, but there were several cars parked outside; Mel grinned at a blue Chevy Cruze that had a Police Box decal on the back windshield. *Very apropos*, he thought as he pulled the door open.

If the name hadn't already told Mel that Ray was very much the same man he'd known in college, the interior would've reassured him. Everything about this place, from the Snake Plissken mural to the burger names, put Mel back into those crowded college dorm rooms where he and five or six friends would crowd onto a futon or curl up on the floor to watch cheesy 80's action movies on an old CRT TV. It made him feel old to realize that when he was in college, Netflix was still mostly a DVD subscription through the mail. That thought fled his head as he realized the woman in the back booth was the same redhead he'd seen at the Pancake Hut the night before. Ray was sitting with her, and she was crying.

Chapter Eleven

LEAH'S NIGHT HAD NOT gone well after Nessa dropped her off from the concert.

Alan had greeted her at the door with thunderclouds rolling behind his eyes. "Why are you so late?" he'd demanded as she walked in. "I thought you'd be home more than an hour ago."

"Nessa and I stopped for pancakes," Leah said. She wanted to roll her eyes or sound exasperated, but she only felt tired. After the freedom she'd felt at the tail end of the concert, it just wasn't in her to get mad. She wasn't even sure what to be mad about yet, aside from the fact that Alan was angry at her. Opening the cupboard and pulling out a glass, Leah pushed it under the spigot in the front of the fridge. It wasn't so much that she was thirsty, but she wanted something to do with her hands while Alan fumed. Some distant part of her recognized it as the chipped topaz glass which was originally part of a set that they'd been given as a wedding present. Its partner had broken a long time ago, and even though this one was chipped, she had never gotten rid of it. "There was also an encore, so I'm not sure why you thought I'd be home earlier."

"I wish you'd stop hanging out with *her*," Alan sneered, making the pronoun sound somewhat vulgar. "She's a bad influence on you."

While Leah had known that there was no warmth between her husband and her friend, Alan's verbal attack took her by surprise. "What?"

"She's trying to break us up. She always has been. I know she has you fooled, but I can see it. It's in the way she keeps getting you to go to those juvenile conventions and these stupid concerts. You'd have grown out of this shit by now if she didn't keep dragging you in,"

Alan's tone was not only indignant, but slightly smug. He had a look on his face like he'd just made a point that couldn't help but wake Leah up to what she'd been missing.

Well, in a way, he wasn't wrong.

"You think that Nessa is the reason I haven't 'grown out of this shit'? Alan, you used to love 'this shit'! 'This shit' is how we got together in the first place! Your brother is still into 'this shit'! How the fuck do you think I feel when you call the stuff I love shit? How the fuck would you react if I suddenly accused your friends of trying to break us up? Wait, I don't even know any of your friends, because they're all 'buddies from work' that I wouldn't be interested in meeting!" Leah wasn't even really paying attention to the words as they sprung from her mouth, but as they flew forth, she realized it was true. Alan had been keeping her separate from his work life. "Wait... you think I'm embarrassing. It's not that I wouldn't be interested in meeting them, you're embarrassed that they would find out I'm nerdy."

Alan's face changed from triumphant anger to only slightly petulant. He rolled his eyes, "I wasn't going to say it, but yes, Leah. I find it embarrassing that my wife hasn't grown up. You still wear those stupid geek t-shirts like a fucking uniform. My colleagues with stickers on their cars have them because they have kids. Kids will never be our excuse, though, will they? Because you can't have them, and I think you're even happy about that! Why be a mom when you'd have to grow up to do that?"

The glass in Leah's hand fell to the floor and shattered. She wasn't even entirely aware if she'd dropped it or flung it. She didn't even care. "You dare... After all these years, you dare... You let your mom dictate decisions that affected both of us, even though we could've paid her back with interest by now if you cared to...You quit jobs without telling me! You let me pay off the majority of our bills for years, until she gave you an ultimatum. Then, when you finally get what she's willing to call a 'real' job, you buy a car we can't afford yet on the day you get hired! You insult my friends, my clothes, and tell me that I'm too embarrassing and juvenile to meet your work buddies that you've known for all of five minutes. Then you shit on me for not being able to have your fucking kids like I'm some sort of faulty brood mare..."

Leah's vision was blurred by a shield of burning, livid tears. She felt like stabbing something, but luckily for Alan, she was grown up enough not to give in to her base desires. "You're wrong about Nessa, by the way. She told me to sit down and talk to you, *like adults*, about the state of our marriage. Instead, I come home from the best birthday present I received this year, to get dressed down in a tantrum thrown by my husband because he thinks *I'm* the childish one."

She and Alan didn't move from where they seemed rooted to the floor. It was out there, now. All of it. The years of resentment and change. Somewhere, in the depths of her heart, Leah still loved him, and that was why it hurt so much. If she'd fallen out of love before it reached this point, his words wouldn't have hit so hard. Echoes of similar pain drifted over Alan's face. Once they moved, this wasn't just an argument that they had when she got home and they were both tired. It wasn't something that they both dreamed and would forget in the morning.

"I think we should get a divorce," Leah said, knowing that if she didn't say it soon, Alan might. Somehow, she felt it would be so much worse if he said it.

Alan nodded and grabbed an overnight bag off of the dining table. It had been there since she opened the door, but somehow it hadn't occurred to her that it existed until the moment he grabbed it. "I'm going to stay at Troy's tonight. He's already expecting me."

Leah still didn't move from her puddle of spilled water and broken glass until the sound of Alan's Lexus made it out of the driveway and the garage door was humming its way shut. Then she carefully walked around the scattered shards and retrieved a broom and dust-pan from the laundry room section of the garage before she set to work sweeping up the pieces.

WAKING UP IN AN EMPTY house, and an empty bed, had been achingly strange. It wasn't like the occasional business trip or out of town convention that Alan hadn't followed her on. There was a sense of finality to the emptiness. A part of Leah still hoped that Alan would burst through the door, holding a bag of doughnuts and a rose bouquet, begging her forgiveness, and telling her that it was all a big misunderstanding. She knew it wasn't, and he wouldn't, but the hope was there.

Her phone rang with his ringtone, and he told her to meet him at such and such an address. He'd made an appointment for them at 9:30 with a divorce lawyer. Leah breathed a mental sigh of relief that they'd never bothered to get a joint checking account. The one time she'd brought it up, Alan had refused, saying that it made no sense to open a new account that far into their marriage. He'd pay for the house and his car, and she could pay for electricity and her car. They were on the same insurance plans. That'd have to be dealt with, but aside from the house, they didn't have much to divide. Leah spent an hour going through each of the rooms and making a list of what she wanted to keep: her car, her bank accounts, her computer includ-ing desk and chair, the game systems and television, her clothes, her books and DVD/Blu Ray collection, a few of their boardgames, and that was about it. All of their furniture was made up of pieces they'd purchased together; sometimes new, sometimes second-hand, but al-ways together. She didn't even want to fight him for the house. It was *their* space. In her head, it would always be *their* space. Leah didn't want to live with the ghost of man that wasn't dead.

Texas was a no-fault state, so the fact that Alan had phoned her was something of a concession. His lawyer, a sturdy man wearing a crisp, button-down shirt that strained a bit around his beer belly and a thinly striped tie, asked them if they wanted mediation. Alan didn't look at the lawyer or at Leah. Leah just passed her slip of things she wanted to keep to the man, and said, "This is all I really want. He's welcome to the house."

The lawyer read over the list and made a few notes. His thinning hair wisped in the breeze of the fan behind his desk as he passed the list to Alan, who scanned it, and hesitated. "Give her the autograph collection. It means more to her," he said after a moment. "Otherwise, seems fair."

A lot of documents were processed and signed. Each of the documents was explained in so far as necessary (sign on this line and initial here) as it was pushed toward her, but most of it just seemed to turn into buzzing as it floated through Leah's ears. Yesterday, she'd been looking forward to a concert. Today, the concert was over and her marriage had ended. The ink would be dry by lunch.

"You'll have at least sixty days to appeal, should things change, and you wish to remain married. We will be sending you each a copy of the paperwork by mail. Ms. Koziel, please let us know once you have a new address in place," the lawyer said. "Once again, I'm officially Mr. Koziel's lawyer and this is being filed as uncontested. I'm not allowed to offer you any legal advice, Ms. Koziel."

Leah's latent neurons fired into place and she pulled her wallet out of her purse. She always had one of Ellen's cards on hand, and this seemed like a good time to use one. "Actually, if you would, send the paperwork to my lawyer's office. She'll make sure my affairs are in place. It all looked good to me, but, you know..." she said with a shrug.

Even though Alan's lawyer was officially not allowed to give her legal advice, he seemed relieved when she passed him the card. Ellen's specialty was actually criminal law, but he didn't know that off of the card. Leah would have to let her sister know that her divorce paperwork would be inbound. She knew Ellen wouldn't mind. Even though Leah was the older sister, she had standing orders that she was to call Ellen for so much as a parking ticket, and Ellen never thought that Alan was good enough for her big sister. Thinking over the last few years, Leah felt that her super kickass little sister might have had a point.

As they left, Alan told her to take her time packing. "Up to two weeks, if you need it," he said.

Leah got into her car at 10:48 a.m. She pulled out her phone and saw three missed calls. Two were from Troy, and one was from Anthony. No texts, and no voicemails. Dialing Troy's number, she felt her stomach twist. She had wanted to call him the night before, to find out when exactly Alan had decided he was staying over, but after cleaning the glass, she'd just crawled into bed.

"Leah, is it true?" Troy's voice was angry. Hurt.

"Yes. Alan and I are just leaving the lawyer," Leah wanted to start crying, but she could tell that Troy wasn't feeling sympathetic.

"So you did cheat on my brother?"

"What! No! Is that what he said? I thought you were asking if it was true we were getting a divorce!" Leah was stunned. She was glad she hadn't started the car yet, because she would've yanked the steering wheel into someone or something had the car been in motion.

"So there's nobody else. This just happened," Troy demanded.

All at once the spark that had occurred at the concert sprung into her mind, and a deep flush of shame ran through her body. "There's nobody else," she managed, though the emotions were starting to clog her thoughts and tighten her throat.

"Oh my god," Troy said from the other end of the phone. "Leah, I wanted so much for him to be lying, but I... I don't believe you.

I... We're done. You're not my sister anymore, and certainly not my friend. A friend wouldn't do that to my family!"

Before Leah could protest, the phone went silent. She tried calling back three times, but it kept going directly to voicemail. She wanted to call Anthony, but she was afraid that he'd heard the same story from Alan, staying at Troy's and all. Nessa had told her that she would be busy until noon and wouldn't be able to answer her phone. *Ellen or Mom and Dad*, Leah thought, but they all lived far enough away that they'd feel horrible about not being close at hand. Her mom and dad would probably load up the car if she tried to talk them right this minute. If she told them about Troy's accusation, her dad might even try to bring his bat'leth, even though it was purely decorative. Ellen *would* bring the bat'leth. And probably some lube and firecrackers, besides. It was sorely tempting to call Ellen. Leah still needed to let her know about the paperwork, too. She just wasn't ready for the big "I told you so," that a conversation with Ellen would include.

Instead, Leah started up her car and drove to Escape from Philly Burger. She didn't know the owner personally, but he was the friend of a friend, and that seemed like the best she was going to get at the moment.

"HEY! YOU'RE NESSA'S friend!" the owner greeted Leah as she stepped up to the counter. He was maybe an inch taller than Leah, and his build was that sort of wiry, muscled look that she usually associated with mechanics. A momentary curiosity about his life before opening this restaurant allowed her enough brain capacity to respond with something other than outright weeping.

She managed a miserable nod and a bit of a smile.

"You look like you've been put through the wringer," he observed. With a quick assessment, he pushed away from the counter. "Got a little time? I'm not a bartender, but you look like you could use someone to talk to. I'll draw you up a milkshake and you can tell me about it, between customers."

"Thank you," Leah said, with more feeling than even she was expecting.

"Don't sweat it," he gave her a bit of a goofy grin. "I've been down and out before. Didn't catch your name the other day."

"Oh, right. I'm Leah..." Even as she offered her hand, Leah cut herself off before giving her last name. It hadn't even occurred to her yet that she might not be calling herself Koziel much longer. Did she want to go back to her maiden name?

The man behind the counter didn't seem bothered in the least by her omission. He gripped her hand firmly, and said, "Ray. Nice to meet you, Leah. Chocolate or triple chocolate?"

"Triple?"

"Standard chocolate, I start with chocolate ice cream. Triple, I throw in chocolate chips and syrup, for a little extra something," Ray grinned. "It's my wife's favorite."

"Triple," Leah said. For a moment, Leah entertained the idea of inviting Ray and his wife to the next session in Troy's game room; then reality seeped its way back in and she felt the dejection and betrayal all over again. She herself would likely never sit in that room again. Ray instructed her to take a seat in the back booth that she'd been in before, and he would meet her with the shake.

Once she was nestled in the booth, Leah couldn't hold back the tears any longer. They started to splash down her cheeks like jellybeans in a dispenser. Ray had barely settled himself, placing the shake in front of her when the door chimed. Ray gave her an apologetic look, his brown eyes crinkling at the corners.

When he looked up, his face changed from sympathetic to outright astonishment. "Holy shit! Mel! Mel Abrams? What the hell are you doing here?" He sounded both astonished and happy. He jumped out of his seat and all but ran across the shop to give the man standing there a huge bear hug.

Leah sipped at her shake, enjoying the way the chocolate melted over her tongue and seemed warming despite being part of something inherently cold. Her divorce was probably going to make her gain twenty pounds, but she didn't feel like that much mattered at the moment. She might care when she didn't fit in her favorite pants anymore, but that would be at least a few months down the road.

If Ellen saw those papers before Leah called her, there would be hell to pay. At the very least, she'd need a head's up. While she was alone in the booth, Leah pulled up her sister's number and sent a quick text: *Expect my divorce papers to come to your office, probably today. ♡ you. Will call later, promise.*

After a few more seconds, she sent another: *Haven't told Mom yet.*

Ray and the newcomer were talking more quietly now. Something about college in Indiana, but Leah was trying her best to be polite and not eavesdrop. It was hard enough having come here when she didn't really know Ray; having him abandon her for someone he hadn't seen in a long time was just emphasizing to her how ridiculous it had been for her to come crying to him in the first place. She could have gone to buy boxes and start packing. She could have driven down to Galveston and just watched the waves lap at the beach for a few hours, and maybe she would've already called Ellen and her parents. Maybe she should've called Anthony back and gotten that over with.

While she was ruminating on her next step, which she thought should probably be to pay for actual food and give Ray an outlandish tip for being so understanding, Leah became aware of that buggy sensation of being watched. Ray and his friend were still talking, but his friend was looking at her like he'd been hit by a bus. He looked oddly familiar to her. Had they met and she was blanking out on his face? It was weird how much she felt like she knew him; his short brown hair was only slightly too curly to be called wavy, he had a thin frame, and he was taller than Ray by almost a full head.

If I weren't married, I'd find him downright adorable, Leah thought, right before it occurred to her that she *wasn't* married. Even that realization pained her, but it helped her to recognize the new-comer. It was the guy that Nessa had pointed out in the Pancake Hut after the concert.

"It seems you have an admirer," Nessa had said, after refusing to let Leah pay for her portion of the bill. Leah had caught the guy looking, but still thought it more likely that Nessa was just trying to distract her from the discussion of payment. As upset as she might have looked last night, and as upset as she knew she looked now, he probably wasn't brimming with admiration. *For the best*, Leah sighed. *I'm a fucking mess right now.*

The door chime went off and a group of seven people started piling through the door. Ray, seemingly feeling that he shouldn't leave either of his unexpected visitors alone, towed his college friend over to Leah's table and made hurried introductions. "Leah, this is my good friend, Mel. He and I were in the same gaming group back in college. Mel, this is Leah. She's having a really bad day, so can you keep her company? Duty calls." Without waiting for either of them to respond, he rushed through the doors that led into his open kitchen.

"I'm sorry," Mel said, his cheeks coloring slightly as he started edging back. "I don't want to intrude on anything. The last thing you probably need is a stranger, right?"

"No, it's okay," Leah heard her own voice responding. She hadn't been aware that she'd made the decision that this guy was okay, but she'd been willing to talk to Ray who was a virtual stranger. Why not switch him out for this Mel guy that apparently was fond of gaming and probably liked one of her favorite bands, what with the timing of his Pancake Hut visit the night before? "I honestly don't know Ray all that well either. Were you at the Magical Space Skeleton Army concert last night?"

Mel had a flash of emotion cross his face at the question. Hesitation? Panic? It passed too quickly for Leah to quite register it. "Yes," he said. "I was there. Did... Were you there?"

Leah nodded, and gestured toward the seat Ray had vacated, "Please, sit. It's weird having you lurk over my table."

Chapter Twelve

TALKING ABOUT THE CONCERT would be hazardous, given Mel's horrible poker face, but it was obvious that Leah's mind was elsewhere. He hated to see anyone cry, let alone someone he was attracted to, whether they were married or not. "So, what brought you to see Ray?"

"Oh, you know... Life falling out from under me. Nothing huge," Leah attempted a smile but it fell flat. "Sorry. I was trying for brave humor, but that sounded melodramatic even to me. You can't possibly want to listen to me cry about my problems, though. Didn't you come here to visit your friend?"

Mel wanted to reach for her hand, but he didn't know this woman well enough to guess how she'd take it. He glanced at the kitchen where Ray was flipping burgers and dunking the fry basket next to his line cook. The door chime announced another table of customers. "Ray seems busy enough at the moment. Look, I'm a total stranger. You don't know me, and I don't know you. Instead of looking at that as a hurdle, how about we treat it like an opportunity. You can tell me whatever you want as long as we're in this booth, and I'll take it to my grave should you wish it. No judgement, no strings. I live in the Midwest, so you probably won't even see me again. Here," Mel pulled out his phone and turned it off. "I'm at your mercy."

Leah let out a laugh that stroked Mel's nerves like a finger on a kitten's back. He wanted to hear it again, but he pulled himself away from that desire. *Married,* he reminded himself, even as Leah said, "You must have some sort of white knight syndrome or something. What could you possibly get out of hearing me complain?"

There was no clear answer to that, so Mel just shrugged.

A moment of silent appraisal passed between them, while Leah seemed to be weighing his offer.

"Okay, I'll tell you all about it," she said. "But only..."

Leaning in closer to the center of the table, Mel waited for the ultimatum that would ruin this moment. Was this the point he'd reached with every woman since Stephanie where he couldn't even imagine being friends with this person? He didn't want that. There was something about Leah that he found very comfortable. Even if he couldn't be with her, he liked being near her.

"Only if you let me buy you lunch," Leah didn't smile, but the sides of her mouth tugged at the corners like she wanted to forget how miserable she felt.

Awash with relief, Mel agreed. Leah made him stay put so as not to lose their booth while she got in line. She came back almost immediately to ask what he wanted. The smell of burgers frying permeated the air, making it hard to choose just one, but he had to go for the Weird Science burger when he saw the name. It took all that he had in him not to start humming the song.

Reading from the menu, Leah seemed entranced by his selection. "Turkey, beef, and bacon patties, mixed with Old Bay seasoning and a touch of dill. Topped with white cheddar, ranch, pickles and extra bacon. Dude, how did I not see that last time? It definitely sounds bizarre enough for that name."

She got back in line, spoke with Ray for a little bit, pulled out a twenty and stuffed all her change in the tip jar, plus a few extra bills. Mel grinned and turned back into the booth so she couldn't see him watching. It seemed Leah was the generous type, which made Mel feel loads better about her and whatever it was she was about to tell him. As she was sitting down, she slid the receipt where they could both see the big number printed at the top. "Don't let me miss our food, okay?"

With an affirmative from Mel, all that was left was for Leah to launch into her story. Which she did. She told Mel about meeting her best friend at a sandwich shop during her freshman year, and how he had introduced her to his brother, Alan. She talked about how they had dated for a couple of years, and how she had imagined that was going to be the way they were for all the years to come. Then she talked about the jobs, and how Alan had started to change into a person she didn't know so well. A loan from Alan's mother, and a fight between the brothers, segued into how Alan had slowly started pulling away from the things that they had in common. When Leah got to the part about how she and Alan had been trying to have kids, Mel felt a little uncomfortable, but then tears started forming as she poured out the story about her infertility and Alan's reaction. *I may have a bit of that white knight syndrome*, Mel thought, as all he wanted to do was wrap his long arms around Leah until she could forget all about it. That wasn't the end, though, as she continued on to how Alan had ambushed her the night before, and how it had all ended with a visit to a divorce lawyer that very morning.

Ray had delivered the food to their table quietly enough that Leah hadn't even seemed to notice that she'd already eaten most of her fries until she stopped talking. Mel felt as though a spell had broken and it no longer shielded their table from the rest of the restaurant.

"Sorry, I'm sure that was way more than you thought you were asking for." Leah bent her head down so that her bangs drooped over her eyes.

"Hey, I volunteered, right?" Mel said. He grinned and took a bite of his burger. The burst of smoky, cheesy, sour spice nearly made him go cross-eyed with flavor euphoria. He offered her his food. "If talking about it didn't help, take a bite of this. You'll forget about everything, I promise."

Leah looked at Mel quizzically, though she did accept the proferred sampling. Her eyes bulged a bit as the cacophony of flavors flooded her mouth, and Mel was privately pleased that she'd let him share. Jessie was the only woman outside of his family that had never complained about possible germs when he just wanted someone to taste something. "That is probably the best burger ever," Leah said. "But, seriously, are you this nice to everyone? You just spent," Leah checked her phone, "nearly an hour listening to me vent about my life."

"In exchange for probably the best burger ever," Mel pointed out. Before Leah could accuse him of ducking the question, he continued, "In all seriousness, though... No, I'm not this nice to everyone. I like you. Not that I'm about to ask you out on the same day you get divorced, or anything."

For a few awkward moments, the words just hung in the air. Mel couldn't believe he'd just come out and said something like that. *I like you*, had just rolled off his tongue as though the words had been planning a prison break and found their opportunity. He wanted desperately to find a way to suck them back out of existence. Fear kept his eyes suction cupped to his cardboard tray of food.

"You... like me?" Leah's tone of voice was unreadable.

Mel wished he had the guts to meet her eyes, to look her in the face, but the situation was just so impossible. Not only was she so freshly divorced, but he'd mounted the initiative to search for his Spark only hours before. *Jessie keeps saying I'm a creature of commitment, too*, Mel stuck a fry in his mouth and chewed miserably.

"I don't think I've ever had anyone come out and said it like that before," Leah said. "'I like you.' A girl could use one of those every now and then."

His eyes were suddenly free of their death grip on his plate. Mel looked up and met Leah's small, shy grin with one of his own. While it wasn't the same as the lightning bolt of a spark that made him want to tear up the continent, this small moment in a lost friend's cafe was more of a connection than Mel had felt with anyone in a very long time. There had to be something he could offer, after everything Leah had shared with him. *I can't tell her about the band. Jessie and Betham would kill me... But I could tell her...*

"In the spirit of fairness, would you like to hear one of my secrets?" Mel asked.

Leah pushed her mostly empty tray aside and leaned in across the table, "Lay it on me."

"This is something that only my parents and a handful of government employees know. Not even my best friends are aware of this," Mel said, pitching his voice extremely low. He was bending in, too, close enough that he could feel Leah's breath moving the hairs on the back of his wrist. "It's a pretty big secret. Are you sure I can trust you?"

"Are you the Batman?" Leah's voice was nearly a whisper. It tickled his brain like an ASMR video, and the playful twinkle in her eyes that had held so much hurt earlier made Mel feel that what he was about to tell her was completely worth it.

"No, I'm Merlin," he told her.

"You're an Arthurian wizard?" she started to laugh but checked herself. "Please, tell me this is a joke."

"No, I'm not an Arthurian wizard," Mel reassured her. "I know how that sounds, trust me. But my name really is Merlin. My parents were, well, are extremely nerdy people. I started going by Mel in school after the Harry Potter books and the LOTR movies came out and people started calling me Dumbledore or Gandalf, teasing me about my secret magical schemes, etc. I think it bothered me more because I really wanted the stuff they were teasing me about to be true."

Leah surprised him by nodding. A look of true understanding was cast over her features. "I made the mistake of letting my classmates know that I was named for Princess Leia after I watched the original trilogy for the first time. I was in the first grade. All the way through high school, I had kids come up to me asking if I'd kissed my brother lately or bought a gold bikini. There was this one jackass that thought it was funny to harass me with lightsaber innuendo."

Mel grimaced and shook his head, even though he wasn't really shocked that there was someone who had done so. He'd heard plenty of barbs about wizard's staffs and wands before he'd changed school districts. Betham and Jessie had never been in any of his classes. If they had learned his real name, neither had ever felt the need to mention it.

"So, obviously, I get the childhood trauma of being named for something outlandishly nerdy, but honestly, the more I think about it, I really like the name Merlin," Leah said. "Have you ever considered going back to it?"

"I've never really thought about it," Mel responded. "I've been Mel for so long, I don't think it even occurred to me."

Another silence drifted over the table. Mel looked over his shoulder and realized that Ray was no longer working, but his college friend was still keeping a respectful distance out of some internal sense of discretion. Turning his phone over, Mel realized that it was still turned off. "What time is it, anyway?"

Leah looked at her own phone, and let out a long sigh, "Time to get back to reality, I suppose. It's 12:40. Thank you, Mel, or possibly Merlin. You've made what should be a horrible day into something... Not so bad." She gave him a smile and began to slide out of her side of the booth.

He wanted to stop her, or give her his number, contact info, anything. Feeling like his tongue was wrapped inside of a taffy puller, Mel let out a garbled attempt at all of these at once that sounded something like, "Waroh heala!"

"What?" Leah actually paused and turned back to him. A small rush of victory coursed through Mel's system. Mel hadn't expected her to tell him she liked him, what with the timing and all, but he was certain that if she didn't like him, she would have kept going.

"I know I'm not local, and you've got a lot on your mind right now, but I'm going to be in San Antonio in January. If you happen to be in the area, or I don't know, head up to Indianapolis for Gygax Con next year, maybe you'd like to let me know?" Mel said.

It felt like a small eternity passed while her eyes searched his, seeming to weigh his suggestion and his merit at the same time. In equal parts, Mel wished he could read her mind and was very happy that he couldn't tell what she was thinking. Finally, she extended her phone, open to the notepad app. He might not make it into her contacts at all, but she would have whatever info he wished to give her. After a moment of thought, he decided that a phone number would be too personal, and he didn't check his social media without prompting. Email was really the only option left, so he typed it in without another moment's thought. He hit the save button and handed the phone back to her.

Leah slipped the phone into her pocket, gave him one last glimpse of a smile, and left Mel behind at his now very empty table

Mel wasn't left alone with his reflections very long, though, as Ray slipped into the vacant seat with his own box of loaded fries and a fork. "So, how'd it go?"

Chapter Thirteen

LEAH'S PHONE WAS RINGING before she even managed to close her car door.

It was Anthony.

For almost a full loop of Hedwig's Theme, Leah debated whether or not to answer. Her discussion with Troy still stung, even though her lunch with a man named Merlin had dulled the sharpness of the pain. *Best to get it over with, like pulling off a bandage*, Leah sighed, and she swiped the green phone icon.

"You, me and Nessa, later tonight, her place. We're going to get our Wood for Sheep on," Anthony said without so much as a hello.

"What?" Leah almost dropped her phone in surprise. "But, I thought..."

"Please, Leah. We're your friends. Alan can say what he likes to soothe his poor bruised ego, but no one that really knows you is ever going to believe you capable of cheating," Anthony said.

His voice was so matter-of-fact and boisterous that Leah wanted to start crying again, though this time it wasn't an urge fueled by bitterness. She shook herself out of it. There had already been too many tears in the last few days. It was getting irritating. "But Troy..."

"Troy," Anthony said, his voice took on an odd tartness that Leah didn't think she'd heard him use before. "I don't think that he really believes Alan, deep down. He just needs his brother to be the good guy. He's gotta get through family Christmases and Thanksgivings and family dinners where his mom criticizes the both of them for whatever she feels like bringing up. Anyway, don't worry about what Troy thinks. He kicked me out this afternoon when I told him to shut up about the whole mess."

A coldness took root in Leah's gut. She'd known that her split with Alan was going to change things. Hell, her conversation with Troy had solidified that in her head the moment she walked out of the lawyer's office. She just hadn't anticipated the lines to be drawn that quickly, or in those directions. She'd imagined that Troy and Anthony would remain inseparable, as they had after their breakup. "Oh my god," she whispered. "I can't believe he did that."

Anthony didn't respond to her whisper. Either he realized it had been more reaction than commentary, or he hadn't heard it. That was a brief pause on his end of the line. "Anyway, I checked in at a midrange hotel for the duration of my stay. Not nearly as nice as Troy's guest room, but I didn't figure Nessa would want both of us crashing at her place."

Leah's inner travel agent kicked into gear at this, "I can get your booking moved to somewhere much nicer for roughly the same price, if you want. I've got a few favors built up with several hotels in the area. I can probably even get you a few meal vouchers."

Laughter carried through from the other end of the phone, "I'm already settled in here, but I really do appreciate the offer. Don't worry about what you can do for me, sweetie. I was calling to let you know that I'm here for you."

"Feel like helping me pack?" Leah asked, the question ending in a sigh. She hated the idea of packing almost more than she hated the idea of leaving her house.

Leaving was something that happened at the beginning of every trip. Lock up, walk down the path, and get in the car. Packing made everything real in a way that not even signing the divorce papers had seemed to; there was a finality to her stuff exiting the house. "I can pick you up on my way to get boxes."

NESSA CALLED WHILE they were on the way back from the storage place that sold boxes between the hotel and what had been Leah's house. When Leah pulled up, Nessa was waiting by the front door, wearing her scruffy jeans and a ratty old shirt. She gave Leah a hug almost as good as one of Anthony's. "Are you okay? How are you feeling?"

"I'm..." Leah paused to assess and realized that she had reached an almost comfortable numbness. "At the moment, I'm not that bad."

Leah unlocked the door and let her friends into the house. Unasked, they remained silent as she ran her hand over the burgundy countertops that had greeted her so often. There was a crack forming in the cement that held the sink. That would be Alan's problem, now. It seemed fair to let him discover it.

The television and consoles were coming with her, but Leah sat down on the old, threadbare couch which had followed her and Alan from their first apartment all the way to this house. In the early days of their relationship, it had been where they marathoned the whole of Babylon 5 and SG-1. Leah still remembered the first day that Alan had declined to sit next to her. He'd sat at the table, put on a pair of headphones and stuck a DVD into his old laptop. She couldn't remember exactly what the movie he had watched had been, but she remembered seeing the Blockbuster logo and being hurt that he hadn't even told her he was stopping to rent a movie. That had been in the old apartment, just after Troy had moved out and before Alan had gone to his mother for the loan. In hindsight, that was the beginning of the end, but the Leah of then hadn't recognized it. At the time, it had just hurt.

Her sense of numbness was now twisting in her chest. This officially sucked.

That was when Anthony and Nessa pulled her off the couch and began peppering her with questions about what to start with and what she was taking. Leah had to climb out of her own head to tell them what they were allowed to take and how much to leave. They set up base in the master bedroom, making boxes at the foot of the bed.

"Seriously? None of the kitchen stuff?" Nessa asked. "You aren't taking the spatulas or the bread maker?"

"I never used the bread maker," Leah said. "It was a wedding present."

"You should call up your lawyer and sue him for all of the forks. Let him keep the rest of the kitchenware, but make him eat his salads with a spoon," Anthony grinned. "Hell, leave the lawyers out of it. Just take his forks."

That idea was just dumb enough to make Leah laugh, which, naturally, had been the point. "I'm not throwing almost twenty forks into my clothes. That's a horrible idea, since I'm not going to have a chest of drawers or anything. I'm going to be living out of these boxes for at least a few weeks."

"Ooh! I know! Take the towels! All of them! Except maybe one hand towel," Nessa suggested. "I'm sure Alan wouldn't even think to check before he took his next shower."

Leah actually considered that suggestion seriously for quite a while. She was going to take some of the towels and a few blankets to pad the television and her computer during transit. As much as it would entertain her, though, she didn't want to have a big, bitter battle with Alan. The last year or so of their marriage had been bitter enough. At this point, she just wanted to get out. "I'm taking all of the board games, so could one of you get those out of the hall closet?"

Anthony volunteered, leaving Leah and Nessa to fill boxes with Leah's clothes. "So what are you going to do after you move out?" Nessa asked.

"I thought I was moving in with you...?" Leah had a moment of panic as she thought Nessa was reconsidering her offer of a roof. Nessa's small second bedroom was set up as a craft-room and had one full wall displaying costume props, but it was better than nothing. Luckily, Nessa owned a trundle bed that would save Leah from buying a bed immediately. Buying new furniture was something Leah wanted to wait on until she had a new place to call home.

"That's already settled, and I'm by no means already asking you to move on," Nessa said reassuringly. "No, I mean, are you going to continue being a travel agent? Go back to school? Maybe start a travel vlog?"

"I could go on a trip..." the thought struck Leah with nearly as much force as the spark she had shared with Lancel♡t. *Was that really only last night?* She shook the thought away and focused on the new realization. Alan was no longer going to tell her they couldn't go places, because she could go without him. The entire world had opened up to her, and something inside her ignited at the possibilities.

WITH ANTHONY AND NESSA helping, Leah managed to get all of her things together much faster than she had thought possible. It helped that all of her stuff was already more or less separate from Alan's stuff. They had separate spaces on the bookshelves, her DVDs and Blu-rays were mostly on the bottom of the media shelves because she was shorter, and the office was primarily her space.

Going through the house, Leah saw more and more of how much she and Alan had really drifted away from each other. When they had first moved in together, they had laughed about how they both had copies of "Die Hard" and they had put them side by side. Now, as she packed away her copy, it was mixed in among her movies, but his copy was inaccessible on the high shelf. They hadn't watched it together last Christmas. *Definitely a flawed marriage*, Leah's lips twisted into a tight parody of a smile at the thought. *Should've known then.*

Nessa drove a silver 2016 Toyota RAV4 Hybrid because she needed the fuel economy and the carrying capacity for her costumes when she opted to drive to a convention. That meant that most of Leah's stuff was only going to take one trip.

Her clothes had gone into boxes, mostly, but she'd packed a few pairs of jeans, a handful of shirts, bras and underpants, and one pair of pajamas into one of the suitcases along with her toothbrush, the newly opened toothpaste and what little make-up she owned. It wasn't that Leah initially felt she needed to put that stuff into a suitcase, so much as she wanted to take a suitcase, but after Nessa praised her for her foresight, it seemed like a really good idea.

It was depressingly early when they finished. Leah checked her phone and realized two things. It wasn't even technically evening yet, and she still hadn't changed her phone's background pictures. Her laughing, happy face with Alan's next to it looked back up at her. Those two people had existed in another world; that world was gone. She would have to fix her phone. Later. In the meantime, Leah dipped into her email and checked that she didn't have any client issues pending. People on cruises didn't often contact her, but with at least three clients out at sea, it was better to be sure.

As much as she was looking forward to a vacation, Leah realized she was going to have to book it at a time that her clients were all staying home, unless she wanted it to be a working vacation. She hadn't stayed in touch with the people at her old office, or she could've asked someone to trade off with her and just make sure her clients were looked after in exchange for her doing the same for them. September or October would likely be good months for her to travel. It was before the family-oriented holidays, and in the middle of hurricane season there were far less cruises booked (even though they were way cheaper and cruise ships were pretty good about not sailing into storms).

Leah didn't specialize in cruises, but they did tend to give her a much higher commission. Cruises and tours. Did she want to go on a tour of England or Japan? Book a cruise and see some islands? She'd been dreaming about the possibilities for ages, but she'd always envisioned going with someone. Who could she get to go with her in maybe a month's time?

"When was the last time you ate?" Anthony asked. "Please, tell me you didn't skip lunch to start packing."

"No, I had lunch," Leah said absently. "I wanted someone to talk to and I thought... Well, I thought you were going to accuse me of stuff, like Troy, so I went to Escape from Philly Burger. Nessa has a friend there, and I... Anyway, I had lunch."

"You talked to Ray about your divorce before you called either of us?" Nessa asked. She didn't sound affronted so much as confused. "Did you think I was going to believe Alan? After our talk at the Pancake Hut last night?"

"No," Leah said. "It was just, you weren't going to be free until noon, and it was 11:30. I had to talk to someone in person. I needed to see a face that, well, wasn't Alan's... You know? But I didn't really get a chance to talk to Ray. He was busy with customers."

"So you just sat there alone?" Pity was starting to swell up in Anthony's voice.

Leah really didn't want pity at the moment. It was easier to deal with the jokes and suggestions to steal things from Alan's house. *Not even* the *house anymore*, Leah realized. *It's become Alan's house in my head already. I think I preferred it as* the *house. I've got to get out of here.* "I actually did end up talking to someone. A D'weasel. Actually, Ness, we saw him at the Pancake Hut last night."

"Your admirer or the other one?"

"His name was Mel," Leah said. The suitcase was the last of what was left in the house. She picked it up and started walking toward the door for what would likely be the last time. "He was the one you pointed out to me."

"Her admirer," Nessa told Anthony.

Heat was starting to build in Leah's cheeks, even as Anthony clapped her on the back and gave her shoulder a squeeze. "Honey, that right there. That's why we don't believe Alan's crap about you cheating. You had lunch with a stranger and you're turning bright red. Cheaters don't do that. I've dated enough of them to know."

"I'll tell you guys all about it as soon as we get my stuff over to Nessa's. I don't really want to be here when Alan gets home," Leah said.

"Can we take all of his toilet paper?" Anthony asked.

Leah stopped with her hand wrapped around the doorknob. She had paid for that toilet paper, after all.

PULLING INTO THE CUL-de-sac behind Nessa's Hybrid, Leah wondered whether to follow Nessa all the way into her carport or just park in the normal spot. *There'll be time later to sort that out, and it's not like I'm used to parking in a garage*, Leah thought as she pulled as close to the curb as she could.

It was almost surreal coming to Nessa's house with all of her earthly belongings in tow. There was still a part of her that didn't really believe that she was going to stay here. At the end of the night, she'd pack everything up again and go home.

Home, the word caught in her mind like a tortilla chip lodged sideways in her throat. She'd been careful not to even think about it while packing. Leah had only been thinking in terms of *house*: the *house*, Alan's *house*, her old *house*. For years, home had been wherever

Alan was—even when being together seemed more like a habit than a relationship.

Anthony pulled the door handle and hopped out of the car. Before Leah had even unbuckled, he was opening the back and taking the box with Leah's game consoles up to Nessa's front porch. Nessa opened the door to her house from the inside, exchanging a smile and a few words with Anthony before beckoning to Leah.

Leah had a few false starts getting herself out of her car. Going into Nessa's place was one more step down this road that seemed so *wrong*.

Yes, she and Alan had been horrible together, getting worse all the time, but that had been familiar. The world now seemed vaguely alien and unsettling. It was like she'd walked into the Upside Down from Stranger Things, or an early season of the X-Files. Everything looked normal, but it wasn't. Even her friends seemed off to her.

Troy, she realized. There was still a part of her that was looking for him to show up, to apologize and hug her, and tell her that he knew Alan had been making shit up. The part of her that had seen the divorce coming hadn't anticipated the rejection of her best friend, Alan's twin brother. He hadn't just rejected her, but he'd also rejected Anthony because Anthony had stuck up for her.

A small spot of warmth flared as Leah really absorbed that. Anthony had defended her against Alan's accusations without even talking to her first. He'd stood up for her even in the face of Troy dismissing him from his house and possibly his life. She'd always liked Anthony and his rib-cracking hugs, but she hadn't realized how true a friend he would really be when things went to ash around her. Leah used that warmth to propel her out of her car. Grabbing the other box in her back seat, she lumbered up to the door that Nessa was still holding open.

Nessa lived in the bottom left of a quadplex that was rented out by her uncle. As one entered there was one large open area that was clearly meant to be divided into a living room and a dining space. The dining space was set up with a green screen photo area instead of a dining table, and a large wrap-around computer desk against the wall that held the kitchen passthrough. An odd sort of nook/corner held a fireplace that was there more for tradition's sake than any real need for it on the Texas coast. There was a television, much smaller than the one Leah had brought with her, mounted above the living room fireplace. A cozy, cream loveseat was situated facing the TV, with a plush chair, that was almost the same size as the loveseat, facing the rest of the room. From the place where the computer desk met the living space, there were bookshelves all along the wall stretching to the door.

"Will your uncle care that you're letting me crash here?" Leah asked. Anthony had already disappeared down the hall next to the kitchen, likely to deposit her first box in the secondary bedroom.

"As long as you don't trash the place, I doubt he'll say anything," Nessa said. "We're family, so it's not like there's much of a formal lease. He basically gave me a key and told me not to be more than five months behind on the rent or he'd have to tell my parents."

"Really?" Leah couldn't imagine anyone in her family being that laid back about funds, and she'd always considered her dad to be one of the most chill people on the planet.

"If any of the neighbors asks, tell people that we pay a thousand dollars a month for rent, but Uncle Alcide really only charges me six-fifty. He gets a bundle package on utilities, so even after electricity and water, I'm only looking at about eight hundred a month. If you don't mind the weird wiring in certain areas, it's a really cozy little unit," Nessa said. "I'd dread the day I moved out, except that I'm actually doing well enough with followers, sponsors, etc., that I could manage a real space of my own."

"Don't get comfy is what I'm hearing," Leah grinned to take the bite out of her words and shifted the box she was holding. It was pretty light, and for a moment she forgot what was in it. She set it down on the loveseat and opened the lid only to see some towels and toilet paper. "Oh, right... I guess this one goes in the bathroom."

Chapter Fourteen

MEL DIDN'T REMEMBER to turn on his phone until he needed a ride back to the hotel. He'd parted ways with Ray after about half an hour of chats that were done in quick spurts between customers. Ray only chided him about his obvious crush on a newly divorced woman for a few minutes before asking what it was that Mel did these days. Even with an old friend like Ray, Mel stuck with a partial truth. He'd told Ray he was a songwriter and had only enough success to be known in certain circles on the internet.

After that, they'd talked about Ray's family, and the move from Philadelphia. Ray's wife had grown up on Galveston Island, moved to Philly as a teenager, but had been homesick for most of her adult life. Rather than offering to take a trip, which is what she'd expected Ray to offer, he'd embraced the idea of moving to a new city and opening the burger joint he'd dreamed about since high school. Their kid was young enough that a new city, while daunting, was quickly her favorite place in the world because she had a new bunch of friends and a new school that was much newer than her old school.

Even though Mel was happy for Ray, he couldn't imagine how hard it would be to raise a child with his hectic, career focused schedule. *How hard is it to find a woman that doesn't want kids?* he mused. The thought led him to his Spark. What if that was doomed to fail at the offset because of something like kids? Part of him wanted to call off the hunt before it even began. What if he found the Spark and then Leah sent him an email? How dumb was it that he gave Leah his email address on the same day that they launched the search for his Spark anyway?

Maybe that was me trying to self-defeat, Mel thought. *It's not like Stephanie was my last girlfriend. She was just my last real try at a relationship.*

He could list the others on one hand, but it wasn't a great list. The first after Stephanie had been Malati, whom he had broken up with because he didn't like the way her dad looked at him. Next, he'd dated Kennedy, whose temper had been a major deal-breaker. She'd thrown things and screamed when a waiter gave her the wrong order. After that, he'd been with Aya for a grand total of three days.

Jessie and Betham hadn't said a word about any of those, but then, they didn't know about most of them. He hadn't even bothered to mention those girls' names to his two best friends. Mel wondered whether he should mention that he ran into Leah, again. Odds were good that Jessie wouldn't be too happy if she found out that he was giving his email to other women when she had already started helping him find his Spark.

He would tell them about running into Leah, Mel decided. There was nothing wrong with him spending time with a woman that he'd probably never see again, and it wasn't like anything untoward had happened. The idea of finding his Spark still sent flutters through his stomach and down his spine.

Still, he mused. *I told Leah I liked her. That's not something I just...do. I wonder if that Spark broke something inside of me.*

THE MAGICAL SPACE SKELETON Army performed in Austin and Fort Worth before heading back to Indianapolis for a two week touring break.

A touring break didn't mean they weren't busy. Mel thought he saw more of Lady Bug and Frimmydukes during those two weeks than he saw of Jessie and Betham. They were in the middle of filming a new music video, which meant long hours and a lot of extra people.

Frankie didn't have anything to do with the film crew, but she still showed up to watch during her spare hours. Betham was directing, and it was always entertaining to watch him point out certain angles with the camera and instruct the stage crew while wearing his Frimmydukes costume.

Their film crew were professional enough to pretend not to notice that they were being ordered around by a masked alien with elf ears, but it was still pretty funny. It was the video for Defenders of Mars, and most of it was being filmed in front of a large green screen.

During his down time, Mel was still trying to come up with his lyrics for the new album. He still had a bunch of titles, but not much else. He was lost in a maze of lyrical thought when it started misting on him as he walked between his car and his apartment.

The mist was intensifying, becoming more of a drizzle. A tiny mewing sound penetrated his musical fugue. He turned and saw that a tiny black cat, still a kitten, was sitting between the wall of his apartment building and the lip of the roof. It was mewing piteously, as though to ask someone to take it somewhere dry. Mel met its jade green eyes for only an instant before it came romping toward him despite the wet.

"I don't have any cat food," he told the kitten.

With its eyes still turned up toward his face, the kitten gripped his jeans with one unsteady leg and stretched a single white paw with delicate pink pads up toward him. Whatever resistance Mel had melted into the drizzle that was well on its way to becoming a proper rain. He bent down and scooped (quick glance) her up. "Okay, you can come with me. Fair warning, I've never had a cat before. I'm not sure what I'm doing."

Purring, the kitten batted at his nose.

Once Mel and his guest had made it in the door, he set the cat down on his couch and called Jessie. Betham had already told him that it wasn't a good night for hanging out because he was going to be busy helping edit that day's filming.

"I thought you were going home and working on lyrics?" Jessie said by way of greeting.

"That's still probably going to happen," Mel said. "Thing is..."

Big green eyes looked at Mel imploringly, so he sat down next to the kitten and started stroking her while she pushed against his hand as though to tell him he still wasn't petting her enough.

"Thing is... I seem to have a new kitten," Mel finished.

Jessie laughed on the other end of the line. "Oh, Mel... Alright. I'll grab some stuff for you on my way over. Does your new kitten have a name?"

Mel winced as the kitten grabbed his thumb with her tiny needle claws and proceeded to rub against his thumb. He couldn't help but smile even though the claws kind of stung. She was so freaking cute, it was impossible not to smile. "I think I might call her Dot, like, you know, Animaniacs?"

"Seriously?"

"I have the whole series on Blu-ray," he admitted. "She's got the whole 'and I'm cute,' thing."

"Of course she does," Jessie said. "She's a cat."

"I meant Dot," Mel said. "It's a thing, in the show... She calls herself cute a lot. There's even a song about it."

"I'm yanking your chain, dude," Jessie grinned hard enough that Mel could hear it through the phone. "I'll be over in about half an hour, maybe longer with the rain."

ROUGHLY AN HOUR LATER, Mel opened his door to welcome Jessie and what looked like half of the pet aisle. "Holy shit," Mel took the biggest bag out of Jessie's arms and let out a grunt as the weight caught him by surprise. "What's in this?"

"Dried clay flecks for your kitten to poop in," Jessie said. "Also known as litter. If you actually look at the words on the front, that's even what it says: kitty litter. I know you're new to this, but that's a pretty basic cat thing."

Mel let the snark slide. The bag was very heavy and he had no idea how long she'd been carrying it. Adding in the fact that she was here after a full day of filming for their new video, Mel would probably have let her get away with punching him in the face without warning. "How much do I owe you for all of this?"

"Call it fifty?" Jessie said. She pitched most of the bags down onto his table and started sorting through them. "Okay, before we start on Cat 101, where is she?"

As quietly as he could, Mel walked back over to the couch. He wasn't sure why he was trying to be so quiet, since Jessie's knock at the door and the subsequent clonks, rustles, and talking hadn't seemed to bother Dot at all. She was curled up into a little bundle, her white paw gripped around her tiny, smug face. Mel had thrown on a random episode of Animaniacs so Dot could see her namesake while they'd waited for Jessie to arrive. It was paused on the intro for their second episode. Even though the kitten didn't really look much like the Dot on the screen, he thought he'd nailed her for personality.

Jessie followed him over to the couch and let out a breathy sort of "Awww," as she gently stroked Dot along the spine. Dot, as though sensing that she was being cooed over, rolled over and stretched, exposing her furry black belly and putting her paws in the air. "Okay, I can see the whole Dot thing, now. Even without," and Jessie made a hand motion encompassing Mel's frozen television screen. "Didn't even need the show reference. She's a black cat with a white spot. Dot just fits."

"Yeah, but... that's boring without the show reference. We're comedy musicians. We shouldn't be boring," Mel argued. He kept his tone light because he could tell she wasn't serious.

"Point," Jessie said, scratching Dot's stomach and chin. A deep rumbling purr began, seeming incongruous with the actual size of the cat emitting it. "Getting serious, though, we're on tour right now. What are you going to do as far as cat sitting? Have you been looking for a vet yet? What's your apartment policy on pets?"

Mel's mind just buzzed at him. He hadn't been thinking about anything past bringing in a kitten out of the rain. It had been wet, his apartment was warm and dry. After calling Jessie, he'd pretty much stopped planning. He suddenly worried that Dot might be hungry, though she seemed satisfied to just sleep on his couch at the moment. "What am I doing? I've never had a cat. My dad was allergic, so the closest I ever got was a goldfish named Skoodles!"

"Skoodles?" Jessie started laughing so hard she fell from her squat next to the couch and started rocking on the floor. "Skoodles! I love it! Why have I never heard about this before?"

"Never came up," Mel shrugged. "Jess! Forget about Skoodles for the moment; we're discussing Dot."

For some reason, this made Jessie laugh even harder. Where the sounds of doors opening, shopping bags, and strange thumps hadn't phased the kitten, Dot rolled into a half-sitting position and gazed bemusedly at the laughing human that had stopped petting her.

Mel rubbed his face and stood up from his own crouch. He wasn't helpless, he reminded himself. Jessie had given him some advice just by asking him questions. Pulling out his phone, he looked up his apartment complex and checked the website for their pet policy. He would have to go in during office hours and declare his cat. They'd tack on something called pet rent, and he'd have to make a safety deposit of some four hundred dollars. "Whoa," he said. "Four hundred dollars, just to have a cat live with you?"

That seemed to sober Jessie up a bit, though she remained sitting on his floor. "That's pretty standard, from what I've seen. When I got Eevee, my rent went up by about twenty bucks a month, but my deposit was only three hundred."

Eevee was a brown tabby that had caught Jessie's eye almost three years before when one of Frankie's road crew guys had found a box of kittens. The road crew kept three and found homes for the rest. Jessie hadn't really discussed the details of caring for a kitten with Mel previously, but he'd been on the receiving end of a lot of cat pictures until Jessie had made the cat its own webpage.

Frankie and Izzy had adopted one of the other cats from that litter, and his name was Axl. Axl didn't come up much in conversation, being more Izzy's cat than Frankie's. That gave Mel an idea for what to do when they had to leave for tour gigs. "I'm going to see if Izzy will come by to check on Dot while we're on tour. What do you think is fair for a pet sitter? $20?"

"Try asking her, or you could look it up," Jessie shrugged. "I usually board Eevee with my vet, but she's older. Better immune system."

"Do you like your vet? Can I take Dot there or is it weird to share a vet?" Mel asked. "Is that one of those weird things like wearing the same shirt as somebody?"

"I do like my vet," Jessie said. "I can send you her contact info when I get back to my place. We're only doing a half day tomorrow. If you explain the situation, she may even be able to fit you in tomorrow morning."

Mel felt better, now. Even if nothing was in its final phase, he was no longer imagining that Dot was going to have to go to a new home just as he had decided to take her in. Plans were forming in his head: vet appointment, apartment office, call or text Izzy and see if she'd mind feeding Dot when he was out of town. Jessie seemed to be watching him as he processed all of the things he had to do and weighed them against his bank account. He still had to give her fifty dollars for the stuff on his table.

"To your bank account? Or would you prefer cash?" he asked.

"Whichever's easier," Jessie said, still looking at him with that indecipherable expression.

"What? Why are you looking at me like that?"

Tilting her head one way, then the other, Jessie finally shook it and stood up. "I just had something occur to me. Why haven't you asked about your Spark woman yet? It's been almost a week since I put it up on our social media accounts and we've been getting some good fan photos."

Ducking his head so that Jessie could see his face, Mel started pulling stuff out of the bags on the table. "I... don't know. It's too soon, right? I thought it'd take a lot longer to piece something like that together."

The truth was that Mel hadn't asked about it because he'd been poring over their social media accounts on his own every chance he got, and he knew that despite a lot of people having pics of him bursting through the doors, the shots of the fans had been maddeningly unhelpful. Most of them were blurred or hands silhouetted against the stage lights. He hadn't asked because he was pretty sure he knew what the answer was going to be, and he wanted to stay ignorantly optimistic.

"You're right, mostly. It is going to take longer. The public forums certainly haven't had what we're looking for, though I've been doing what I could to encourage the types of pics we need. I've liked a lot of selfies in front of the stage before the lights went down this week. Maybe that'll encourage the Houston D'weasels to use our hashtags for the pre-concert stuff. Then we can piece together a bit of who was standing where," Jessie reasoned. "Also, we've had a lot of people who heard that we wanted crowd pics emailing us directly. We've got some very photogenic fans, FYI."

A small smile spread across Mel's face. The foreboding shadow of disappointment walked away, probably with its own cloud of discouragement. Jessie wasn't just trying to make him feel better, she was still working away at the Gordian Knot that finding his Spark had become. If she still thought there was a way to figure it out, then it was way too soon for him to give up. Mel knew that he needed to be patient with this problem, but telling himself to be patient and actually *being* patient were very different beasts.

"Good to know," he said after a silence that was just a tad too long.

"So what are you doing on your end? Have you figured out how to rig a giveaway or something yet?" Jessie asked. "Because I'm not going to be the one putting all the work in on finding your new woman. I'm willing to help out a friend, but I'm not willing to toil on a project that you're not putting any effort into."

"Honestly, I've been staring really hard at the fan pics, and I forgot about that part," Mel admitted. "I'm sorry, Jess. I wasn't trying to coast on your efforts."

Rolling back onto her knees, Jessie scooped Dot up into her arms. The kitten lazily blinked and purred as though she'd been planning on this from the beginning. "So long as you've been doing something," Jessie said. "That's all I wanted, was to know that I'm not working on something you already forgot about."

"No," Mel said. Even the memory of that one touch still tingled. He wanted to feel it again, properly, when the other person knew him for who he was, and he could look into their eyes. "I haven't forgotten."

"Good," Jessie smiled. "Then it's time for me to school you on how to care for this adorable little fluff ball."

Chapter Fifteen

FOR THE FIRST FEW DAYS, Leah thought that living with Nessa felt like going to a convention that was out of town. Anthony was still in town and even though Leah would work her usual hours, the three of them would go to his hotel and play games in the lobby or hangout at Escape from Philly Burger. Ray wasn't usually there in the evenings, they found out. Her fondness for the place was in no small way tied to the fact that it had provided her with a safe haven on that first day of her divorce.

When Anthony left, though, it started to really sink in that this wasn't just a temporary situation. Even though she'd known it was coming, Leah wasn't prepared for the actual physical longing that hit her after the second week. It was like a part of her body had been removed. She spent long hours at night in her room, not sleeping but staring at the pictures she still had stored on her phone, wanting to call Alan even though she really didn't want to talk to him. He hadn't even texted her about the toilet paper. That was probably for the best, since she didn't know how she would've responded, even if the text had been an angry one.

Telling her parents and her sister had been hard, mostly because they were so damn supportive. They wanted to know if she needed any money, if she wanted to come stay with them, or if there was anything they could do. Ellen wanted to go after Alan legally, and rip his world apart. She offered to call Troy and chew his ass out over the phone, too. Leah had convinced her that it wasn't worth it, but only just. There was a part of Leah that wanted to turn her sister loose on the two men that had scorned her after years of love and friendship.

Nessa tried to let her house guest have some space, but Leah could see that she was making her friend worry. There was a period of time where Leah lost track of the days. It was only through work that she noticed the dates on the calendar at all. She spent two weeks in the same pair of pajama pants, not even caring that they were starting to smell. If she could've lived on nothing but ice cream and brownies, that was all she would've eaten.

Leah started to wonder if Nessa even really wanted her in the house. She started contemplating the offer her parents made to let her move in with them, again. They hadn't changed her old room at all since she had moved out, or Ellen's either. It would be like moving into a time capsule, or an alternate universe, where Leah had never met Alan or Troy and had never gotten married. Except that she'd be older, worn down, and there would be those people that *knew.* Old acquaintances would start conversations with, "Oh, and I heard about what happened with you and that husband of yours. Such a shame. What happened?"

Even the Magical Space Skeleton Army had trouble getting her out of bed, though she was pretty sure their music was the only thing keeping her going. "Dweeb Weasels from Space" was her alarm tone in the morning, and she wouldn't stop working. Sometimes, she kept working deep into the night so that she couldn't stare at the pictures of her life before.

There were times when she fell asleep, after staring at the pictures, that Leah felt like she was in her old bed, not alone in the dark. She wasn't even sure it was Alan that she missed, or just the presence of another person in her life. Sure, she missed the old Alan, the Alan that made her laugh and had gone out of his way to be with her. Leah didn't miss the Alan he'd morphed into over the years, the one that she'd divorced. It was beyond weird to her that the two Alans were technically the same person.

It was the middle of September when someone knocked at her door on a Saturday while she was streaming Doctor Who. She'd binged her way through all of the Ninth Doctor and a good portion of the way into the Tenth Doctor the night before. Leah debated whether it was worth getting up to answer her door when it was opened anyway.

Leah had been expecting Nessa to walk in and demand that she leave. She didn't expect to see Ellen, with her arms crossed, looking as livid as the time that Leah had beheaded her favorite doll with the vegetable chopper. (Leah had been reenacting the French Revolution and Ellen had said that doll wanted to be the queen. Leah had been grounded from Charles Dickens books for two weeks and forced to buy her sister a new doll.)

Ellen was taller than her older sister by almost three inches and had a strong nose and a stubborn chin. Her ashy blonde hair was styled into a very neat pixie cut, one that she had adopted after an occasion where the wife of a convict had jumped her in the courthouse bathroom.

The woman had gotten ahold of Ellen's hair and tried to bash her into a sink. It hadn't worked, and the bailiff had entered the bathroom to find Ellen sitting on the woman, restraining her with an arm bar maneuver. A day or two later, Ellen had gone to the salon and gotten her hair shortened so that it wouldn't provide anyone with a convenient handle for her skull. Things like that incident didn't scare Ellen; they made her fight harder. Right now, looking at Leah lying on her borrowed trundle bed, wearing an aging pair of pajama pants, Ellen had on her fighting face.

"Am I in trouble?" Leah asked.

"Get up, get showered, get dressed, and meet us in the living room," Ellen said, her tone brooking no arguments. Even their mom didn't bother to contradict Ellen when she used that voice. Leah wasn't sure if the lack of answer was confirmation or not that she was the one Ellen was mad at, but whatever it was, she didn't want to make it worse.

As Leah showered, she realized she was in worse condition than she thought. Her hair still felt unclean after the first lather, so she shampooed it a second time, and then a third. She scrubbed at her skin until it was pink and a little tender. Remembering the anger that had burned in Ellen's eyes, Leah shaved just about everywhere for good measure. Slipping on her favorite pair of pants was a little confining, but she was pleased to learn that they still fit at this point. That was probably Nessa's doing, since she seemed to be making sure that Leah ate real food from time to time.

Even though she was getting dressed for real, Leah still pulled out one of her depression t-shirts. It was a black Snape shirt that had a silver doe and the words "Never forget." It was a size too big and had been a gift from her father two or three Christmases back.

When Leah finally emerged, Nessa and Ellen both gave her fierce hugs and then led her to Nessa's computer chair. "Nessa called me and said you hadn't come out of your room at all in over a week," Ellen said. "Have you seen Alan's social feed?"

"No..." Leah said slowly, looking from her sister to her friend. Her stomach was starting to sink all the way through her seat and into the floor beneath her. Whatever had brought her sister here from her home up in Dallas had to be bad. That was easily four hours of solid driving. "Why?"

Ellen and Nessa exchanged a look, as though they were discussing how best to handle her. Nessa's expression was sad, but not surprised, while Ellen looked like stone if stone got pissed. Without a word, Ellen spun the chair to face Nessa's computer. "Best if you just see it," Ellen said.

Nessa tapped the spacebar and her screen saver (an extremely old-school maze graphic which Leah recalled being super popular in the '90s) gave way to an open social site. It was Alan's, which Leah had been expecting, but he wasn't distraught or sad or any of the things that Leah could have called herself during the last few weeks.

Rather, he looked as happy as he did in the old pictures that she'd been staring at in the late hours of the night, and he had his arms wrapped around a woman whose hair was professionally dyed blonde, with all the highlights and lowlights that were designed to make hair look more natural than real hair. Her makeup was applied with the finesse of someone that had been wearing it since they were thirteen, and she was wearing high heels with her skinny jeans.

If this woman had any trace of nerdiness, it was buried deep within her fashionable shirts and designer handbags. The first picture had been posted on the previous Saturday, while Leah had been binging her way through all the Monkey Island games she had downloaded. Even Guybrush Threepwood's antics had failed to make her feel any better, but Alan had apparently found something that made him feel better. Someone, anyway. Someone named *Brooke Bailey*. Even the woman's name seemed like it had been picked out of a catalogue.

Some people may have gotten even more depressed. Her husband, ex-husband as soon as the paperwork was processed, was already dating the type of woman he had wanted Leah to turn into. This was the type of woman that he thought he deserved. Leah felt a bit of vindictive curiosity amidst a swirling cloud of anger. What did they talk about together? How long had they been seeing each other? There weren't enough pictures for her to think they'd been together before the split, but Alan certainly hadn't let his sheets cool before finding a replacement. Scrolling down, Leah couldn't find herself mentioned at all since the split. Only a single post on the day of the divorce that read: Single again.

Ellen and Nessa just watched as Leah absorbed the information. It made sense to her now that Nessa had called for backup. With as little as Leah had been interacting with the world, Ellen was the obvious person to knock her out of it, since Troy still wasn't talking to them.

Another realization struck Leah. *Troy knows about Brooke Bailey. He's liked some of these photos.* Not only had Troy not called to warn her that his brother was moving on, but he was publicly approving of her replacement. Troy was never going to call and ask to be friends again, as a part of her had still been hoping.

She'd been wrapped in some sort of relationship penance as well as mourning, with a hidden longing in her subconscious mind that Troy would find out how poorly she was dealing with the breakup and come back to her even though she and Alan were over.

Well, if Alan's allowed to move on, Leah's inner voice seethed, *there's absolutely no reason for me to spend another second moping in my pjs.*

"How do your calendars look for October?" Leah asked, closing the window that still held Alan's smug face. She swung her computer chair around and faced Nessa and Ellen. "I'm thinking it's time I book myself a cruise."

AFTER SOME DISCUSSION, the three women agreed on a seven-day cruise that made stops at three different ports: Mahogany Bay (Honduras), Belize, and Cozumel. They booked two adjoining balcony cabins for the week of Halloween.

Although Leah had been expecting to find a cruise with numerous excursions for Dia de los Muertos festivals, it seemed like the really big celebrations didn't really happen in Cozumel. There was a celebration after dark in the main plaza, but their ship was due to pull out of port by seven o'clock.

Still, Nessa was extremely excited about the costume ball that would happen on the ship, and she was set on trying some of the local cuisines at their ports. Ellen was looking forward to being away from her office with people that knew their way around a board game. It made Leah happy that both her friend and sister were genuinely excited, that they weren't just going with her out of a sense of duty, but what excited Leah the most was the fact that she was about to *go somewhere*.

Leah made sure that her website had the dates blocked out and double-checked that the vacation dates were clearly marked on her social media calendars. Locating her bathing suit in the wall of boxes that still made up one half of her bedroom seemed like a lost cause, so she ordered two new ones off of the internet.

Instead of hibernating in her room, Leah made it a point to go out into the living room and spend time chatting with Nessa and taking a turn in the kitchen every couple of days to cook something. They both spent a lot of time on YouTube watching packing videos and travel tips. After the third or fourth video, Nessa announced that she was making a run on the Daiso down the street and Leah was coming with her.

That shopping trip lasted almost the entire afternoon as Nessa had to talk Leah out of buying most of the snack aisle; even so, Leah came out with a couple of boxes of Pocky, one Hokkaido Cream bun, three glass bottles of soda, and a bag of clothespins. Nessa's haul had been much more practical, being comprised of smaller bags to separate and compress her clothes so they would take up less space in her bag and some of her own colorful clothespins. Most of the videos had suggested clothespins for tacking your towel to the back of your chair while sunbathing or swimming.

On the way back from the Japanese store, they also stopped at a Target for a travel fan and a travel pack of disinfectant wipes, because most of the videos also suggested one or the other.

So this is what this side of things feels like, Leah thought as she packed her one suitcase and then took everything out to repack it.

Even though she'd talked several of her clients through travel nerves before, she hadn't actually experienced them firsthand. Thoughts about Alan and Troy took a backseat to a sudden rush of dreams where she was standing on the dock, watching as her ship left port with Nessa and Ellen waving at her sadly. Some of those dreams were just sad, while others were realistic enough to wake her in the middle of the night.

On one memorable occasion the two themes merged, and Leah had a twisted nightmare about her upcoming trip. Alan was on her ship with a distorted plastic version of Brooke Bailey on his arm. The Brooke doll had jerked her head weirdly in Leah's direction and Alan had started laughing an odd, bellowing laugh that sunk into Leah's skin like ice. He'd pointed at her from across an empty deck that didn't even have safety rails. Leah had started running, while the wind picked up and lightning broke the sky. Something grabbed her by the ankle, and she was pulled upside down toward a face that both was and wasn't Troy's. A hateful sneer climbed the muscles around his nose and his eyes flashed a sickly yellow in the storm. "No," he said, and flung her body down toward a dark, waiting ocean. Leah had woken in a cold sweat, only to find it was four in the morning. It took her another hour to get back to sleep.

That same night, she had another dream where the guy she'd vented to, Merlin, was dressed in wizard robes. He captured Alan, Troy, and the odd Brooke doll in a DeLorean and sent them to a park full of dinosaurs. Most of that dream evaporated in the light of morning, but she woke up feeling oddly refreshed, despite the remembered nightmare.

During the days leading to their trip, Ellen called Leah nearly every night. It was the most Leah had heard from Ellen since Leah had left for college. Her sister had worried college would change Leah's personality. After a week free of binge drinking and college parties, Ellen had relaxed. This time, Leah wasn't entirely sure if Ellen was checking on her big sister again, or if it was because Ellen had also been bitten by the travel bug.

"Don't worry about bringing any games," Ellen greeted her sister one evening.

"Hello to you, too," Leah said, amused.

"Seriously, no games. I've got a plan," Ellen said.

"Should I be worried?" Leah asked. "Because, I've gotta say, I'm a little worried."

"Have you checked in on any of the apps that let you meet people on the ship before you set sail?" Ellen asked.

Leah had been sitting on the couch, absently watching Nessa sew a hem on one of their Halloween costumes. As soon as Ellen asked about the shipboard apps, Leah put her on speakerphone. "No, I can't say that I have. Why do you ask?"

"I found a couple that wants a group for roleplaying on the ship. The wife is willing to be the GM and I've been talking to her about some of her past campaigns. I told them I'd ask you guys."

Nessa looked up from her sewing and quirked an eyebrow at Leah. She looked amused even though when she spoke her tone was acerbic. "So by asking, you meant telling us that we were going to participate?"

"Yeah, basically," Ellen said, not at all flustered. "I mean, as long as you guys are cool with it," she added belatedly.

"Any particular system?" Leah asked. She wasn't entirely adverse to the idea of gaming with a married couple. It meant that the likelihood of being hit on was much less great, and five was a much better gaming number than three. Even though she'd known the answer, Leah had invited Anthony on the cruise. He couldn't take that much time off after the semester started without a much better reason than because he wanted to go cruising.

Ellen was actually quiet for a little bit before answering. Interpreting the silence with her years of sisterly experience, Leah knew that meant one of two things: either Ellen wasn't answering because she thought Leah was going to disapprove, or Ellen wasn't answering because she had actually wanted to keep it back as a surprise. "It's going to be a horror-based game, similar to Call of Cthulhu."

A flutter of excitement and dread tickled through Leah's torso. She recalled the haunting image of Troy's face from her nightmare and added some images from dreams that she'd had after reading through the entirety of Lovecraft's Mythos when she was younger. "How similar?" she asked.

"...very similar," Ellen said after an even longer pause.

"How very similar?" Leah prodded.

"...exceedingly similar. Maybe even excessively similar."

"It actually is CoC, isn't it?" Nessa asked.

The lack of confirmation on Ellen's end of the phone was pretty telling.

Chapter Sixteen

IN THE WEEK LEADING up to Halloween, Mel felt like he could feel the Sword of Damocles hanging over his head. He was squeezed into his space on the Magical Space Skeleton Army tour van, staring at a laptop that housed just about as many lyrics as it had back in August. Betham and Jessie hadn't looked very happy when he told them he still needed more time. If it hadn't been for the fact that his quest for his Spark had bolstered their numbers of D'weasels turned patrons and overall fan satisfaction, Mel thought he'd have to start worrying about replacements and dismissals again.

It wasn't like he hadn't written anything in the last two months. He'd just deleted most of it without showing it to his bandmates. While that made him feel slightly more productive, it wasn't exactly helpful. Back in August, the November deadline that they'd agreed on for finishing their new songs had seemed ages away. The new songs had to be finished and polished by December 8th, when they had booked time at the recording studio.

Mel wished that he was sitting at his table in his apartment, with Dot trying to steal his chips. Not that he'd had any better luck staring at his laptop there, but at least Dot provided a distraction from his unrelenting writer's block.

"Still no love, bro?" Betham asked, pulling himself up from the floor where he'd been laying. The tour van had bunks that could fold down when people wanted to sleep, but they were claustrophobic nightmares that everyone tried to avoid if there were other options. There was a small table on the other side, with a long stool that could only loosely be termed a bench. If Mel were ever to develop a beer belly, he doubted that he'd be able to fit where he was currently sitting. With Betham next to him, the space seemed even tighter. Betham didn't have to try very hard to notice that the screen Mel was looking at was blank. "Dude, I think you may be thinking too hard. Just release your thoughts. Let 'em talk to you."

"Betham, you sound stoned."

"Yeah, but I'm not wrong," Betham smiled at Mel, a glint of self-aware humor shining in his eyes. "You're treating this whole Spark thing like it's a chore. You're not letting yourself think about the possibilities if you stop focusing. Back in high school, we made a band that zeroed in on other people's songs, and we never got anywhere. When we started up again, we didn't get hung up on making it. We were just having fun. Let yourself have some fun, dude. Even if it sucks, you'll still enjoy the ride."

"Stop focusing," Mel said. "Right. That's much easier said than done."

Betham shrugged, and sank back down onto the floor. "If it helps, I brought my handheld. You could play some games, catch some pocket monsters. Usually helps me Zen."

Oddly enough, Betham's suggestion to stop focusing on Mel's Spark did yield something, though it wasn't words. It was that afternoon that he'd spent at Ray's burger diner with the divorcee. Leah hadn't emailed him, but that was hardly surprising. All they'd talked about was her ending relationship and some stuff about growing up with difficult names.

I grew up without a name on a planet I didn't really know.

The words seemed to have arrived all on their own. Mel couldn't really recall writing them, but there they were. He looked down at his hands and back up at the screen. What else had they talked about? He didn't remember words as much as the way her hair framed her face. She'd been to his concert and asked if he was a D'weasel. Suddenly, all Mel wanted to do was write something that would make the woman he'd talked to smile, even though her life was probably still really dim. He'd always had a talent for making people laugh, so he jumped into the idea of making a song to make one random fan, one that he'd liked, happy.

My old planet's gonna regret that they let me go.
Even if I don't remember them, they're gonna know my face!
I'm blasting Outer Space!
I'm blasting Outer Space with a Song!
I'm rocking the human race!
Fuck you, Outer Space!

Words poured out of him onto the page. Mel barely even noticed when Betham pulled himself up on the bench again and started reading over his shoulder. It was only when Betham started tapping out chords on an invisible keytar that Mel really came out of the writer's trance and saw that he'd gotten down an entire song.

"Hell, yeah, bro! I knew you just had to get out of your own head!" Betham said. "Blasting Outer Space, I love it!"

If Mel ever saw Leah again, he swore to himself that he was going to give her the biggest hug, whether he'd found his Spark or not. Stephanie was no longer the only woman he'd ever written a song for, and now that that was true he could feel another song burning its way through his fingers. It was time to pay tribute to the Burrito Gods.

HALLOWEEN IN NEW YORK City was very similar to and yet completely unlike going to New Orleans for Mardi Gras. Like New Orleans, there were costumes, parties and parades with skulls and skeletons prominently on display, but not so many beads or body parts (which wasn't to say there weren't body parts). One of the other things the two holidays in the two cities had greatly in common: Mel felt very out of his element.

While Jessie more or less disappeared after they gave their concert the night before Halloween, mentioning something about a list of parties that she intended to hit, Betham and Frankie were going to take a ghost tour and then wind down in a Halloween themed bar. On the first of November, they were all due to meet up back at the hotel, get in the van and go home.

Even though Mel liked Halloween, he didn't really like spending time on his own in New York. Something about the size of the city and being on his own made him feel lonelier than he normally did. When he was younger, he'd always imagined that being in New York would make him feel like he'd wandered onto the set of Friends or Seinfeld, or any of the other shows that seemed to be based in New York. Instead, he felt like he'd wandered into the Deep Roads of a Dragon Age game. It smelled of decades of exhaust, unwashed bodies, clashing perfumes, clinging cigarette smoke and other smokes.

"Dogs and cats living together, mass hysteria!" Mel muttered to himself. He'd watched the original Ghostbusters after he got settled in his hotel room the night before to try and get more into the spirit of the holiday, but it hadn't seemed to help.

"Did you say something about dogs?" a boy, probably six or seven, plopped himself onto the couch next to Mel. Sitting in the lobby of a hotel sometimes led to very odd conversations in Mel's experience, but unaccompanied kids were often the weirdest. Mel started looking for the boy's parents, hoping he wasn't about to have a Kevin McAllister encounter.

Wrong season, his brain interjected.

"That's my mom, over there," the boy pointed to a woman in a long red trench coat that was standing in line at the front desk. "She told me to sit down where she could see me, and to shut up because I was being a nuisance. What's a nuisance?"

Mel wasn't sure he wanted to field that question. He still hadn't answered the first question the boy asked.

"My mom is upset because we won't get to see the dog parade this year. She said it got cancelled. Were you going to see the dogs?"

It didn't seem to bother the kid at all that Mel hadn't said a word. Mel finally gave up, "No, I wasn't going to see any dogs, but it's a shame about the parade. A dog parade sounds pretty cool."

The boy just looked at Mel now, with his mouth open, showing two gaps where he was missing teeth. "I've seent your videos! You're that one man with the helmet!"

"What?" Mel asked, suddenly paying far more attention to the conversation than he had been before.

Small, stubby fingers pointed at him. "I knowed your voice! You're the guy with the helmet! Mom! Mom! It's the guy with the helmet!" The kid launched himself off of the couch and ran toward the woman he'd identified as his mother previously.

Getting to his feet, Mel walked out onto the street before the kid could drag his mother over to the couch. He'd never been identified by his speaking voice before and the incident unnerved him. What if more people out there could pick up on who he was by voice alone? He pulled out his phone and started texting Betham and Jessie to let them know what had just happened.

Almost immediately, his phone buzzed.

Jessie: *Don't worry about it too much. Just smile and say something like I get that a lot, or just say what?*

While Mel was still trying to decide how to respond to Jessie's advice, he got a response from Betham.

Betham: *Bro, that's one precocious youngster! No worries. It's not like he got your name just by looking at ya.*

Mel knew they were right. He was overreacting to what had been a relatively minor incident. If that kind of thing happened at a convention where a bunch of fans were constantly on watch with their cameras ready, that would have been a much bigger deal. As it was, he'd been identified as the guy with the helmet, which could describe any number of people. Mel wasn't even the only singer that wore a helmet. Odds were good that the kid's mom wouldn't even pay much attention to "that one guy with the helmet." Especially given that it was Halloween.

Suddenly, Mel felt much more inclined to celebrate the holiday. He could visit a costume rental shop and be someone other than Lancel♡t for a day.

Chapter Seventeen

LEAH WATCHED NERVOUSLY as her backpack disappeared into the scanner. She hadn't packed any contraband booze or anything illegal, but she was still nervous about being separated from her stuff. Even though she'd heard about this process often, this was her first time going through a security check. Most of the people around her seemed very blasé about the whole thing, as though a security check was the most boring thing in the world. For Leah, this was the final hurdle in what felt like a many years long dash.

"Okay, step through," the female security officer beckoned Leah through the metal detector. With pursed lips and sharp eyes, the woman looked as bored as most of the passengers, but in a more gruff sort of way.

One long stride took Leah through the metal detector. *If you didn't know what it was,* Leah thought, *they kind of look like big doorways that don't lead anywhere. In a sci-fi setting, they could easily be the portals onto the ship. Just walk through, and they don't even have to dock.*

Watching people struggle to put twelve packs of soda back into their carry-on, Leah was glad that she, Ellen and Nessa had bought the drinks package. It was more expensive, but ultimately way less hassle. Maybe on a different cruise, some day in the future, Leah would want to be frugal. On this occasion, her first real trip outside of the U.S., Leah was willing to splurge on convenience. She started to wait for Nessa and Ellen to catch up to her in the hall, but when she saw a guard give her the stink eye, Leah quickly moved on to the waiting room.

Ellen had arrived at Nessa's the night before so that they could all drive into the port together. Nessa had driven, since her RAV4 definitely had the most trunk space. They'd pulled into the Galveston port parking garage far too early and spent a pleasantly anxious (mostly on Leah's part) couple of hours perusing the Strip. Leah had tried to distract herself in the candy shop by getting a strawberry malt, but she was nervous enough that most of the ice cream melted while she fiddled with her straw. More than half of it had remained in the glass when Nessa suggested that they go ahead and get in line.

"Leah, relax," Ellen said when she caught up with her sister. Her own bag was easily twice the size of Leah's and held extra copies of all of the paperwork that they needed for each port. Ellen had insisted that she would take care of anything that required someone to be organized for the week. It wasn't that she didn't trust Leah with it, since she'd booked her own trips through her sister ever since Leah had gotten her license. She just wanted Leah to spend her vacation having fun. "We're here, and you're fine. You're quivering like a puppy."

"Am I?" Leah asked. She noticed that she was gripping the strap of her backpack hard enough that she was leaving fingernail imprints in her palm. "Okay, I'm fine. This is good. I'm good."

"What's going on?" Nessa asked. Her raven hair was braided and clipped up to keep it out of the way of her own backpack.

"Nothing, really, I'm just... I can't believe we're really here, that this is finally happening..." Tears were threatening to make their way past Leah's defenses. *Not today*, she told herself firmly. *I'm not going to cry today, not even happy tears.*

"Well, I think it's time to start believing," Nessa said. "According to the last announcement, we can go ahead and board."

TRANSITIONING FROM the gangplank to the ship was a thoroughly weird, almost magical experience. Somehow, the plexiglass and aluminum tunnel that hooked into the ship didn't prepare Leah at all for the interior of the ship. She could see the water between the ship and the dock, hear seagulls calling over a hum that sounded a bit like a vacuum cleaner in the next room, smell the tang of salty sea air, and then suddenly she couldn't. Instead of metal and water below her, she was in the atrium of a lush hotel with plush carpet sinking beneath her feet. Jubilant music was welcoming her aboard, as well as smiling crew members. Someone was laughing loudly from the group ahead of them; a bellowing, heartfelt, infectious laugh that brought a smile to Leah's face.

"They're serving lunch on the Lido deck, if you ladies would like. Deck 10," one of the smiling crew members suggested.

"Okay, thanks," Leah responded.

After they'd gotten past the entryway, Ellen asked, "Okay, so did we want to head up top for lunch, go exploring, or go swimming?"

"It's October," Nessa protested. "Are we really sure we want to go swimming in October?"

"Sun's out, and this is Texas," Leah pointed out. "I'm going swimming!"

"Nessa?" Ellen asked, managing to pack an entire question into two syllables.

"Oh, I'm in," Nessa said. "I just thought someone should point out that we're not in the tropics yet."

Since none of them had actually worn their swimsuits, they had to find an unoccupied bathroom on the Lido deck (which happened to have the pool was well as the buffet and a few orbiting restaurants with tacos and burgers). Leah tried not to feel self-conscious about the extra pounds that she'd acquired during the last few weeks. She'd always been pretty average as far as weight anyway, but now she was leaning toward the heavy side of average. Next to Nessa, who never seemed to gain any weight, and Ellen, who stayed active enough that calories just burned away as soon as food went through her lips, Leah could practically hear her thighs grumbling to the people they passed that she'd been eating her feelings. *Not about to do myself any favors on a cruise ship, either*, Leah sighed. *Ah, well. I'm not looking to impress anyone here, and it's not like Alan's going to ever see it.*

Anger and shame sizzled through Leah's being. She wasn't supposed to think about Alan during her cruise. This was for her, and not about him. Anything she did or didn't do, he was not to be a consideration. If she got a tattoo in Mexico (unlikely), it would be her version of a Jolly Roger with a lightsaber crossed with a wand, and with a d20 in place of a skull. Possibly a dragon's head instead of the d20, if it was a cute dragon. It would not say "Screw Alan!"

Ellen pressed a strawberry margarita into Leah's hand the moment she came out of the bathroom. Leah raised a questioning eyebrow at her sister, who didn't drink often, if ever.

"Just a hunch," Ellen said. Her black bikini was garnering attention as they walked across the deck, and even Leah's tankini, with its pink and purple tropical flowers, was drawing a few eyes.

They joined Nessa at the water's edge. She was wearing a one piece that was royal blue on the top, black on the bottom with a decorative buckle that made it look like she had a belt around her waist. It was definitely inspired by dresses from the 1950s. It almost made Leah wish that she cared enough about shopping to find something like it, but not quite.

It didn't seem like the pool was the place for a margarita, so Leah took a long sip and set it under one of the empty deck chairs and set her backpack down next to Nessa's. "Have you tried the water yet?"

"No," Nessa said. She dipped one toe into the pool and came back up to her original position. "I'd call it cold."

Leah didn't bother with sticking her hand in to verify, she just ran toward the edge of the pool and jumped tucking her legs in as she hit. Aside from not yelling, "Cannonball!" it was about as good a cannonball as she had managed when she was twelve and in peak cannonball condition. Unlike those days, the water's temperature seemed to register immediately, and she wanted to rethink the decision. "Ohmigod, cold!" she sputtered as she came to the surface.

"I told you," Nessa chuckled as Leah rubbed at her arms ineffectually under the water.

Ellen jumped in right next to her sister and let out a bit of a whuff, but she didn't start shivering or hopping around to try and warm up quicker. "It's not so bad. Once we start moving around, we'll adjust. Unless, you want to give up and go get food?"

For a moment, Leah did consider it, but she was already starting to feel better. She knew that if she got out of the pool now, it would sour her mood. Thoughts about how the first thing she decided to do on this vacation had been a mistake would start to taint her attitude toward the rest of her trip. A great trip could turn into a disaster a lot more easily than a mediocre trip could become a fantastic one. Leah had dealt with a fair number of customers that had let those moments that decided the tone of a journey dip in the wrong direction. "Let's swim for a bit longer."

Nessa stepped down into the shallow lip, and then slowly sank into the water. She made an effort not to express her discomfort, but she was making some very odd faces on her way in. "Warm thoughts, warm thoughts, warm thoughts," she chanted to herself.

THEY STAYED IN THE pool for about half an hour, playing Marco Polo just for kicks. Leah spent most of her time being it. Nessa's hearing was like a radar; she zeroed in on Leah no matter how quietly Leah tried to sneak past her. Ellen was athletic enough that she would nimbly slide out of the way whenever someone got close to her, and then get to the other side of the pool before they could try again. After that, they climbed into the hot tub to regain a bit of the warmth they'd had previous to their pool dip.

"So, I get it if you don't want to talk about it," Ellen said, leaning back against the edge of the tub with her ash blonde hair plastered wetly to her skull, "but what happened with you and Alan?"

Leah debated whether to cut off the conversation or not. She wanted this trip to be about her, not him, but evading her sister's question felt like a similar moment to the one she'd had after jumping into the pool. Refusing to talk about it would be that moment where she'd look back and realize that the bitterness won, but it wouldn't be just a trip that got messed up. It would likely be several years of her life, wasted on a man that wouldn't even care.

With a deep sigh, Leah closed her eyes and said, "I guess we just fell out of love. All those little things that bug you about a person... While we were in love, I didn't notice them. Then there were the times when I couldn't help but notice, like the time he quit his job without talking to me, or the time he bought a car without talking to me. When we found out I couldn't have kids, he kept acting like it was my fault. It seemed like he thought I went out of my way to do it to him, or something. I don't know. That night, when everything came to a head, he accused me of being too childish. He asked when I was going to give up being a nerd and focus on reality."

"Holy shit," Nessa breathed. "That was the talk you guys had after the concert?"

"Yeah," Leah watched the inside of her eyelids glow red as the sun beat against her from the afternoon sky. The bubbles from the jets in the hot tub burbled with a metallic hum as she remembered the knife-cutting sear of Alan's words against her heart. "Yeah, that was the one. I told him I wanted a divorce. He went to stay with Troy. The next day, he told me to meet him at a lawyer's office."

"The next day?" Ellen said. Leah heard the water move as Ellen sat up. "He had an appointment ready for the next day?"

Deep down, Leah had known what that meant as well as Ellen did. She hadn't wanted to talk about it before because she knew what that meant. She liked the idea that the divorce had been her choice, and not something that Alan had already planned on. But there was no way that he'd have managed an appointment that quickly without some pre-planning. The argument had been to assuage his guilt about having fallen out of love with his wife. While she was being honest with herself, Leah admitted silently to some surprise that he'd felt enough guilt to have that fight. She could have come home to a letter, or he could've sent a text. Leah could have come home to find nothing at all, just a bunch of Alan's stuff missing. *No*, Leah thought. *I think he wanted to keep the house. Too much of a status thing.*

"I know, Ellen," Leah said, realizing she'd been silent for a little too long. "Trust me. I know."

"Fuck him," Nessa said. "I always knew he was a prick, but I have to admit that I underestimated his level of douchebaggery."

For some reason, that made Leah start giggling. Her giggles grew into a giddiness that had nothing to do with the margarita that still sat half-finished under her backpack. Suddenly, Nessa started laughing, too. Ellen tried to stay stalwart and angry on her sister's behalf, but when Leah paused between giggles to give her a genuinely happy grin, Ellen couldn't remain stoic.

AS SOON AS THE ANNOUNCEMENT was given that rooms were ready, Nessa made a beeline for the elevator they'd taken up to the Lido deck earlier. She wanted to jump in the shower as soon as possible. Ellen and Leah came behind her, much more calmly. As much as Leah wouldn't mind a shower, she knew Ellen wasn't going to take very long. Because they had two cabins, Leah and Ellen had offered to let Nessa have a bathroom to herself. There had been a token protest on Nessa's part, but seeing as she had more hair and makeup than the two sisters combined, it took very little persuasion. Likewise, there had been a debate as to who was going to be given the largest bed, because they'd only requested separate beds in one room. Nessa and Ellen had wanted to give Leah the king-sized because it was her vacation. Leah wasn't sure she wanted a big bed all to herself. There were nights when she couldn't sleep because she felt the lack of a physical presence in the bed next to her. She'd spent the better part of eight years with someone sleeping next to her and her body missed Alan's body, even if she was starting to adjust to his absence mentally. They finally agreed to a rotation. Ellen would get it for the first two nights, Nessa would get it for the next two, and Leah would get it for the next two. On the final night, they would draw straws.

Before showers were had, Leah and Nessa pulled out the disinfectant wipes and scoured all the surfaces they were likely to touch during the course of the cruise. Ellen made herself feel useful by finding all of the outlets available in the two rooms, pulling in the luggage from the hallway, and stashing the snacks and drinks that the cruise line put out to entice people into spending extra money. Finally, Nessa said she had cleaned enough, and she jumped into her chosen bathroom. Ellen pulled out a pair of flip flops from her backpack and got into the other shower.

Leah debated sitting down on one of their couches and seeing what the cruise actually had on their television networks, but the call of the balcony was too great. Their rooms were facing the dock, so at the moment, there wasn't much to see but the tops of the cruise terminal and the city of Galveston. Still, it was an angle of the city that Leah hadn't seen before and she felt the swell of excitement growing within her again. Soon, so very soon, she'd be on the ocean, heading to a place that she'd never seen before. Even though they'd talked about going to the launch party, Leah suddenly felt that she'd much rather see the launch from right here. She wanted to witness the moment she left the life she knew behind.

DURING THEIR FIRST official sea day, Ellen led the way to the ship's library where they were supposed to meet the couple that was looking for gamers. All that Ellen had told Leah and Nessa about them was that they were married, and they were from Portland. Leah wasn't really sure what she was expecting, but it definitely wasn't what met her eyes as Ellen ushered them into the library.

There were only two people there, and they smiled expectantly as Leah, Nessa and Ellen walked in. "You must be our group!" the woman said as Ellen ducked around to give them both a hug.

Leah knew that her parents were every bit as nerdy as she was, that there was no age limit on gaming, but somehow, she just really hadn't pictured the mystery Cthulhu couple as being older. She smiled at the strangers but knew they'd noticed her hesitation.

"Don't be intimidated by our good looks," the husband gave her a good-natured wink. He had a bit of a Latino accent and his once black hair was mostly steel at this point. "My name's Ruy Delgado, and this is my wife, Bobbi Delgado."

Bobbi Delgado was a big woman. She was easily six inches taller than her husband, who was roughly equal to Leah's height. Some people shrink with age, but if Bobbi had started shrinking, she must have been a giant to start with. Leah guessed that the woman had some Viking heritage, because her silvery hair looked like it had started as a snowy blonde. It wasn't just that Bobbi was tall either; she was broad. The first word that popped into Leah's mind upon looking at her was "Tank."

"I'm so happy to finally meet you, girls," Bobbi said, sweeping Leah into a hug. "I just know we're gonna have the best time. So, don't tell me... Red hair, same eyes, you must be Ellen's sister, Leah."

Managing to squeeze out a small, "Yep," Leah met Ellen's amused gaze. Her sister had known that this was going to be an awkward meeting and hadn't whispered so much as a hint of a warning. If Leah had laser beam eyes, Ellen would've looked less amused. Except that if Leah had laser beam eyes, Ellen would probably have an impenetrable shield or armor skin or something. Stupid hypothetical super genes.

Nessa didn't seem flummoxed, but she met all sorts while working conventions. As Bobbi gave Nessa a hug, Nessa found something to comment on and the two were soon deep into conversation. Ruy edged closer to Leah and Ellen, even though his eyes never left his wife. His expression was soft, full of love and contentment. "I'm really glad you girls agreed to do this with a couple of old farts like us. You've made Bobbi so very happy, you have no idea."

"It's no trouble. This is Leah's first time on the ocean, so it seemed like a good time to scare her off of it," Ellen said, grinning to show that she didn't really mean anything by the verbal prod. It was just her sisterly love showing.

Nessa and Bobbi finished their private exchange and rejoined the rest of the group.

"Since we only have a week on this ship, and I figured you girls wouldn't be too keen to play on excursion days, I hope no one objects too strongly to playing a pre-made character. I've left the character details open, so you can choose your name, height, gender, whatever, but all the stats, classes, equipment is finalized. I've got a reporter, a librarian, a private eye, and a college student," Bobbi said, pulling a messenger bag out from behind the chair she'd been sitting in. From the depths of the bag, record sheets, pencils, a large dice bag, and a very old rulebook. "You girls may be more familiar with a newer ruleset, but Ruy and I've been playing this one for some time, and it works well enough for me."

Leah, Ellen and Nessa reassured Bobbi that they were fine with the arrangements as they set about procuring their own chairs. Ruy requested to play the college student, which drew some gentle chuckles as Bobbi handed him the sheet with an expression of jocular exasperation. It was easy to see their dynamic as a couple. An aching sort of longing pushed against Leah's heart as she watched them. This was the kind of couple she had imagined she and Alan would turn into one day. This was the kind of couple she still wanted to be a part of, she realized, just no longer with Alan. The thought shocked her. It was the first time she'd contemplated moving on, but the conviction grew as Leah watched Ruy and Bobbi smile at each other. Love still existed. It was out there. It would still take her a while to be ready to find it, but she was suddenly aware that she wanted to search.

THEY GAMED IN TWO-HOUR increments, because that was the longest Bobbi could sit down at the table before her back started giving her trouble. Leah was playing the private eye, while Ellen was the reporter and Nessa had opted for the librarian. Bobbi's game was set in a coastal town, in the same time period that Lovecraft had lived, but it wasn't pulled directly from the Mythos. They were investigating a billionaire/philanthropist that had sudden gone missing while on holiday. Leah's character was hired by his estranged wife, Ruy's college student was out to find the man that was supposedly his father, Ellen's reporter had her eye on a piece about how the Golden Boy of Maine wasn't so Golden, and Nessa's librarian wanted to find out where the millionaire had gotten his hands on the pile of moldy, old tomes that he'd recently donated to her library's historical section. As expected with a Lovecraft-themed game, the search uncovered a cult, a plenitude of horrid creatures, and a plot to sacrifice the innocent and the less innocent to bring forth an elder god.

In between gaming sessions, Leah had time to explore the ship, read on her balcony, and spend time with Nessa and Ellen. It felt bizarre getting to know her friend and her sister all over again, after having spent six years being friends with Nessa and having been sisters with Ellen for Ellen's whole life. So much of the last eight years, a large part of her brain had been devoted to knowing the ins and outs of a single person, that there were times Leah felt she was also getting to know herself.

She'd anticipated having to distract herself constantly in order to banish the sense of loneliness that draped around her like a bathrobe since the divorce, but oddly enough, Leah's favorite time of day was the morning. Ellen and Nessa would both sleep until almost 9:30, but Leah would wake up before the sunrise. She arranged with room service to bring her iced orange juice, coffee, and a bagel every morning at 7:30. They left the tray in the hallway, and Leah would quietly retrieve it. Once her breakfast had been delivered, she'd go out onto one of the two balconies (whichever one was next to Ellen's bed, since she was the heavier sleeper), and just spend some time watching the water as the sun crept into the sky. Sometimes, flying fish darted across the water, and one time, there was a dolphin. Mostly, though, it was just her and the ocean.

IN MAHOGANY BAY, ELLEN convinced Leah to go ziplining. Nessa had declined, telling Leah to have fun but she'd meet them at the bottom of the course with a few ready plates of jerk chicken. After gearing up, signing a waiver, and riding to the beginning of the course on the back of a pickup, Leah couldn't blame Nessa for bailing. Ellen had been the first on the line, hanging upside down just because she could.

"She's done this before," the guide said. "Okay, who's next?"

Leah felt obligated to follow her younger sister's example, even though it felt like her morning bagel was trying to climb back up her throat. She stepped forward, nodded as the guide showed her how to use her gloved hand to slow down, cautioned her never, ever, ever to put her hand in front of the pulley that she was clipped to, and then she was thrown out of the tree. The small metal wheels whirring and the wind whipping past her face barely had time to register while she kept her feet up like she'd been instructed. Branches reached up toward her from the lower canopy and Leah had visions of oddly industrious jaguars leaping out from the trees below her. Then, she was on the next platform, and that guide was pointing to where Ellen was waiting.

"What did you think? Fun, right?" Ellen gave Leah the exhilarated smile of an adrenaline junkie.

"Maybe. Has there ever been a jaguar attack on someone riding a zipline?"

"Not that I've heard of," Ellen said. "They're usually smarter than that. If a jaguar did try to pull down someone on a zipline, odds are they'd die too from impact."

"Thanks, sis. Now I feel loads better," Leah grimaced.

"Don't mention it."

WHILE THEY WERE IN Belize, they ended up being in the same tour group as Bobbi and Ruy. It turned out that Ruy knew more about the Mayan ruins they were visiting than the tour guide seemed to be able to tell them. He'd whisper asides and point out places that had been excavated since the last time he and Bobbi had been on this particular tour. He had been a history professor at a private university and spent a lot of his free time continuing to research the ancient civilizations of Central America. He was as animated and energetic in teaching as Bobbi was while GMing. After the tour returned to the port, Bobbi insisted on buying her gaming group lunch, and taking a load of pictures to go on her social media.

That night, when they returned to the ship, they had to start getting ready for the Halloween costume party. Nessa insisted on doing everyone's makeup, because she was planning on putting a lot of shots up on her Insta.

"I thought you were on vacation, though," Leah said. She wasn't trying to whine, but her voice did still carry a bit of a plaintive note.

"A professional cosplayer is never off on Halloween," Nessa responded. "Now give me a duck face so I can see your cheekbones."

Leah sucked in her cheeks and pursed her lips while crossing her eyes and flaring her nostrils. There was a flash from Ellen's phone, and a cackle of laughter. "Hey!" Leah tried to get away from Nessa, but Nessa practically sat on her to keep her from escaping. "Ellen, you better delete that!"

"You're just lucky none of us has the internet package, or this baby would already be uploaded," Ellen laughed. "Better yet, I'd give it to Nessa for her 'gram."

"Ellen!"

"Leah, do you want to be Poison Ivy, or do you want to be a demented Picasso? Sit still," Nessa said, releasing an impatient breath through her nose. Leah stopped struggling. Ellen was already dressed as She-Hulk, having procured a green bodysuit and a green wig. Her white dress wasn't a perfect match for the one from the comics, but it was close enough for a non-professional. Nessa was going to work on Ellen's face as soon as she was done with Leah's.

Nessa's costume was on a completely different level, even though she'd made Leah's costume, too. She was going to be Wonder

Woman, and it looked like she'd raided Gal Gadot's wardrobe after the movie had finished filming. With Ellen and Leah both sporting mostly green outfits on either side of her, Nessa was going to look like one very lethal rose. Her fans would absolutely love it.

COZUMEL WAS LEAH'S favorite port. Ellen and Nessa had both agreed to try out the mini-subs with her, which were basically little underwater scooters with attached diving helmets. They went out at 9:30, despite it meaning that Ellen and Nessa had to get up early.

After a brief safety lecture, they were allowed to get into the water. Leah dove down and came up into the helmet. She held her nose and popped her ears like the instructor had directed and then waited for the others in the group to get settled. Looking around at the ocean floor from her bobbing little underwater motorbike, she felt like she could've been on another planet. Once the guides signaled that they could get started, she followed the leading scooter as they puttered through the water. The sun above looked like it was trying desperately to find her through the twenty feet of ocean that didn't normally separate them.

Unbidden, Leah suddenly had the Defenders of Mars pop into her head. If the blue around her had been red, and she was surrounded by air instead of water, it would have made more sense. *Oh well,* she thought. *If I have to have a song in my head, there are definitely worse ones.*

The scooters were approaching an intersection with a school of silver scaled fish. As though this was an everyday occurrence, the fish parted around the alien vessels and kept heading wherever it was they felt they needed to be. A guide in scuba gear floated next to Leah and checked that she was doing okay through a questioning thumbs up. Leah nodded and gave an affirmative thumbs up in response.

Bobbing along in the surreal oceanscape with Defenders of Mars sounding in her head, Leah couldn't help but remember the spark she shared with Lancel♡t. It was highly unlikely that the man behind the mask had felt anything even remotely like it. Even if he did, what was he like? There were all kinds of rumors that Lady Bug was dating one or both of her bandmates, or that Frimmydukes and Lancel♡t were lovers. In general, Leah didn't pay much attention to any of it. The band chose to remain anonymous, and part of that had to be privacy. There were those fans that just didn't know when to back off; Nessa's official address was a P.O. Box for a reason. The odds of her ever meeting Lancel♡t face to face, let alone recognizing him should she be that lucky, were astronomically low. No, even should she be ready to move on, the idea of being with Lancel♡t was little more than a pipe dream.

A sea turtle swept its flipper-like legs through the water, gliding only feet above Leah's helmet. She watched as it eclipsed the watery rays of the sun. *I think I'm going to move*, she realized as soon as the shadow passed from her gaze. *I've never lived anywhere but Texas in my whole life. I'm not exactly swimming in earthly belongings right now. There really won't be a better time. I'll give it a month or two to figure out where I'm going, and let my divorce finalize, but then I'm going to find a new city. Everywhere I go in Houston, I remember something that I did with Alan, or something to do with Alan. I want a fresh start.*

When they puttered back to the boat only fifteen minutes later, Leah felt like she'd been gone for a decade. Everything looked fresher, newer, cleaner. It wasn't that the world had changed, she realized after a moment spent blinking in the sun of the overworld. She had changed, and that changed everything.

Once the three women were back on land, Leah suggested that they go find some authentic Mexican food. They ducked into a place that served tacos, guacamole, and chocolate margaritas advertised on a sandwich board outside. Since she was about to tell them about her big, life changing decision, she offered to pick up the bill. Naturally, that immediately made Ellen suspicious.

"What are you up to?" Ellen asked as the bowl (more like a vat) of guacamole arrived.

"What do you mean?" Leah attempted to maintain an air of innocence, but it only served to make Nessa look at her skeptically as well.

"I mean: what are you up to?" Ellen said, enunciating each word so much that it sounded like five different questions at once. "You're acting like you feel guilty about something."

Leah hesitated, then shrugged. It was true, after all. She did feel guilty, after nearly a month of crashing at Nessa's place, to just suddenly decide she wanted to leave her friend behind. "I decided to move away from Houston," Leah admitted.

"Back to Mom and Dad's?" Ellen didn't look like she approved of the idea, even as she asked. She still wasn't happy about the fact that Leah hadn't wanted to fight Alan for the house.

"No," Leah said. She took a sip of her chocolate margarita and made a face. Somehow between ordering and taking a sip, she'd forgotten that it wasn't a normal margarita. She made a mental note to ask for a soda the next time they saw the server. "I actually have no idea where I'm planning on going yet. I just know that I want to go somewhere new."

"A fresh start," Nessa supplied.

"Exactly!" Leah agreed. "I need to find a place where I'm not about to see Alan and his Barbie doll girlfriend sitting in our old booth or remember the time that Troy and I went shopping somewhere. I don't need constant reminders that I got a divorce. I want to just be Leah, again."

For a long moment, no one spoke, even though there was crunching and chewing in the absence of discussion. *Even in tragedy, no one can ignore a good guac*, Leah thought, scooping a hefty mouthful onto her chip. *I'm pretty sure that's a universal truth.*

Finally, Nessa looked up from the chip she was contemplating. "Did you need a change of company as well as a change of scenery, or would you mind having a roommate tag along?"

Several blinks accompanied Leah's attempt to mentally process the question. "Are you serious? You would want to come with me?"

Nessa shrugged, "The timing is actually really good for me to relocate. I know Uncle Alcide would never kick me out, but my cousin Monica is about to hit twenty-one and they could both use the space. Besides, I've been wanting to get a bit farther from home for a while now."

Springing from her seat, Leah rushed around the table to hug Nessa. Leaving Nessa behind was really the worst part of her decision to move. Nessa's offer to come with her meant that now Leah's only real regret was going to be that she wouldn't be able to go to Escape from Philly Burger anymore.

"So," Ellen waited until Leah had gone back to her seat to swipe the rest of her sister's chocolate margarita. She took a long swig before making the same face as Leah had after her first sip. With a shake of her head, Ellen continued, "that's vile. Are you still buying us lunch?"

Chapter Eighteen

A WHINY, PLEADING MEOW broke through Mel's concentration. "I just fed you," he told Dot, trying to get his head back into the problem at hand. He couldn't actually *fix* a contest, because if that got out it would do untold damage to the fan base. Mel genuinely liked the D'weasels as a whole and didn't want to do anything that would hurt Betham and Jessie's careers either. Instead, he had to come up with a contest that gave them a lot of data but a prize that wouldn't take too much time or energy away from their upcoming album.

Prize ideas:
Prop from one of our video sets.
Autographed t-shirt and poster.
Private Q and A after a concert.
Sneak peek at the newest video.
Something less lame.

Mel pushed away from his laptop as Dot continued to make sounds that urged him to believe that she was the most pitiful and neglected creature on the planet. "Alright, already," he said as he went in search of the kitten. "What do you want?"

Dot was in the kitchen, staring plaintively at her water bowl. It wasn't that the dish was empty because it was nearly full. She seemed to be upset because of the collection of cat toys that were currently submerged. Mel looked at the water dish, and then back at Dot. "Dot, why do you have mice and jingle balls in your water dish?"

The answer he got was a playful twist of Dot's head as she reared up and tried to bat at one of the jingle balls that was still floating. She danced around the bowl, decided that the water presented too much danger, and plopped back down to look up at Mel beseechingly. Mel wasn't sure whether to pick her up for a cuddle or sigh with exasperation. He fished the handful of cat toys out of her dish and freshened the water. As soon as the jingle ball was free, Dot mewed to let him know that was what she was after. Mel tossed it down the hall and began drying the rest of the toys off with the hand towel by the sink. As he was doing so, he heard a jingle and then a small plop. Sure enough, the jingle ball was back in her water dish.

"Really?"

Looking up at him with expectation, Dot sat next to the dish and waited.

"Is this a game now?"

Dot still waited, the expression on her whiskered face one of supreme smugness. He'd had Dot for a couple of months, and the one thing that Mel had learned from his time as a cat owner was that he had no real way of winning this battle. Either he'd throw the toy again, and this would continue, or he wouldn't, and Dot would stare at him for the rest of the evening like he'd wounded her somehow. "Alright," he sighed and plucked the jingle ball out of the water dish, "one more and then I'm going back to work."

There was a toss, scampering kitty feet, jingle, and then another plop. Mel was already heading back to his laptop when Dot gave a meow that was almost as demanding as it was pleading.

Mel closed his eyes and sternly told himself to stay put. He'd already spent a good portion of the afternoon with Dot and the laser pointer. Yet another part of his day had consisted of tossing a feather back and forth on a string. He was trying to make it up to her that he had been gone so much in the past couple of months. She was warm, fed, and he'd plucked her off of the streets, but he still had a tendency to disappear for days at a time, which the kitten wasn't entirely pleased about. Despite the reputation cats had for being standoffish, solitary creatures, Dot seemed to want attention pretty much every moment that she was awake.

"Dot, if you want attention, why don't you come help me work?" Mel asked. He didn't really think she understood the question, but sometimes when he talked to her, she actually did come to him.

Not this time, however. She bounded out of the kitchen and dashed across the couch fast enough that she had to use her claws to stop on the arm, and nearly fell off of it. Then she started bathing her back foot like that had been her plan all along.

"I don't know who you think you're fooling," Mel said. It seemed that the kitten distraction break was over for the moment, so he went back to thoughts about the contest.

He'd figured out the basics of asking for entries: a short video DMed or emailed to the band's main account that included a ticket stub or proof of purchase of some sort, and why the D'weasel felt they deserved the prize. The video had to include a name and contact information. All the standard legalese followed: Void where prohibited, legal age, personal information wasn't to be used for solicitation, etc. That part was easy enough, though it would mean a lot of time for someone, slogging through all of the fan submissions. There was no way that any of them would be able to tackle it until after the current tour had ended.

Very deliberately, one tap at a time, Mel deleted *Private Q and A after a concert* from his list. It irked him to do so, because of the options, it had been his favorite. Of course, his daydreams had the object of his search winning and the Q and A turning into some sort of love confession with him dramatically whipping off his helmet and having an epic time-stopping kiss. The likelihood of that fantasy was very low, because the only way for the object of his search to be the winner would be for their video to be something like, "I deserve to win this prize because I felt a spark when I touched Lancel♡t on the floor of the show in Houston, and hey, here's my very conveniently placed VIP ticket that shows I was definitely the one."

While he was fantasizing, he may as well picture that the encounter was taking place on his personal spacecraft.

As Mel was about to delete the rest of his list out of pure frustration, his phone began to buzz and crawl across his table to the Rush song, "Roll the Bones." Only Betham had that particular ringtone, fitting as well as it did to the combined passions that fueled Betham's being.

"Hey, B, what's up?" Mel asked as he answered.

"Bro! How goes your special proj?"

Mel pulled his finger away from the backspace where it had been hovering since before he grabbed the phone and he stuck that hand under the arm holding the phone, as though Betham could tell from his voice that he'd been about to pull the plug out on said project. "It's... coming along," he said, hating that he didn't even sound convincing to himself.

"Bummer, dude. Not actually calling to check up on ya, though. Jess and I are goin' to hit the family mansion for the big turkey carve and wanted to know if you needed a lift to your parentals."

A sigh of relief made it out of Mel's mouth before he could stop himself. He wasn't going to have to put up with the big family event this year, with all of the well-meaning family prodding about his job as a musician.

Outside of his mom and dad, no one really knew what he did. That meant during most family holidays, he had to endure through an average of five job offers, and several lectures on how he'd never be able to start his own family if he didn't buckle down and make something of himself. This year, Aunt Wanda had told everyone that she was bringing her latest boyfriend, and Mel's dad had no interest in meeting yet another of his sister's conquests. Patrick and Sloane Abrams were coming to see their son for Thanksgiving this year, with the excuse of wanting to see his new kitten. "My mom and dad are actually coming to stay with me for a few days, but thanks for the offer," Mel said.

"No worries, mi amigo," Betham said. He disconnected without so much as a goodbye, but Mel was used to that. Even before his stint in California, Betham hadn't been one for extended partings. Once he was done with a conversation, he tended to just walk away or hang up. Some people got offended by it, but it never seemed to bother Betham what people thought of him. Mel had gotten used to it, even though he'd taken it poorly at first.

It made him wonder what habits his potential Spark had, and whether they'd be deal-breakers. It wasn't the first time the thought had crossed his mind, but as he went back to staring at the list of possible prizes, he did worry about it harder than usual. This project had started in August, it was now November, and Mel and his bandmates hadn't come any closer to solving the puzzle. What if they did find his Spark, and she was worse than Stephanie? What if she *was* Stephanie?

Burrito gods, please, don't let it be Stephanie, Mel shuddered.

"MEL!" SLOANE ABRAMS practically hopped into her son's arms as he opened the door for her. Patrick Abrams was struggling with a massive suitcase that was far and away too large for a four-day weekend. "Are you sure we're not putting you out? We can still get a hotel if you'd like to have your own space."

Even though Mel didn't really have a guest room, since his second bedroom was taken up with a bunch of Magical Space Skeleton Army paraphernalia, he shook his head. "I don't mind giving you and Dad my bed for a few days," Mel assured her. "I'm going to go help him unload, so if you want to greet Dot, I think she's behind the couch. There are some treats in the cookie jar on top of the fridge."

Mel's mother was tall enough not to need a footstool to pull down his cookie jar, which happened to be a housewarming gift from his parents. It was shaped like the Death Star and was more often used as a catch-all than for actual cookies. Right now, though, it proved to be the only container in the apartment that Dot hadn't been able to pry open.

When Mel reached his father, Patrick Abrams paused in his struggle with the suitcase long enough to give his son a proper hug. Mel returned the greeting but couldn't take his eyes off the enigma of the suitcase and its current position. "How did you guys even get it in there?"

"Your mother somehow managed to put it in the backseat all on her own," Patrick said. "She said that if she could get it in the car, she was sure that I could get it back out."

The suitcase was one of the large ones that could hold Princess Vespa's hairdryer three times over. Mel wasn't sure that it couldn't double as its own apartment, and yet, somehow, his mother had stuffed it into the backseat of her Mini Cooper. "Maybe she put it in empty and then packed?" Mel suggested.

His father let out a grunt of not-quite agreement. "Maybe your mother has magical powers."

"Wouldn't one of us have noticed by now?"

"Depends, I suppose. We could have noticed already, and she may have used them to make us forget," Patrick grinned.

"That would be pretty messed up," Mel said.

"Well, you'd be the authority on secret identities," Patrick shrugged and went back to trying to pull the overstuffed suitcase out of the tiny car.

Mel stood there for a moment, stunned. He'd been under the impression that his dad was proud of Mel's success with the Magical

Space Skeleton Army, but that comment had felt a bit barbed. "Dad?" was all he could manage.

With a sigh, Patrick let go of the handle he was pulling on and leaned against his wife's car. "I wasn't meaning to get into this first thing as soon as we got here."

"Get into what, exactly?" Mel asked. He was suddenly pretty sure that his mom's leaving the bag to his father had more to do with distancing herself from this conversation than an eagerness to meet his cat. The idea that she had some sort of mystic power seemed less far-fetched.

"First off, I want to be clear that this is in no way a dig at what you do for a living," Patrick said. "Understood? Your mother and I are extremely proud of you. You work harder than just about anyone we know, and we love what you do. Our friends think we're nuts for following a band of kids that sing about nonsense as earnestly as we do, and my students are always weirded out when they see me outside of class wearing Magical Space Skeleton Army t-shirts. I love you and support you no matter what, though. Even if you weren't doing as well as you are, I'd be happy that you were doing something you love."

It took a while for Mel to process that entire speech, but eventually he nodded. "Okay, I understand. Sort of. This isn't about attacking my job?"

"Exactly," Patrick went back to trying to yank on the handle of the suitcase, as though that speech had somehow cleared everything up.

"Um... Dad? If that's not what we're talking about, what are we talking about?"

His father sighed again and gestured to the opposite side of the car. "Can we talk while we work, then? I'd like to get this inside before it gets any darker out."

Obligingly, Mel went around to the far side of the sunny yellow Cooper with its hard, white top. He got the impression that his dad was actually wanting the enormous suitcase between them more so he didn't have to look Mel in the face as he said whatever it was that he wanted to say. Once the door was open and Mel was using his shoulder to try and shove the suitcase through the other door, Patrick Abrams started speaking again.

"Mel, your mother and I love you very much. We... *I'm*," Patrick amended, making it clear to Mel that his mom had objected to the idea of bringing the concern up at all during the holiday. "I'm just concerned that you're letting this whole identity thing close you off from the rest of the world. You haven't had a significant relationship in close to five years, and every time we talk to you, it's Betham and Jessie, Jessie and Betham. You might mention this Frankie person that Betham's been dating for a while now."

"Two years," Mel supplied.

"There you go, two years," Patrick said. "It's not that we're after grandkids, not that we'd mind if you decided to give us some, but I just wanted to be sure you weren't closing yourself off to some potential happiness by being too concerned for your privacy."

Completely unintentionally, Mel started laughing. It just seemed so absurd that this was what his father had been working up the nerve to talk to him about when Jessie and Betham had sat him down for the same talk almost three months earlier. "I'm sorry, Dad. Trust me, I'm not laughing at you, just... I've got quite a bit to fill you in on."

MEL SAT AT HIS TABLE, his laptop stowed in anticipation of the holiday feast that would take over the table the next day. His mom had never cared much for turkey, so Mel had three guinea hens thawing in his fridge. He was going to make dinner for his parents, since they'd driven to stay with him this year. He had the stuff to make twice baked potatoes, green bean casserole, mushroom gravy, cornbread dressing, and two frozen pies. Mel was pretty decent in the kitchen, but baking wasn't his strong suit. Even though he had to get up early from a night of sleeping on his couch, it still felt good to have his parents staying with him.

"I brought board games," his mom said. "We could play something while you catch us up on your latest news."

Exchanging a look with his dad, Mel realized that he would basically be rehashing everything they just talked about in the car. Patrick Abrams shrugged at his son as though to say, "If you don't tell her, I'll just do it later."

"I hope none of them got damaged while we were trying to get the suitcase out of the car," was all that Patrick said out loud.

"Nonsense," Sloane Abrams grabbed her keys from her purse and headed out the door. "I put the important stuff in the trunk. Back soon!"

"I don't think I'll ever understand that woman," Patrick said, looking fondly at the spot his wife had just exited. "If I live to see one hundred years, she'll keep me guessing to my dying breath."

"Knowing Mom, she'll enjoy every second of it," Mel grinned and picked Dot up off the floor. She gave a startled squeak, and then immediately began purring. Dot was getting noticeably bigger, but she still hadn't grown into her paws. Jessie had claimed the size of Dot's paws indicated that she'd get to be roughly ten pounds. It was hard to imagine such a small creature getting that big.

Patrick watched as his grown son cuddled the black kitten with one sock, grateful that he'd brought plenty of allergy medicine for the long weekend. "You're sure about the not giving us grandkids thing?" he asked. "You'd make a good father. Almost as good as me,"

Patrick's voice almost cracked despite the jovial tone he was trying to achieve.

Mel let Dot down as soon as she started to struggle. As much as she loved a good cuddle, she was still a kitten and there was much romping to be done. While Mel's parents were staying with him, his door was closed to her, a thing without precedent. Piteous meowing echoed down the hall as she requested this atrocity to be rectified. It took Mel a little while to respond to his dad's unexpected compliment and the question attached. "I'm not inherently against kids, but I just don't see it in my future. Even if this whole Spark thing works out for me, which, here's hoping, I'm going to have a lot to deal with just fitting that one more person into my life."

The door nudged open and Sloane reappeared, laden with four bulky game boxes. "We've got some options," she said. "Something easier, something harder, or something in between and possibly Lovecraftian?"

Only Mom would refer to a Lovecraft game as being the medium difficulty, Mel thought. Out loud, he said, "Let's go with Lovecraft. It's been a while since I went insane."

IN THE MORNING, MEL woke up and started preheating his oven. While that was starting, he started on a pan of scrambled eggs and bacon. His kitchen wasn't huge, but he knew it well enough to navigate cooking a small feast for three. It helped that most of his time spent cooking was generally for three. A flash of a memory, the D'weasel, Leah easing her sorrows by tearing into a cheeseburger, popped into his head. If he ever found the Spark he was looking for, he'd have to learn to cook for one more, and that person may be able to eat more than he did. Well, that would be a happy challenge for another day, he decided. Even so, the thought made him smile.

"Something smells good," Sloane Abrams came tottering out of the hall wearing a bathrobe over her flannel pajamas. It didn't surprise Mel that his mom looked bundled up against the cold. The temperature had dipped below freezing the night before, and Sloane had always been the first to grab a sweater when he was growing up. Even though she wasn't quite as lean as the men in her life, she was definitely not built for winter.

"I figured we'd need a good breakfast, since it'll take me until 2:00 or so to get done with our actual Thanksgiving food," Mel said. "Toast or bagels?"

"Toast, please," his mother smiled and began rummaging around in the cupboards. "Where's your coffeemaker?"

"Don't have one," Mel responded. "But I knew you and Dad wouldn't be able to deal without your morning cup, so I got you something." He opened the fridge and pulled out a six pack of bottled coffee.

"Well, it's not what I would've chosen, but it'll do," Sloane said. "This says cold brewed, but I'm gonna heat it up."

"Mugs are in the cupboard next to the pantry," Mel told her. "Just hit the 'Add 30 seconds' button on the microwave."

Sloane kissed her son's cheek and ruffled his hair. "I raised such a good boy."

As soon as her coffee was suitably warm and she was situated in the seat she'd laid claim to the previous day, Sloane broached the subject of the Spark and Mel's search. "So, the thing you were telling us about last night. You haven't the slightest inkling who this person is? Only that they are likely from Texas?"

"Yeah, basically," Mel wasn't really focused on his conversation, but plating the mound of eggs and bacon before they had a chance to burn to his best frying pan. "The Texas thing is only a guess, though, since it happened in Houston. We've had people come from all over the world to concerts in some very unlikely cities."

"So, why this mystery woman and not, say, someone closer to home?" Sloane asked. "I know you and Jessie are just friends, but surely there are plenty of nice local girls available?"

"Mom," Mel started, and then paused trying to find the words. "When you met Dad, what drew you to him?"

It took Sloane a little while to answer. It was odd to think about just how long ago their meeting had been. She'd been married to Patrick for so long that she'd spent more of her life with him than without him. Thirty-five years, and she couldn't imagine it being different at this point, though it nearly had been. "I... I mostly liked the fact that he wasn't trying to date me," she admitted. "I was one of three nerd girls on campus and I got a lot of unwanted attention. Your father didn't try to gain my affections at all. One day it was raining, and he lent me his umbrella. Nothing else. There wasn't a phone number written inside of it, and he didn't tell me his name. I had to find him in order to return it."

"Right," Mel said. "You were drawn to the pursuit. I've got countless women that send Lancel♡t all kinds of nude photos and we all receive unsolicited undergarments in our fan mail. My desire to find this person I sparked with isn't about finding someone the easy way. It's about finding someone that's the right fit. I didn't even realize I was in a downpour, and then I suddenly found myself with an umbrella. That's why I've got to find this mystery woman."

Sloane nodded slowly, finding herself with unexpected tears in her eyes. A plate of scrambled eggs, bacon, and toast slid in front of her and she felt a quick squeeze around her shoulders before Mel returned to the kitchen. She lifted her fork and poked at her eggs a bit, waiting for her son to come to the table with his own plate and a can of Coke. "Since that's the case, I have a few suggestions for this contest of yours."

Chapter Nineteen

DECIDING TO MOVE AND getting ready to move were two completely different propositions. For starters, Leah didn't have a hard time packing, since most of her stuff was already in boxes, but Nessa hadn't even begun to pack. Another issue was that Leah didn't have the slightest idea of where she wanted to go. She liked living next to the coast, but she wasn't sure that she wanted to move from one coast to another. California appealed to her, but it was so expensive. The more she looked into Seattle, the less she wanted to go there. She did think it might be fun to visit, so she put it on a separate list, along with California.

There was something about Indianapolis that kept drawing her to it. Maybe it was the proximity to Anthony, or that Gygax Con was there. Looking into apartments, it was far more affordable than trying to move somewhere along the East or West Coast. There was no way that she could've known that before she started researching, but it was definitely something to keep in mind.

Yet another complication was trying to manage it within Nessa's schedule. Nessa had requested that they wait until after AXES at the very least, because it would be much easier to drive from the current house than flying in from somewhere else in the country.

Leah was trying to be as patient about the delays as Nessa had been with Leah's hibernation just after signing her divorce papers, but she wasn't quite as graceful as she desired.

An accidental evening encounter at a grocery store, when she came face to face with Alan and Brooke Bailey, had pushed her mental moving date forward. Even though Leah would have preferred to exchange nothing more than a brief nod, Alan hadn't been satisfied to leave well enough alone. He had pointed her out to his new girl-friend and the two of them had ambushed her while she was waiting to check out.

Brooke Bailey had smugly talked about how they had met standing in line to a movie theater, waiting to see a horror movie. She'd been so scared to see such a movie, and there he was, about to go in alone! How could she not invite such a brave and lonely soul to sit beside her! It was all Leah could do to stand still and listen to the blonde woman gush about Leah's ex-husband. Alan sealed off the encounter by leaning in to give Brooke a huge kiss, his eye opening to catch Leah's reaction. Any residual feelings that Leah may have imagined she had in reserve for Alan had reduced to nothing but cinders by the end of the encounter.

"How the hell did I spend eight years with that douchebag?" she demanded when Nessa opened the door for her. Leah's key hadn't been cooperating when she was attempting to unlock the deadbolt.

"Love is blind?" Nessa guessed.

"Blind, deaf, and naive," Leah huffed. "Guess who was buying condoms, chocolates and grapes at the grocery store?"

"Not Tom Hiddleston," Nessa said.

"Definitely not Tom Hiddleston," Leah agreed. "Not only was Alan there, being *supremely* Alan, but he was there with his new girl-friend and she was doing that thing where she's pretending to be nice."

"Ah. Yes, the thing where if you try to call attention to it, it just looks like you're a paranoid bitch that's still hung up on the guy," Nessa shook her head as she slid back into her computer chair. She was in the middle of editing a new batch of photos for autographs. "I've encountered it myself. I was a rookie at the time, and I made the mistake of warning the guy because I believed him when he said we could be friends. Some people can, but we could not."

Still feeling a warm pocket of rage boiling around her rib cage, Leah carried her grocery bags into the kitchen. If she hadn't been waiting on Nessa, she wouldn't have had her nose rubbed in Alan's new happiness. Leah resisted the urge to open and slam the door of the fridge a few times. Nessa had legitimate reasons for delaying, and there wasn't any reason to lash out at her for Alan's bullshit.

Popping the top on a fresh pint of Chocolate Fudge Brownie helped Leah's mood considerably. Cold, silky chocolate ice cream with chewy bits of brownie lent her a sense of perspective. Alan being a dick was nothing new, and the fact that he was dating someone like Brooke Bailey had nothing to do with Leah. The reason it tore at her was just that she'd been so certain that he'd loved her at one point, but the longer she thought about it, and the more encounters like this occurred, the less Leah was convinced that it was true. That hurt more than being alone—the realization that her husband, the man she'd thought was her other half, never really felt more than luke-warm toward her.

"Maybe I'm looking at this wrong," Leah said, taking the pint with her as she plopped into the nearly couch-sized chair. "I've had it in my head this whole time that Alan took up eight years of my life. Maybe I should be happy it only took me eight years to break out of what could've been a life sentence. I mean, had things been different, we'd have kids right now."

"Just let me know when you're ready to move on," Nessa said. "When that happens, I have something to show you."

"Oh?" Leah asked. She knew she was fishing for information a bit prematurely. Getting over Alan and being ready for something new were not the same thing. Leah knew herself well enough to realize that a rebound relationship was the last thing she wanted, especially after recognizing Alan's lack of emotional depth.

Nessa seemed to agree with the unspoken commentary. "Nice try, but not yet."

THE ANNOUNCEMENT OF the Magical Space Skeleton Army's new album, the release of their video for "All Hail the Defenders of Mars," and that they had some big contest in the works all came just when Leah needed it most. She had been dreading Thanksgiving ever since D-Day. Since AXES wasn't until January, moving was not the convenient excuse to stay home that she'd been hoping for. At least she and Nessa had made a decision on where they were moving, so between that and her recent cruise, hopefully she could turn the tide of conversation as much as possible.

If it was just her parents and Ellen, it wouldn't have been *so* bad. This year, however, the whole Walsh clan was having a big potluck at her Uncle Scooter's. Uncle Scooter was actually her father's uncle, making him Great Uncle Scooter to Leah and Ellen, but no one ever called him that. Even though Grandma and Grandpa Walsh were older than Uncle Scooter, he was the one that most of the family deferred to when it came to calling in a family gathering. Part of it was that he had more kids. Grandma and Grandpa Walsh had Gerald (Leah and Ellen's father) and Doug. Uncle Scooter had ten kids, the oldest of which was the same age as Leah's dad, while the youngest had been born a year after Ellen. The other part was that he owned an actual ranch outside of Abilene, which meant that he had the room for the whole family to gather in one spot.

Leah normally went to her parents' house to ride out with them when Uncle Scooter was having a big family gathering. Despite her daughters being fully grown, Daphne Walsh still drove her old minivan most of the time. Even with Alan, Ellen, and Leah, they'd had room for more people in the car. This year, though, Leah wanted the freedom of having her own vehicle. She didn't want to be trapped at the ranch until her parents were ready to flee.

Daphne Walsh wasn't taking well to the idea of her oldest daughter asserting a bit of independence. "I just don't like it. You're going to drive from Houston to Abilene on your own? That's a six-hour drive, and then you're going to spend the whole day eating before driving home?"

"I was actually still planning on staying with you and Dad until Sunday, if that's still okay," Leah said. "The drive from my house to Uncle Scooter's is only one more hour than my drive to your place. I'm going to get plenty of time to recover while we eat and mingle, and then it's only another couple of hours to your house. I've driven farther than that in a day."

"Well, of course it's okay. We're looking forward to seeing you, sweetie. Your father can't wait to show you all his projects, and we've had several new games come in. Honestly, I just don't see why you can't come a day early and leave with us. Your sister is coming over on Wednesday."

"You guys live like half an hour apart," Leah tried not to roll her eyes. Her mother would somehow sense it through the phone.

"Alright, well, if you're *sure* that's how you want to spend your holiday," Daphne's tone very much implied that she wouldn't want to drive that much on a holiday and couldn't fathom why her daughter would want to do such a thing. At one point, that tone would have worked on Leah. Before her divorce, she couldn't stand the idea of disappointing her mom like that. Since the divorce, though, Leah felt like she'd learned a lot about what she could tolerate.

Once your world crumbles on you a couple of times, you find out what you're really made of, Leah thought as she exchanged goodbyes with Daphne. *Mom's still going to be there. Even if I told her I was absolutely not going this year, she'd still be there. It's just weird for her that I didn't head back home after Alan and I split up.*

Even as she thought it, Leah realized how true that was. Daphne had called for a week straight after the divorce, not that Leah had picked up the phone. Leah had gotten a number of voicemails, emails, and text messages that were just that: requests for Leah to move back in with her parents so her mom could take care of her.

It wasn't that Daphne Walsh wasn't aware that her little girl had grown up so much as she was a Mama Bear that couldn't stand to see her baby hurting. And Leah had been hurting. She'd been hurting in a way that she didn't want to share. Leah hadn't wanted witnesses to her pain. At the time, the pain had felt real in a way that the rest of the world hadn't, and Daphne had been part of that shadow reality where happiness and love still existed. When Leah had emerged from her crucible of torment with Ellen's help, her mother had left a single message of self-crimination, moaning about how she should've been the one to pull Leah out of her sulking.

Leah wasn't sure what Ellen had said to their mother after that, and she wasn't really sure she wanted to know. The calls had stopped though, and Leah was grateful. It was hard enough to handle her own emotional fallout without having to explain her state of being to a woman that had never gone through the things that Leah had gone through in the last year. Daphne had the best of intentions, but she'd married Gerald, her high school sweetheart and had had two planned pregnancies with no complications. It wasn't that Leah's mother led a charmed life, and Leah knew there had been plenty of things that her mom had sacrificed for her daughters. Those sacrifices were just not part of Leah's pain, and Leah wasn't much interested in comparing. She just wanted to get through it.

Thanksgiving was going to be rough.

"I WAS SO SORRY TO HEAR about you and Alan," yet another cousin said, a thick southern drawl making the words feel even more like a slap than the last five times Leah had heard it. "He seemed so nice, too."

"Thanks," Leah said, trying to edge away before the inevitable follow up.

"So what happened? Why didn't it work out?"

Even though everyone at the ranch was family, Leah didn't understand why it was that everyone felt entitled to the whole unraveling story between a couple that were basically strangers to them. Not one of these cousins or uncles or aunts called Leah for birthdays or sent her a text just to chat, and yet everyone she'd encountered had known about the divorce. It was probably on her dad's social feed or they'd friended Alan at some point over the years.

Leah hadn't posted anything about her divorce, really. She'd switched her status and then posted some of her cruise pics, ignoring her personal messages and looking at the page as little as possible. Every page she had that wasn't tied into her work accounts had a similar amount of attention paid. Social media was not something she'd much enjoyed before the divorce, and nothing that had come after had improved it for her.

Well, nothing save the updates on the Magical Space Skeleton Army. *New album is due out by February*, she thought. *Pre-ordering starts Christmas*. It became her inner mantra to deal with the relentless wave of cousins and questions.

The other thing that helped her deal with the invasive questions was imagining what she could start telling people. "It was my rampant use of steroids," or "Latent homoerotic urges," had been two of her favorites. Of course, telling her family either of those things, or that she had married Alan as part of her cover for a secret mission that was no longer classified (new favorite that just made the list), would only make a new set of problems for her later.

Every so often, one of the extended family *didn't* ask about the divorce. They just nodded and sipped a drink with a wave of uncomfortable camaraderie until the tide of people swept them away again. Eventually, Leah recognized that these were the others of her ilk, those that were divorced and either hadn't or wouldn't remarry. Only five of them existed besides herself. Hers was the freshest wound, and thus the most discussed, but each of them had the well-meaning oblivious poking at the hurt. Something about these encounters was oddly soothing. It reminded Leah that she wasn't alone. Others had survived what she was currently navigating.

Ellen managed to find her in the center of the familial storm and pulled her from the eyewall into the outer edge. Leah couldn't imagine Ellen having to go through a divorce, but then, anyone that managed to date her sister for more than a couple of months was a man of unwavering constitution or maybe the most laid-back individual that ever lived. Perhaps that was why she couldn't imagine Ellen getting divorced; it was very hard to imagine her sister getting married.

"How are you holding up?" Ellen asked, handing Leah a frosty cola can as she rummaged through the cooler for the elusive Dr Peppers.

Leah wasn't feeling picky enough to hold out, so she popped the top and took a long swig of generic soda. The next can, she decided, would not be generic. This stuff had an aftertaste. "Wishing I was back on the ship, honestly. Things seemed much easier at sea."

"That's the thing about vacations," Ellen said. "You always come to the point where you have to come home. Have you talked to Dad and Mom about moving yet?"

With a shake of her head, Leah pretended to study the nutrition label on the side of her soda can. She knew that Ellen wouldn't rat her out, even if she didn't tell her parents about the move until it had already happened, but that didn't mean that Ellen agreed with Leah's prolonged silence on the matter. "Not yet. I'm going to, though. I thought I might bring it up this weekend."

"Not a bad time," Ellen said. "I'm going to be there, so you'll have back up when it comes to talking to Mom. You may even try talking to Dad first. He never liked Alan, you know."

The grip Leah had on her can nearly faltered with her shock. "I had no idea. Dad never said anything to me. He got kind of quiet whenever Alan was around, but I thought that was just because Alan didn't talk much to him either."

Gesturing toward a stockyard fence, Ellen indicated that they were still too close to the edges of the cloud of visiting family members. Any moment, their parents could make their way through the onslaught of people and descend upon the sisters' conversation. The fence was across the river of swarming younglings that had no interest in the adult happenings only yards away. Leah and Ellen had to dodge a few of the kids on their way to lean against the planks that sometimes contained a few horses but currently only held a field of grass and horse dung. "He didn't want you to know, but Alan said something to him at some point that made him feel like this was only a matter of time."

"What did he say?" Leah asked. She wasn't sure how she felt about the fact that her father had apparently seen her divorce coming before she had. Surely, he should have warned her? *But would I have believed him?* her inner voice asked. *Maybe he knew that I wasn't ready to hear it, and he didn't want to hurt me. Maybe he didn't feel it was his place to say anything, and what if he had been wrong? How would I have dealt with the knowledge that my dad didn't like my husband?*

"Dad wouldn't tell me that," Ellen shrugged. "He was concerned enough that I was going to tell you about the rest of it. He was right, of course. I would've told you exactly what Alan had said, but then, Alan and I were never shy about disliking each other."

"Alan never liked Nessa or Anthony, either, and they were the two that were there for me after things fell apart. I'm starting to think he didn't like people based on how much they cared about me," Leah said.

Whatever Ellen thought about that, she kept to herself. Leah had a guess as to where her sister's thoughts were heading and didn't really want to follow them all the way down that road. There were reasons that Ellen wanted to right the wrongs in the world, and while they hadn't touched either of the sisters firsthand, they'd been closer than they liked.

One of Ellen's friends in high school had dated the wrong guy. He'd slowly cut her off from her friends and then started hurting her. It had taken a broken collar bone and a blackened eye for people to realize something was really wrong. Ellen hadn't been able to save her friend. The guilt had stayed with Ellen and driven her to become the driven criminal justice lawyer that she was. She wanted to stop the hurt in the world.

Leah cleared her throat and threw back the rest of her soda. Alan hadn't been abusive, at least, not physically. Toward the end, there may have been some emotional stuff, but Leah wasn't sure if that was truly abusive or just the pressure of trying to stay in a bad situation. In truth, Leah didn't feel qualified to make a judgement. It had been a bad marriage, she knew that much. That was bad enough, in her estimation. She was out of it now.

"I think I need another drink," Leah said. Ellen nodded and finished off her Dr Pepper. They both could use a distraction, and it looked like Uncle Scooter was about to dip the turkeys in the fryers.

AFTER ONE PLATE OF turkey, stuffing, sweet potatoes with marshmallows, and some sort of cheesy rice with something green mixed in, Leah was ready to hit the road. It said something about her day that she wasn't even certain she wanted to wait for the dessert table to be declared fair game. Ellen came to her rescue, snagging a whole pumpkin pie in a travel tin when no one was looking. Someone whose entire career was about justice was awfully sneaky when the mood suited her. Leah wasn't about to complain though, when her sister was more than willing to share her pilfered pie.

They found Gerald and Daphne in the center of a large group of people watching as one of Uncle Scooter's middle children attempted to ride the mechanical bull. Their dad's cousin was well lubricated, despite it only being about three o'clock in the afternoon, and several of his siblings were making bets as to whether or not he'd stay on long enough for the bull to turn on.

"Leah, you should get out there," her dad said, clapping his large hand around his daughter's shoulder. "Tanner's not going to take too long."

"Actually, Ellen and I were thinking about heading out," Leah said. "I was up early to get out here, and I'm starting to run down a bit."

Daphne clucked her tongue as though she wanted to start in on a lengthy, "I told you so," but held back after a glance from her husband. Gerald was a very gentle man and loved his family. He wasn't fond of bickering amongst the ranks, though, and he definitely didn't care for it on a holiday.

"Well, we'll be sorry to see you go, but you're both staying with us so it's not like I won't get to see you for a bit," Gerald told Leah, turning the shoulder clasp into a proper hug. "You be careful on the road, now. If you get tired, let that sister of yours drive. If we're still out about 9:30 or so, make sure Eowyn and Eomer have food."

Eowyn was a blonde tabby cat that Ellen had saved from the side of the road when she was seventeen. The cat was roughly ten at this point, and she had firmly claimed Gerald as her human. After the sisters had both moved out, Daphne had brought home a chocolate lab and named it Eomer, claiming that it was going to be the cat's new brother. Oddly enough, that really was the dynamic between the now grown Eomer and Eowyn. If someone wasn't convinced that her parents were as nerdy as she claimed, the fact that both pets had collars that resembled the One Ring made for a pretty convincing argument.

"Will do," Leah agreed, eager to be off.

IT WASN'T UNTIL THE next day that Leah really got a chance to talk to her dad away from the masses of family and the anxious ears of her mother. Waking up on the same bed that she'd spent most of her childhood on, Leah saw her father's large frame filling her doorway. He raised one finger to his lips and beckoned her to follow him out to his garage. While there was technically enough space in the garage for two cars, that was not where the cars lived. They were banished to the carport outside of the garage while her father had furnished the large, weatherproofed space with all kinds of wood-working tools and silicon molds.

Gerald Walsh, with his ruddy complexion, large frame, and hair as red as his oldest daughter's, didn't come off as the biggest nerd in the world, but that was only before people got to know him. After they found out that Leah and Ellen were named for sci-fi heroines, that his animals were named for LotR characters, and that he made cosplay props and gaming figurines in his garage, they were usually inclined toward Leah's view of it. He was the *biggest* nerd in the world. And his wife and daughters loved him for it.

My dad is the type of guy I thought Alan would be, Leah realized. *Growing older and nerdier with me, like my mom and dad have done.*

"I don't want your mom seeing this until it's done," Gerald said, keeping his voice low so that it didn't carry to the bedrooms of the house. "It's supposed to be a Christmas present."

Shutting the door behind her, Leah stepped down the one carpeted stair that led into her dad's workshop. He led the way over to his project shelf. As long as Leah could remember, the shelf had housed a stack of two by fours on the top level, which she'd always assumed were tossed up there for some forgotten project from long ago. Gerald Walsh never responded with more than a shrug when he was asked about their purpose, and most people soon forgot about them. It had never entered her head that this was by her father's design. He pulled on the outer edge of the wood pile and the whole thing came down as a single unit. That was when Leah noticed the hinges on the side hidden against the wall.

"Dad, has that always been a box?"

"Oh, yeah. This was one of the first things I ever made in here, but that's not what I brought you in here for," Gerald said, a bit absently as he placed the box on his work bench. His focus was obviously on the project he was currently hiding inside of his homemade mimic (minus the face-eating bits). "This is what I wanted to show you."

Leah moved closer and saw that the box currently housed an intricately carved staff head. It had three serpent-like dragon heads that wound around and through each other in a manner that left three orb-shaped settings. It had been sanded and stained, small details done in metalwork on two of the heads. Bits and pieces were kept within smaller plastic boxes, along with a selection of enamel paints that would be used to detail the piece once it was closer to completion. "It's incredible," Leah said. "I don't recognize the design, though."

"It's based on the staff your mom described her character having the first time we were in a campaign together," Gerald said. His voice was a bit gruff, the way it got when he was feeling sentimental. "You're probably sick of hearing it, but it was the first time either of us had been invited to game with that group. I was completely new to roleplaying, but your mom had gone to a few of her ex-boyfriend's sessions. The way she described things... It was so vivid that I felt like I could reach out and touch them. That game is where I fell in love with her."

The lump forming in Leah's throat had little to do with her father's story. She'd heard it many times through the years, and she was pretty sure had contributed to her blindness with Alan. Her story was a shallow echo of the story that had fueled her parents' lifelong bond. "Mom's going to love it," Leah managed.

Gerald nodded, and then turned his detail-oriented gaze on his oldest daughter, "Not the only reason I brought you out here, of course. Ellen says you've got something on your mind. And I've been waiting my turn to have a talk with you about your late marriage."

Something about the way that her father phrased it made Leah's rising barriers melt. If there was anyone in the world that she trusted whole-heartedly, it was her dad. Leah found herself hugging him and sobbing on his shoulder without quite remembering how she came to be there. Her father bore the onslaught of tears with his usual brand of gruff stoicism, holding her until she felt completely cried out. It was the first time in over a month that Leah had really let herself cry, fearing to reenter the cocoon of sadness that had first consumed her after the divorce.

Once she was more or less down to a sniffle every minute and a half, Gerald released his daughter from his bear grip. "Better?"

With a nod, backed onto the metal stool that was constantly situated in front of her dad's jigsaw. She was very careful not to accidentally touch the machine, as it had been drilled in her head from a very young age that the equipment in this room was only as safe as her own caution made it. "I'll live," Leah said. "I do need to tell you something, though. I'm getting ready to move to Indianapolis."

"Why Indianapolis?" Gerald sat himself on the wooden stool that he kept next to his work bench.

It wasn't the first question that Leah had anticipated, but it was on the list. "Honestly, I don't know why it popped into my head initially, but after looking into it, there's a lot that makes sense about it. My friend Nessa is going with me, and Indianapolis is pretty affordable. Anthony already lives pretty close to the city, so we could hang out with him on weekends. I'm wanting a fresh start in a city where I'm not going to think about Alan, or run into him, every time I turn around. Alan and I never went that far north back when we actually went anywhere. It's about as fresh a start as I can get, without leaving behind the people that were there for me."

For a long moment, Gerald Walsh sat without speaking. He'd propped one arm against his work bench and shifted his weight so that one leg was still touching the ground. It was the position that Leah's father usually took when he was about to launch himself into motion on a project that he was still planning. His process was a mixture of gathering materials and envisioning, followed by sketching, and then making. While his work was slow and deliberate, Leah realized that her father possessed his own air of potential energy in just about everything that he did. That potential energy was restraining itself as he considered his daughter's reasoning.

Leah waited. While her father wasn't going to be able to change her mind, he might try. She didn't like the idea of having to debate the matter, but she wouldn't sour his views by trying to press him before he'd issued an opinion. This was her decision; however, that didn't mean she didn't want her father's blessing.

Finally, after what felt like an hour had passed, Gerald nodded his head. "It makes sense that you'd want to get away. We all need to start fresh from time to time." As Gerald said this, his eyes darted to a shelf that he'd attached to the wall above his work bench. That was where he kept a lot of his scrapped pieces until the shelf was out of space. Then he'd shove everything on the shelf into a trash bin and start the collection again. He claimed the shelf served to keep him humble, hanging just at eye-level when he stood. "We'll need to tell your mom about this."

Breathing a sigh of relief, Leah was heartened by her dad's use of the word "we."

Chapter Twenty

"BREAKING FOR LUNCH. Back in twenty," Ethan Burgundy, the sound director, said from the mixing booth.

Mel pulled off his headphones and met with Jessie and Betham in the hall. The recording studio had a meager breakroom, but they didn't have time to run down the street and grab food in only twenty minutes. "Could use one of those cardboard sandwich trays right about now," Mel grinned as he reached out to open the breakroom door.

"No sweat, mi compadre," Betham said. "Delayed delivery allowed me to provide sustenance!"

Three steaming Styrofoam containers were laid out on the table along with chopsticks and plastic spoons. Next to each container, there sat a tray of sushi covered with a clear plastic lid. Betham practically skipped into the room and sat in one of the chairs, pulling out the chopsticks and popping the top on his chosen sushi tray. "Pho and fish, bro!"

Jessie and Mel pulled up their own seats and broke out their utensils. Twenty minutes wasn't long to shovel food into their mouths even with everything set up, but the recording studio charged by the hour. Even having booked the whole day, they had no desire to spend more time away from the microphones than absolutely necessary. Recording in a studio was always an odd experience for Mel. He was so used to having his helmet on when he sang that he practically felt like he was naked when they did album sessions. The studio had non-disclosure agreements and a sterling reputation for discretion, otherwise the Magical Space Skeleton Army would never show up sans costumes. Which would've meant that they'd be recording on their own equipment and the sound quality would be more like their first album, with all of the finishing done by the three of them in the dead hours of the night. None of them wanted to do that particular method of album making ever again if it could be avoided.

Once the edge had been taken off their hunger, they had about three minutes for regrouping before heading back into the booth. "By the by, Mel, I've been meaning to tell you," Jessie said. "The thing you came up with for the contest... I like it."

Mel took a swig from his water bottle before getting to his feet to head back toward the sound booth, not quite meeting Jessie's eyes. "Thanks," he responded. He felt a little weird about taking the credit for something that he'd come up with after talking to his mom during Thanksgiving, but his mom's ideas hadn't really been feasible. Sloane Abrams had suggested that the Magical Space Skeleton Army ask their fans for the best fan suggested song title or make up a lyric for the band's next album.

Even with the legalese and a lawyer, Mel doubted that asking for what amounted to unsolicited material was a sure way to face a bounty of lawsuits. Instead, he'd suggested to Jessie that instead of the contest being for a new idea for a song, what if they asked for video submissions about their own material?

Every single song that the Magical Space Skeleton Army sang held some sort of inner narrative, but there were always new ways to interpret one lyric out of the set. The band was working on their fourth album right now. That meant the D'weasels had almost fifty songs to comb through to find their favorite non-title lyric and submit it with a request for the Magical Space Skeleton Army to come up with a song using that lyric as a title. They would feed all of their non-title lyrics into a randomizer and it would select the winning lyric. If there were multiple submissions of the same lyric, the winner within that group would be chosen by lottery. The rules would stipulate one submission per person, and only one entry per submission.

Of course, they would still have to go through all of the videos to make sure that the video didn't hold multiple entries and the D'weasel in question wasn't trying to push through multiple submissions. The winner's submission would be the title of a brand-new song that would have a dedication to the winner in the next album, and the winner would get flown in to attend the first show of the next tour. Granted, the next album wasn't even in production yet, and the next tour wasn't going to be booked until they completed the one they were on. Still, the contest would take a fair amount of time since they'd have to go through all of the submissions themselves. If they launched it on the same day that they started pre-orders of the newest album, they might even have a winner by July.

That was the part that Mel found the hardest to stomach. After five months, his best plan to find his Spark seemed to hinge on even more waiting.

As Lancel♡t, if he made a video claiming that someone at one of the concerts had shared a moment with him and asked the D'weasels to help him find that person, things would go south in a hurry. It had to be the slow, unnoticeable, gentle nudges. Still, when he imagined what could happen in a year, it made him very nervous. In addition, there had been no way to introduce the concert ticket requirement into the necessary contest conditions that made sense. Mel had let the requirement slide out, even though it made things that much harder on his quest.

Nerves had no place in the sound booth, however, and "Blasting Outer Space" was the song they were about to tackle. Adjusting his headphones, Mel tried to reign himself in. He couldn't let Leah down with a mediocre performance on her song, even if she didn't know it was for her. *A year could change a lot of things*, Mel thought a bit more cheerfully. *Maybe our paths will cross again someday, and I can tell her...*

The thought cut off in his own head as the music started. He hadn't been certain where it was headed anyway.

CHRISTMAS WENT BY IN a blur of twinkle lights and wrapping paper, the latter of which was mostly shredded by Dot. Mel's parents were going on a trip to Ireland this year, so Mel found himself alone, watching old movies and eating a cheese pizza for nostalgic reasons. Having a kitten romping through his small stack of presents helped a bit with the loneliness that he felt, but only marginally. When Betham knocked on the door the next day, Mel was both surprised and grateful.

"Bro, so sorry your parentals bailed on your holiday," Betham greeted Mel with a rare hug.

"I thought you guys were spending Christmas with your folks?"

"Well, we hopped in a van with Frankie and Izzy, but Jess caught a bug or something, so we jammed for the Eve with the fam, but then Jess declared herself unfit for human interaction until the passing of her fever. Frankie and Izzy are chillin' at home, but I got to thinkin' about the fact that you were all holed up on your own and decided to enact some merriment upon you!" Betham went back to the door and picked up a sack that he'd apparently set down before knocking. "I come bearing vanilla vodka and stuff to make nachos."

"Sounds like a party," Mel said, though he wasn't really in the mood for the vodka. He would occasionally drink socially, but he was pretty sure the vodka bottle from the last time Betham had decided to surprise him with alcohol was still in his freezer.

"Not looking to get you wasted, bro," Betham assured him. "Just a bit blurred. Assuming I can crash on your couch, that is."

That made Mel pause. He really looked at Betham, instead of the casual notice that he'd been paying his friend before. "Betham, is everything okay with you and Frankie?"

"Yeah, no worries," Betham said, though his voice sounded a little tighter than normal. He ducked past Mel on his way to the kitchen and started to unload his bag of supplies. Mel knew he couldn't rush Betham to share anything his bandmate didn't feel like sharing. It was so rare to see Betham in any mood that wasn't tinged with contentment and mellowness that Mel felt like Betham was on the verge of shouting and throwing plates. There was nothing so overt going on in his kitchen, though. Just a pan being sprayed with cooking oil, and various cans and jars being opened.

Just when Mel thought that Betham was going to leave things unsaid, Betham began talking, "Frankie and I got into it a bit on the way back from Illinois. We ran into one of my exes from the way back and there were some stories that she didn't know about. It's not like I wasn't telling her stuff; it just never really came up, right? I told her it was just some high school stuff, long past..."

Mel translated most of this to mean that the ex that Mel and Frankie ran into was one of two women that Betham had been with prior to graduating. One of them was Betham's first love, and first most other things. They'd gotten into a bit of trouble for shoplifting beers at one point, and at least one count of public indecency. The other option was a girl that had introduced Betham to drug use. Though the romance had only lasted a summer, and Betham had been lucky not to come out of that with any addictions, the experimentation had strained his friendship with Mel and Jessie almost to the breaking point. Frankie usually had a live and let live sort of philosophy, but she had some lines that she just didn't hold with people crossing. She had told them early on that becoming a mother had lessened her tolerance for certain things, even working in the business that she did. Mel didn't even know all of the stories involved with Betham's two exes, but he suspected some of it would definitely fall under Frankie's banner of unacceptable behavior.

"Anyway, she said she needed some time to process things, and whether we could still be us, after," Betham's voice was full of hurt. "I know enough to clear out for a night when my lady needs space. I'm just hoping this one blows over, ya know? I don't think I could stand to lose her, bro. She's the fire in my sky."

Joining Betham in the kitchen, Mel pulled out a Coke for himself and a Sprite for Betham. Neither of them liked to drink their vodka straight, but there wasn't any Bloody Mary mix or lemonade in Mel's fridge at the moment. He did have one can of coffee left from when his parents had been in town for Thanksgiving, but Betham shook his head when Mel offered it. Pulling out two glasses, Mel took the vanilla vodka and gave himself about a thumb's worth but measured out roughly two thumbs of liquid for Betham.

As Betham dumped a can of pinto beans onto the pile of chips, cheese and olives that he'd already piled together, Mel thought about Betham's relationship with Frankie. When Betham and Frankie had started dating, it had completely floored Jessie. She'd told Mel, in confidence, that she'd always figured her brother was going to have to find someone as mellow and chill as he tended to be. The idea that he'd click with Frankie and her no-nonsense attitude hadn't even entered her head. Not to mention the age difference, which was easier not to think about now that Betham and Frankie had been dating for so long. It was a matchup that never should've occurred on paper, but the idea of them splitting was as unthinkable as the likelihood of their hookup had seemed. Mel set the Sprite and vodka close enough to Betham that his friend could reach for it whenever he was ready.

"So, mildly shit-faced and kids' Christmas movies?" Mel asked.

"And nachos!" Betham rose his glass as though toasting the night's activity roster.

"I still have a bit of cheese pizza, too," Mel said. "Feel free to help yourself."

Dot raced into the room, saw Betham's head bobbing in the passthrough and made a dash into the kitchen to beg for whatever scraps she could. When Betham emerged several minutes later, Dot was riding on his shoulder. As soon as he was settled, she ambled down into his lap and meowed at his hand until it began stroking her. Curling up into a bundle of fur on Betham's lap, Dot started purring loudly enough that Mel would've felt a bit jealous of his kitten's affection if he didn't think that Betham needed it more at the moment.

BETHAM WAS GONE BY the time Mel got up in the morning. There was a written note on the table that said, "Izzy talked her down. I don't know what all she said, but my future daughter is a rock star! Thanks for letting me crash, B."

A surge of relief flowed through Mel's system. Not only would Frankie and Betham making up mean that his friend's happiness was secured, but the Magical Space Skeleton Army wasn't in danger of losing their tour manager right before their last concert of the year. The concert was the night before New Year's Eve, but they were going to do a countdown at the end of the night anyway as sort of an End of Tour celebration. It really wouldn't have felt right to have the final Post Concert Pancakes celebration afterward without Frankie in tow.

They also had to start preparing for AXES in San Antonio. They were not only booked for a show, but they were due for signings on all three days and being given a panel. While the Magical Space Skeleton Army had done a few conventions in the past, they'd never been asked to do a panel before. As nervous and excited as that made him, there was something thrilling at the thought of being in Texas again, only hours away from where he and his Spark had encountered each other. He pulled out his phone and texted Jessie a new thought for their AXES social media announcement. What if people at AX-ES with concert tickets got a free autograph?

Chapter Twenty-One

"NESSA! NESSA! DO I have a favorite Magical Space Skeleton Army lyric?" Leah was practically bouncing in her seat on the couch while trying to hold her laptop steady. "I need a favorite lyric!"

Nessa looked up from the costume trunk that she was currently digging through. She'd begun the process of choosing outfits for AX-ES, a process that was far more involved than Leah had believed prior to moving in with a professional cosplayer. While some professional cosplayers were specialists and focused all their efforts on one character, Nessa was a chameleon. She was planning on bringing a minimum of four costumes per day, to better showcase her talents. Her costume choices had a lot of thought put behind their selection, too. Fan favorites had to make up a certain percentage of her wardrobe, but also a fair number of her newer costumes needed to have their live debuts. Leah's head was swimming as Nessa laid out timetables and charted things like flexibility and ease of motion vs location within the con and activities. Maybe some cosplayers were a bit more lax with their scheduling, but it seemed like her friend was much more type A than Leah had ever anticipated.

"A favorite lyric? Like, just one? Because I can tell you your favorite song," Nessa said, before heaving a sigh and shutting the trunk in front of her. "I can't find my Korra hair pieces. How vexing."

"What is my favorite song?" Leah asked. Before the concert, it had been "Then She Puked on Me," but things had been shifting around in her head a lot lately.

"Currently, it seems to have become 'All Hail the Defenders of Mars,' and I'm pretty sure it's because of..."

"Don't say it!" Leah said. She'd been trying to convince herself that her spark with Lancel♡t had been born of a fantasy, just a random daydream that hadn't influenced her day to day decisions in any particular way. Mostly, this was more to protect herself from forming an attachment to a man that she had no way of meeting than because she really wanted to forget it. *But if I win this contest, surely the band will at least high five the person they're flying out to a concert, right?* her traitorous brain insisted.

"...the concert," Nessa finished saying it anyway. She was every bit as bad as Leah's brain, bringing up the incident with Lancel♡t more often as well.

"I didn't want you to say it," Leah glared at her friend.

"You may as well acknowledge that you are crushing on the lead singer, and hard," Nessa said. "I think it's healthy. It'll help you move on from your asshole ex-husband."

"I'm all for moving on with my life," Leah said. Even as she said it, she was pulling up the lyrics of "All Hail the Defenders of Mars" on-line. If nothing popped out at her, she would check every song in the discography until she found the perfect lyric for a new song. Not that she knew anything about songwriting. Somehow, though, she had to find the right one. "That's why we're moving up to Indianapolis. I am literally moving on. I just don't want to fixate on someone that I know I'll never get and close myself off to someone attainable in a real sense, you know?"

Nessa opened her mouth to say something and then seemed to change her mind. Leah still hadn't actually told Nessa she was ready to get out there again romantically, but the day seemed to be getting closer.

The contest deadline wasn't until March, so Leah went back to the tab that held her Magical Space Skeleton Army announcements. She hadn't told Nessa about becoming a patron recently, since she didn't want to give her friend even more ammunition in the Lancel♡t crush conversation.

"They're going to be at AXES, you know," Nessa said, uncannily voicing the same thing that Leah had just come to in her feed.

Leah let out a squeal of delight and jumped up and down in her chair until it interfered with her ability to read. Autographs! And a panel! Their first panel!

"I've got to get into that panel! It's on Saturday at 3:00. Would you be able to come with?" Leah asked.

Before Nessa had gotten out more than a, "May-," Leah was bouncing in her seat again, "I can get a free autograph with proof of a concert ticket! Do you still have your ticket? Or a receipt or something?"

"I knew it!" Nessa said, getting to her feet and running out of the room.

Leah wasn't sure what to make of her roommate's behavior. She wasn't sure whether to follow Nessa or wait for her to reemerge from wherever she'd gone. Nessa came back with a ticket stub and handed it to Leah, grinning like she was the sole possessor of something that would shatter the Konami code. "You knew what?" Leah asked, reaching up uncertainly to take possession of the extended ticket.

"I think somebody's looking for you," Nessa grinned. "The requests for concert pics, the freebies, the contest... You weren't the only one that felt something that night."

"No," Leah denied it, her voice dropping several octaves in disbelief. "He can't be... No... How much sense would that even make?"

"The heart wants what it wants. Sense need not apply," Nessa shrugged, though she was still grinning as she went back to her costume arrangements.

It's all in her imagination, the logical part of Leah's brain argued. *Nessa is seeing patterns in things that are just coincidence.* Even so, Leah felt a warmth in her chest that she hadn't felt in what seemed like eons. She closed her laptop and went into her bedroom to process this newest development in solitude. Should Nessa be right about this, and the Magical Space Skeleton Army was looking for her, it wasn't like she could just go up to Lancel♡t during a signing and say, "Hey, we had a moment back in August. Want to date?"

How embarrassing if he said no. How dangerous, in front of all of those D'weasels, if he said yes. How would she even go about proving something like that? And how did you date a man in a mask? Superhero movies and comic books always made things look, if not easy, less daunting. It was impossible to tell what kind of person Lancel♡t was outside of his persona. She'd been reluctant to admit a crush, and now she was trying to imagine an actual relationship based on Nessa's crazy theory. *This is absurd*, she pulled out her laptop and started going through some work emails to take her mind off of the idea. *Whether she's right or not, I can't do anything about it right now. I'm just an average D'weasel going to AXES, and that's it.*

The warmth in her chest refused to fade despite her inner assertion.

SINCE AXES WAS PRIMARILY a video game convention, the majority of Nessa's cosplay revolved around characters that were either originally from or had been made into video games. She was starting out on what she called "Easy Mode," with Lara Croft, complete with dirt smudges and bloody looking smears. Leah was glad that Nessa's status as a guest meant that they'd received their passes before arriving at the con. Day one, and the registration line was already insane.

Soon the Expo Hall would open, which would cut down on the crowding in the halls a bit. Because Leah was here on a comped badge as part of Nessa's invitation, she wouldn't be eligible for any of the raffles or door prizes, which disappointed her a bit. But the odds of being one of the few winning attendees selected was ridiculously low anyway. *Almost as low as the probability of attracting someone like Lancel♡t,* her thoughts interjected. Leah shoved it away to a back corner of her brain.

Nessa begged off to go make her first costume change now that the booth was set up. She was going to spend a few hours standing near it and posing for pictures and selling autographs. It took Leah a moment to remember that Nessa might need help, but by the time she thought to offer, Nessa was already gone. Looking around the large crowds of people waiting for the con to open its gates, Leah waited for the pang of sadness that she usually experienced when she realized that Alan wasn't there, wasn't coming, and had no part in her life.

It didn't happen. If she could've used her hands to physically check the spot that her Alan wound had been, she would've done so. The lack of pain was so surprising that Leah froze in her tracks; luckily, most of the crowd was confined to their various queues, and no one was close enough to stumble into her.

Because she was motionless, she happened to be looking in the right direction to see a familiar face, though it took her a little bit of thought to place it.

"Oh my god, Merlin?" she breathed. It wasn't until that moment that she remembered him saying something about being in San Antonio for AXES. In fact, it wasn't until that moment that she had really thought about their encounter at Escape from Philly Burger.

Some of those in between moments of not thinking about it had been harder than others. *It's not like you can just forget a total stranger admitting that they like you,* Leah felt her heart palpitating in surprise, and perhaps a bit with excitement.

"Merlin!" she yelled across the room, then realized that name was shared as a secret. He probably wouldn't even register that she was calling him. *Shit, what was it that he went by?*

His lanky legs covered more ground in a single stride than Leah's and she was starting to fall behind. Finding him again in a convention like this on accident seemed highly unlikely and she didn't have his phone number. She couldn't text him and meet up later. Something in her rebelled at the thought of letting this opportunity pass her by. *Damn it! What was his name!* Leah gritted her teeth and shouted, "Merlin!" again, hoping that if he actually heard her, he'd forgive her.

He'd paused, his head slightly shifting in her direction. A group of cosplayers that were dressed as the crew from Mass Effect ambled their way past her, the shortest of which was a Tali that still had a few inches on Leah. On a normal con occasion, Leah would be asking the group for a picture and cooing over the excellent Garrus and Wrex that this group boasted. Right now, she just wanted Shepard to get out of her way, Savior of the Universe or not.

"Merlin!" she tried to jump up so she could see past the crew of the Normandy, but by the time they'd made their way past her, he was gone.

Chapter Twenty-two

MEL FELT LIKE HE WAS forgetting something or hearing something from too far away. He wasn't sure what the feeling was connected to as he made his way through the crowded-if-spacious corridors of the convention center. San Antonio loomed just outside the doors, boasting such historic sites as the Alamo and the first building with air conditioning. Mel enjoyed the Riverwalk, with all of its shops and restaurants, but the number of stairs almost overwhelmed him. He had thought he was in fairly decent shape before they went out for lunch on their first day in town.

Again, he had that feeling, like if he just turned his head, he'd remember something. Just as he thought he caught a glimpse of red hair, a group of Mass Effect cosplayers blocked the walkway as they made their way toward parts unknown. Mel picked up his own pace, recalling that he was already running late for gearing up for their first autograph session. He'd left his helmet in the hotel room, and there was no way that he could do autographs without it. Maybe that was why he felt like he was missing something important, but then again, it could just be a case of pre-signing jitters.

Dreams about being outed as Lancel♡t had plagued him most of the night: from the first dream where someone had stolen his helmet right off of his head and run around the center jeering at him, until the last dream where the kid from New York found him and had the ability to make his costume melt just by touching it. It didn't make him feel any better that he'd somehow woken from those dreams to actually forget the most crucial bit of his Lancel♡t attire.

Being invited to AXES was a huge deal for the Magical Space Skeleton Army. Mel told himself to get a grip. Betham and Jessie were no doubt going to bring their A game, and he needed to match them.

THEIR FIRST SIGNING event was taking place in a small auditorium on an upper level. Normally, this would be set up for a panel or an auction, but it was still the first day of the con, so panels and auctions weren't really on the schedule yet. When Mel arrived at the green room, he found Betham and Jessie fully attired as Frimmydukes and Lady Bug. He rushed to stuff himself into his Lancel♡t costume, embarrassed that his band was waiting for him before they signaled an escort to lead them through the back halls to their signing space. There was one con staff handler already standing uncomfortably at the door to the main hall, trying to pretend that she was invisible and not impressed by being close to celebrities, even minor ones in ridiculous costumes. The woman peeked out through the slightest crack she could manage with a door that size, and her walkie-talkie buzzed.

"Okay, we're ready back here," she responded to the static-laden voice on the other end. Apparently, she had worked a few cons, or security, because Mel couldn't understand anything coming out of the walkie-talkie.

"You guys already have a line," the woman said, opening the door. Feel free to seat yourselves at the table, and if you need more Sharpies, let me or Sylvia know."

Frimmydukes released a whoop the moment he entered the room. To say they already had a line was an understatement. People were wound through the room, smiling at each other with enthusiastic anticipation. If it weren't for the cheer that erupted at Frimmydukes' arrival, Mel would have believed there had been some sort of mistake. It was one thing for people to line up like this and cheer them at a concert, but this was a line where they'd get maybe five seconds of his time in exchange for a couple of hours of their day and an entire pizza's worth of money. He'd been on the other end of this line, waiting eagerly to meet someone that was one of his personal heroes. The thought sobered him and made him feel weirdly giddy all at once.

And maybe, somewhere in this line, my Spark is waiting to be found, Mel thought. With all of the D'weasels that were currently craning their necks to get a good look at him, Mel hoped he wasn't blushing. To hide his embarrassment, he blew a kiss to the crowd. They let out another cheer that rumbled like thunder in the upper corners of a room that was not made to house such a sound.

THOUGHTS OF HIS SPARK all but fled as a familiar face framed by red fly-away hair approached him with a ticket stub and a nervous smile. Mel felt himself grinning like a smitten idiot, but he hoped that it didn't look too different from the I-Love-My-Fans smile that he was giving everyone else. He very nearly said something that Lancel♡t didn't know, which would've made all his dreams from the night before all the more real. Lancel♡t had no reason to know Leah's name.

"Hi," her voice held steady despite the fact that she looked as ready to run away as she was eager. Mel wanted her to speak more, to greet him like an old friend. He wanted to give her the hug he'd promised her when writing her song. Of course, none of those things would make sense to her.

Instead, he responded with his own, "Hi."

It took the coaxing of one of the con attendants to remind them that she needed to select one of the headshots so that the band might begin signing it.

The knowledge that Leah was here, at AXES, made him almost as excited as the panel that they were doing the next day. He was concentrating so hard on not saying her name that he very nearly wrote it before he realized that would also be hazardous. Her badge didn't say "Leah"; actually, it labeled her as NotaDecepticon. If Mel hadn't already been grinning from ear to ear, that would've made him smile. Again. "Who should I make it out to?"

"I... Leah," she said. There seemed to be something she was on the verge of saying, if they just had more time. "L-E-A-H."

Even though they were verging on taking too long, Mel wrote, "To the best D'weasel that ever Weaseled, my Leah, Lancel♡t." It was a bit much, even for one of his signatures, where he liked to play up the heart symbol in his name, but he wanted to tell her so much more; he wanted her to know it was him behind the mask. But that secret wasn't just his. Mel's exposure could unmask the whole band.

He watched as she made her way to Lady Bug's table where Jessie greeted her professionally, but not with any overt familiarity. Of course she wouldn't, Jessie had no idea who Leah was. The two of them had never met with or without the costume. Why should Mel expect his friends to recognize a woman they'd never seen? Somehow, he thought that Leah's importance to him would wash over the others like some sort of aura.

It wasn't until the next D'weasel in line came up to him that he remembered that he hadn't checked Leah's ticket stub for seating information.

Chapter Twenty-three

SHE HAD CHICKENED OUT. Leah clutched her Magical Space Skeleton Army picture through its protective autograph bag that someone had handed her on her way out of the auditorium. Lancel♡t had been exceedingly patient with her clumsy attempt to talk to him, and his note to her was obviously filled with pity for how tongue-tied and awkward she had been.

If Nessa asked her right this minute, Leah was ready to admit it. She had a full-blown crush on Lancel♡t. How in the hell she had thought she'd tell him that she'd felt a spark the first time they touched, though... *He must hear things like that fifty times a day*, she felt herself blushing at the absurd notion of bending over one of those tables to try and whisper into the ears of a man wearing a helmet. Even if she had managed to find the courage, it was probable that he would've just nodded and motioned for the next D'weasel in line.

After the earlier incident when she had tried to chase down Merlin, and now the thing with Lancel♡t, Leah was feeling very let down. It wasn't like she'd really imagined the con going much differently, but somehow, she'd imagined everything going better. Lancel♡t would somehow know, just by looking at her, that she was the one, and he'd find a way to tell her.

With one failed marriage under my belt, you'd think I'd have stopped believing in the fairytale, Leah thought ruefully. *Here I am mooning after the guy that I just spent an hour in line just trying to get to, when every other person in there is probably hoping the same things about one or all of those band members.*

Leah shook it off and tried to enjoy the autographed photo for what it was: free.

THE NEXT MORNING, NESSA convinced Leah to get out of bed early enough to go out for breakfast. Somehow, Nessa had managed to get into her costume without even waking Leah up. Normally, that would've been impressive enough, but Nessa was starting the day as Princess Farah from the Prince of Persia games, with real bits of chain mail and extremely jangly jewelry.

"I'm never not going to be astonished at how easy you make that look," Leah muttered as she trudged along the many sets of stairs between them and the promised stacks of eggs and bacon.

"Like anything else, it's a matter of practice," Nessa said. "Now step quick. This is one of my coldest outfits. If this were any other con, I wouldn't have bothered pulling it out in January."

Despite Nessa's assertion that this was one of her coldest outfits, Leah wasn't too worried about her friend. She was wearing a fleece lined cloak overtop of the ensemble, and though it was chilly, it wasn't freezing. The river itself seemed to be giving off a fair amount of heat, making the Riverwalk warmer than the streets.

"Not even E-Expo?" Leah asked. She wasn't really sure if she was teasing or genuinely curious.

"E-Expo isn't in January," Nessa said after a moment.

"I know. But if it were, would you pull this costume out for it?"

There was a pause that was much longer while Nessa considered the question. "If, for some reason, E-Expo was held in January, and I was invited as a cosplay guest, then yes. I could see myself pulling it out for that. But that's it. AXES and E-Expo."

"I guess it's good to know your boundaries," Leah said.

They found a sandwich shop that had a breakfast menu. Despite it being too early for any of the scheduled con activities, or maybe because it was too early for con activities, there were a number of people in the restaurant sporting badges and a few more cosplayers scattered around the tables. Leah was scanning the faces for Merlin before she was even really aware that she was doing it. Nessa grabbed a couple of menus and pulled Leah along into the line before any newcomers could crowd their way in front of the two women.

"Who are you looking for, anyway?" Nessa asked.

"Is it that obvious?" Leah hid her face behind her menu rather than look her friend in the eye. If it hadn't been that obvious, Nessa wouldn't have said anything. Leah figured her cheeks were probably as red as her hair.

Nessa did Leah the courtesy of not answering her mostly rhetorical question.

The line moved forward, and Leah stepped with it, still buried in her menu. She was reluctant to tell Nessa about the two events that had happened while Leah was on her own. At the same time, if she didn't say something, she felt like she was about to burst. "Okay, okay, okay... You remember that guy I told you about? The one that I met at Escape from Philly Burger on the day of my divorce?"

"Mel something?"

"Mel! That was it!" Leah felt one star move back into alignment. The time was not yet right, but soon, the elder gods could awaken, maybe. "I saw him yesterday."

"Really? Didn't you say he was from out of state?" Nessa asked.

"Chicago or something," Leah nodded. "He was in town for the concert last time, and I think he mentioned AXES and Gygax Con."

"Trust you to remember the conventions better than the guy's name," Nessa didn't laugh out loud, but Leah could tell from the amused crinkles around Nessa's eyes and the way her nose flared that it was starting to bubble to the surface. "Are you sure it was him?"

That was something Leah had been asking herself since her mad dash through the convention center. She'd only seen his face for a few seconds, but she had been so sure of it in the moment. Unless she happened to find him again, Leah wasn't entirely sure she hadn't imagined it. "Not really one hundred percent," she admitted. "Maybe more like ninety-three percent."

When they got up to the counter, Nessa placed her order, and Leah realized that she hadn't really absorbed anything from the menu. She picked the name of something at random and hoped that it wouldn't have powdered sugar or blueberries. Neither of those things belonged on a breakfast menu, in Leah's opinion, but the rest of the world didn't always agree with her.

It was just as their food arrived that Leah convinced herself to stop looking at the door each time it swung open. Naturally, that was when she heard a familiar voice behind her say, "Leah?"

Chapter Twenty-four

MEL COULDN'T BELIEVE it. He'd imagined that he would have to scour the convention looking for her, and probably end up heading home without ever laying eyes on her. Except when he happened to be in costume as Lancel♡t.

When he'd gotten up this morning, Mel had been mildly annoyed that Jessie had blown him off for breakfast in favor of meeting up with some woman she'd met at a con party the night before, but the moment he saw Leah that irritation passed out of his system quicker than tickets to a TNG reunion panel. Leah's head whipped around leaving a mess of hash brown and egg dangling from her fork.

"Holy shit! Mel! It is you!" she started to jump up to greet him, but then seemed to rethink her impulse. There was a very large man cosplaying a barbarian blocking her chair from behind, and it may have occurred to her as it had to Mel that they really hadn't known each other all that long. "I mean... I thought I saw you yesterday, but then I wasn't really sure if it was you or not."

All Mel could think of was seeing her walk toward him in the autograph line. *Shit... Did she... No... Maybe? ...Shit...* "I, um... I..."

"I actually chased you for a little while, but then a bunch of cosplayers got between us," Leah was blushing. Mel's fears and half-formed explanations evaporated, and all he seemed to be able to focus on was the way her eyes caught the light.

There was a delicate coughing sound from across the table Leah was seated at. The dark-haired woman that Mel only dimly remembered as the friend Leah had been with at the Pancake Hut nearly five months ago, wearing a professional level cosplay outfit that Mel didn't immediately recognize, was waiting for an introduction or some sort of acknowledgement. It was probably rare for someone not to notice her immediately, let alone miss her entirely.

"Sorry," Leah said. "Sorry. I'm completely out of my brain, today. Nessa, this is Mel, the guy I told you about. Mel, this is Nessa. She's here professionally, and I'm just kind of tagging along."

Mel and Nessa nodded to each other, but they were too far away, and the place was too crowded for the traditional handshake. There was a slyness to the look that she gave him that made Mel almost as uncomfortable as the moment he'd thought Leah had seen through his mask. Though if he was entirely honest with himself, that moment had been tinged with excitement as well. He wasn't sure why, but Leah made him want to throw down all of his barriers. Even thoughts about his Spark tended to dull when she was around.

"Well, I should, probably go get in line," Mel started to excuse himself, even though leaving was the last thing he really wanted to do. "It was great to see you again!"

As he was starting to turn away, Leah caught his jacket sleeve. It wasn't a firm grip, just enough to get Mel's attention. "Wait, I just told you I tried to chase you down, and you're going to just leave?"

"I'm... I'm here professionally, too," he said. "I'd really like to meet up later, though, if our schedules mesh."

"Maybe the Magical Space Skeleton Army panel?" Nessa suggested. Even though Mel had just met her, he wondered if there wasn't something arch in her tone. "Leah mentioned that you were a D'weasel."

"Unfortunately, I will be working," Mel said. He didn't have to act hard to achieve the level of disappointment that a D'weasel should have for missing something like that. On the one hand, he was elated to know that Leah would be there to see his first panel, but the idea that he could be with her, doing something together almost made the panel into a chore. "I will be free closer to four o'clock. I'll have maybe an hour and a half or so."

"Meet me in front of the Expo Hall? We can go gaming," Leah suggested.

It was all Mel could do not to give out a victory whoop that would've rivaled Betham's entry into the autograph room.

AS EXCITED AS MEL WAS about his designated hang out with Leah later on, Mel couldn't stop thinking about the look on her friend Nessa's face. He tried to tell himself that he had imagined it, that there was nothing to worry about, but he couldn't quite let it go. Had the suggestion of meeting at the panel been innocent, or had she been hinting that she knew something?

Rather than drive himself crazy with jumping at shadows, Mel arrived early to the dressing room that they'd been allotted by the con staff. It had an entrance through the back hall so that people couldn't watch all the comings and goings in order to figure out that three of the normal con attendees were the Magical Space Skeleton Army wandering around as their alter egos, or in Jessie's case cosplaying as the Tenth Doctor. When Jessie arrived, Mel was trying not to pace, which just meant that he was pacing in small worried spurts between pauses.

"Mel, what the fuck are you doing?" Jessie asked. She didn't waste much time watching him but immediately went to her makeup vanity and began transitioning from the Doctor into Lady Bug.

"I... I'm not sure. I saw her, and her friend may know something, but probably not?" Mel said, aware of how nonsensical his sentence was only after it left his mouth.

"Saw who?" Jessie didn't seem all that put off by his nonsense. If anything, she looked a bit excited. "Did you find your Spark? Did we find her?"

"Leah, the woman from Ray's restaurant," Mel said. "She's here. She actually got our autographs yesterday."

"Wait..." Jessie actually looked away from the mirror to lock eyes with Mel directly. "The divorcee that you spent the afternoon with down in Houston is a D'weasel?"

"Yeah. Did I not mention that before?"

"Has it ever occurred to you that she might be the one we're looking for?" Jessie asked.

"But... she was married at the time," Mel said, as though that were all the answer he needed. It had never been more than a passing notion to him that the Spark may not have been available at the time of the concert.

Jessie's expression held something like genuine pity. "Mel, no one can control a chemical reaction. Even the most devoted person in the world can feel something in a touch every now and again. It's not about feeling a thing, it's about how you react. So, how about it? Have you and this Leah person ever brushed hands, hugged each other, anything?"

"I... I can't remember," Mel's cheeks flushed at the admission. "Maybe? She tugged on my jacket earlier."

"Okay, well, that doesn't really answer much of anything," Jessie shrugged and turned back to her mirror. A liberal amount of red powder was applied to her cheeks and forehead, mostly areas covered by her mask. She put the large brush away and started drawing in black freckles and giving her eyes more of a tilt. "If finding your Spark isn't what's got you all agitated, what's up?"

Launching into an extended play by play of his encounter with Leah and her friend Nessa, Mel explained his concerns. "So am I crazy, or does it seem like she knew?"

While he was waiting for Jessie to respond, Betham wandered into the room and started stripping down to his boxer briefs. Neither his sister or Mel paid him much heed. They were bandmates, after all. There were plenty of times that they didn't have access to private dressing rooms. It wasn't exactly comfortable, but it was something they were all more or less used to. "I'm not sure, Mel. Honestly, having not been there, it's a possibility. Equally likely, though, is that she honestly just thought you'd like to go with them. It's not like you can ask her to clarify."

Betham dragged his stool over as soon as he had his body suit and harem pants on. "So what's the dealio?"

Mel told his story again, and Betham nodded along. "Dude, that's a hard call. Could be she's rolled a nat twen' on her perception, or could be some confirmation bias based on your New York encounter with that tiny bro."

"What should I do?" Mel asked.

"Unless she says something, not much we can do," Jessie said, pulling out a lipstick tube and twisting until the nub of pigment was visible. She used black lipstick as Lady Bug, and regularly stocked up at Halloween stores. Mel wasn't sure where she acquired it during the rest of the year. "Best thing would just be to avoid her."

"What about Leah?" Mel asked. "Nessa is her friend. I'm not sure if I can avoid one without avoiding the other."

"Your call, bro. We're not about to make you give up your lady friend, but we can't say you're not taking a risk," Betham said. He spun the stool around back over to his portion of the dressing room and began the task of gluing on his ears.

Turning to his own costume, Mel began to unbelt his jeans. He wasn't really comfortable with the idea of it being his call whether to risk associating with someone that may have identified him. Then again, if his bandmates had told him to avoid her at all costs, he wasn't sure if he would've been able to keep himself from hanging out with Leah anyway. His friends weren't stupid; they knew him well enough not to box him in by asking for promises he couldn't keep. Still, he owed it to the band to keep his secret and theirs.

As he donned Lancel♡t's helmet, he put the potentially heart-rending decision on pause. Lancel♡t had a panel to attend; Mel could make his decisions later out of the limelight.

Chapter Twenty-five

BY THE TIME LEAH AND Nessa met up for the Magical Space Skeleton Army panel, Nessa was no longer Princess Farah, but Vincent of Final Fantasy fame. Leah hadn't actually seen this cosplay before and commented on it.

"I made it during that month that you were still deep in your pit of mourning," Nessa shrugged. Leah got the feeling that Nessa wanted to grin, but it wouldn't be in keeping with the broody persona of her current crossplay. "I'd been wanting to make this one for a while. I knew it would be a big hit, and I was drawn to how warm it looked."

"That being the case, I'm surprised you wore it in the afternoon instead of this morning when you could've used it," Leah laughed.

"I'm efficient, but even I make mistakes," Nessa said. "Shame your friend Mel couldn't make this, don't you think?"

Leah nodded. Despite Mel saying that he'd probably have to work through the panel, she was trying to keep an eye out for him. Of course, if he wasn't in line already, the probability of his getting in was extremely low.

Because Nessa was a guest, they had tickets to the panel already in hand. Several of the people that were being turned away made grumbling remarks about unfair treatment, demanding to know how it was that two women who had just shown up happened to have tickets. Con personnel flanked by con security were fielding the complaints with explanations about pre-registration for certain events being available to people on the VIP list. This led to a new volley of complaints about how some people thought they should've made the VIP list, and how there would be lawsuits and negative reviews.

The unfortunate con staff member that was weathering the deluge of bile did so with a quiet dignity that impressed Leah. Just watching the exchange, she couldn't believe that people volunteered for these positions. Even though she was here on a comped badge, she was pretty sure she'd rather pay full price for a weekend pass than deal with some of the stuff that she'd witnessed the con staffers suffer.

"You girls okay?" one of the con security officers asked. He was an older man with a graying beard and a large gut that rode over the top of his black pants. Even though Leah doubted he could run someone down, he was big enough to be imposing anyway. "Mind if I take a look at your tickets and your badges? I'm sure you're probably fine, but with a complaint on record..." he gave a shrug that wasn't quite casual enough to be believable.

They showed him their tickets and held up their badges. He wrote down Nessa's information first, and then barely glanced at Leah's. Walking a short distance away, he pulled out his walkie-talkie and spoke with someone on the other end. There was a burst of static, a lot of nodding, and then he came back over. "Sorry to bother you ladies," he said, walking away as the other guards escorted the most vocal of the complaining guests off toward someone higher up the chain.

"Is that going to reflect poorly on your status as a guest?" Leah asked.

"Unlikely," Nessa said. "I'm pretty sure that was just them verifying that we were actually on the VIP list, since that one guy was bitching about how we looked too young to be important."

"Seriously? Has he never heard of Millie Bobby Brown?"

Nessa didn't respond to that. Leah hadn't really expected her to say anything anyway. In general, Nessa tried to avoid expressing negative opinions, but she was even more reticent in such a public arena. This was the kind of situation that would likely get spoken of in a lot of quiet corners until something juicier took the focus of the con gossip circle. Nessa Fierro getting called out by a guy while in line to attend a panel was only kind of interesting. If someone heard her bragging about how important she was or saying the guy deserved it, it would get ten times the attention. Leah bit her tongue to keep it in check. She didn't want to cause Nessa any more trouble by saying something dumb that she couldn't take back.

"Are you going to try and ask anything during the Q and A portion of the panel?" Nessa asked.

"I... I'd like to, but I have no idea what I could ask about," Leah said.

"You could ask them what lyrics they'd submit to their own contest," Nessa suggested. "Or you could just get up to the mic and wing it. Maybe bring up something about Lancel♡t rushing the floor in Houston..."

Leah just shook her head as the burning sensation of a blush hovered just under her collar. She wished that she'd outgrown her blushes the way her sister had seemed to, but they'd never gone away. Even when she and Alan had been married, and he'd tried to talk to her about sex or she was the one picking up their condoms before they'd decided to start trying, the blushes had been there. Alan had originally thought it was cute, but toward the end of their marriage, he'd seemed to find them tiresome. One more reason for Leah to be glad that was over, not that she really kept track anymore. "I didn't tell you, but I got my free autograph yesterday. I was a total spaz. I'm pretty sure that whoever is behind that mask saw me as just another starstruck D'weasel in a sea of them."

"Are you a starstruck D'weasel?" Nessa asked. "You were a fan of mine, and we've never had any issues getting past the fan gap."

"Well, no, but we knew each other before we knew each other, you know?" Leah said. "We had a business relationship, too. That kinda made you into a real person in my head, not somebody famous."

"Trust me," Nessa said, an aura of humor soaking the air around her. "If you were to find out who Lancel♡t really was, I think you'd manage to see him as the real him and not just the masked version."

Not sure how to respond, Leah was saved by the doors opening to admit people to the Magical Space Skeleton Army panel. Leah and Nessa made their way to two available seats that were reasonably close to the stage. As the rest of the crowd filtered into the folding chair rows, the doors closed behind them.

The house lights dimmed but didn't turn off. As with the day before, a side door opened, and the Magical Space Skeleton Army poured out into the crowded room as their waiting fans broke out into a cacophony of applause. "Please, welcome to the stage Lady Bug, Frimmydukes, and Lancel♡t!" the moderator said, though it was hardly necessary or audible.

Frimmydukes and Lancel♡t jogged up and down the aisles, giving a high five here or there, while Lady Bug raised her arms in the center of the stage and basked in the adoration of the crowd until they were called to bring order to the chaos. "Lady Bug, if you could just... settle your subjects," the moderator pleaded. "There is another panel in the room next door."

Lady Bug held up her hands in a silence gesture, and the D'weasels obeyed. She lowered her arms and went over to the table, beckoning Frimmydukes and Lancel♡t to join her.

"Okay, so getting started," the moderator said. "You guys are from a planet that neighbors the Dread Pirate Planet Jenkins, but you don't remember anything about it. Do I have that right?"

"That is entirely correct, Steve. May I call you Steve?" Lady Bug said, smiling at the moderator.

"Well, my name is actually Matt..."

"Very good. Yes, Steve, we don't remember a single thing about the planet that we grew up on. All we recall is that when they needed defenders for the planet, somehow they decided that myself and my honor guard were the best they could possibly muster. After some test marketing, the Magical Space Skeleton Army was deemed the fiercest name in the galaxy; although between you, me, and everyone here, I think there may have been something of a kickback involved in that process," Lady Bug sounded like she was delivering light chit chat over a cup of coffee as opposed to some of the most ridiculous backstory elements Leah had personally heard.

"Still, I'm Matt," Matt the moderator said, though he seemed pretty okay with the gag. He was smiling, and it seemed genuine rather than tight and tense. Leah wondered if he'd been asked to play along beforehand. With a band like the Magical Space Skeleton Army, that struck Leah as likely. It wouldn't do to have someone super serious and prone to take offense when dealing with a band that refused to disclose their real identities. "So our first question on this sheet that I'm reading: If you don't remember your home planet, how is it that you remember so much about the Dread Pirate Planet Jenkins and the way that you received your name?"

"That's a good question, Evan," Lancel♡t answered. His voice was a bit huskier and deeper than Leah seemed to remember from the concert. *Maybe he's trying for more of a stage voice*, she thought, and then mentally shrugged it off. It had been five months, and she wasn't sure how well she remembered the speaking bits of the concert anymore. "The answer is that our minds were wiped of all pertinent information before we left our home planet in case we were captured by the Dread Pirate Planet Jenkins. In mid-mind wipe, the machine that was supposed to erase all of our memories of home got unplugged. We retain some of the most recent things prior to getting closed into our ship and pointed toward the enemy."

"Not Evan, or Steve. I'm Matt," Matt gave the audience a grin and then looked back at Lancel♡t. "Okay, so the machine got unplugged, but no one thought, 'Hey, these guys probably still remember some stuff. That might be a problem later,' or anything of that sort?"

Frimmydukes shook his head, "No, Matt. No one seemed to notice, or if they did, we don't really remember it."

"It's... Oh, right. Never mind." Matt seemed genuinely flummoxed at the use of his real name, which elicited more of a chuckle than all of the wrong names had. Leah felt herself grinning. She wasn't really sure what it was that she took from watching this band, but they made her happy. It was like being on the cruise again. There wasn't anyone that she felt the need to impress and she wasn't worried about the crowd of D'weasels judging her. They were here for the exact same thing as she was; a group of creative people in costumes, making stuff up, just to laugh with their audience. "On a more recent subject, the launch of your new album is in February. Is there anything that you guys would like to share about any of the songs or subject matter?"

"One of the songs is rather special, kind of close to my aortic pump," Lancel♡t said. "It was inspired by a very special D'weasel who was going through a rough time. I don't want to say more than that because they don't even know about it. It's dedicated to all of our D'weasels that make time to see us no matter what they've got going on in their lives. You guys are the reason we do what we do."

A new round of cheering rose from the crowd. It was a rare genuine moment that the fans were sharing with their band that jumped around the stage in Spandex, singing bizarre, silly songs while pretending to be aliens. Unless they really were aliens, and this was the most ingenious cover story ever, but Leah had her doubts. At least, she really hoped she wasn't that drawn to someone from outer space. Then again, if they were compatible, what did it matter if they were from a distant incompetent planet of people that did faulty market research?

There were a few more questions from Matt, but they were mostly about things like how long it took to acquire technical skills, how often the band practiced, what music videos the D'weasels could expect in the near future, and if the band felt that they might branch off into other forms of entertainment. The answers were amusing, but stuff that was readily accessible to those who actually bothered to go to the Magical Space Skeleton Army website or were band patrons. Leah found herself just watching the way that Lancel♡t moved, listening to the way he spoke, less than following the actual words that he said. There was something that struck her as slightly familiar about him, but she shrugged it off as being the number of times she'd watched all of the band's music videos. It would surprise her more if he didn't seem a tad familiar at this point.

During the Q and A portion of the panel, Leah tried to think of some reason to stand up and get in line for the microphone. Anything other than, "Hey, did we have a moment...?" which seemed to be the only question that kept echoing through her headspace. A few people tried to ask the ever popular, "Can I have a hug/kiss/handshake/high five?" only to be rebuked by Matt, who would then remind the room at large that they only had so long with the band and such requests were not permitted due to time constraints.

"Are you going up there?" Nessa asked.

"I really want to, but I can't think of a question," Leah admitted.

"Does it have to be music related?" Nessa coaxed. "I mean, the best questions are about them, but unexpected, right?"

"And they get asked if they've met the Doctor all the time," Leah said.

"So don't ask them that," Nessa said. "Ask them about their favorite video games, or the best restaurant they've found on the Riverwalk. It doesn't have to be profound."

Leah stood up, still completely at a loss for what was going to come out of her mouth once she made it through the line to the microphone. She tried to keep from fidgeting, but only succeeded in keeping her fingers still by grabbing the cuffs of her hoodie and pulling them down over her wrists where she had a much better grip. *Something personal, but not too personal. Not their favorite bands, because that's on the patron page. Biggest influence? Trite! While I'm most curious about Lancel♡t, the best questions are ones for the whole band. What the fuck am I doing here?*

Just as Leah reached the point where she was ready to give it up and go back to her seat, she made it to the front of the line. The large guy in front of her had identified himself as Samoan and asked when the Magical Space Skeleton Army was going to make it to Hawaii. His answer had been as soon as they could make it happen. Before Leah could stop herself, she leaned toward the mic and said, "I'm a travel agent, so just let me know if you need help with that."

There was an appreciative chuckle that rolled its way through the audience. People that weren't afraid of the mic were always the best, and Leah had just inadvertently made the list. *Nothing to do but press on*, she thought as she grabbed the first question that formed in her mind. "This is to the whole band. I feel like it says a lot about a person, what star they follow, so I was wondering what star it was that each of you felt you were the most tied to: Trek, Wars, or Gate?"

"Captain Picard, all the way, chica!" Frimmydukes said. The part of his mouth that was visible through the mask's portal held a big smile.

Lady Bug had to turn away from her microphone for a moment to avoid laughing into it, though whether it was Leah's question or Frimmydukes' response that set her off was up for debate. "It wasn't an option, but Galactica. That works, right?"

Leah gave a hurried affirmative, and then she and the rest of the D'weasels waited for Lancel♡t's response. "I think I'd have to say... Babylon Five," Lancel♡t said.

"Dude, she asked for a star, not a space station!" Frimmydukes chastised his bandmate.

"Alright, fine. Firefly," Lancel♡t answered.

"Still not a star," Lady Bug shook her head. "Try again."

"Farscape," Lancel♡t tried.

"Not quite," Leah said, wondering when Matt the moderator would cut them off.

"Okay, okay... Final answer: Galavant." Lancel♡t crossed his arms as though that really were his final say, and then just before anyone else could break in, he leaned really close to his mic and did what Leah thought of a pillow talk whisper, "It's Wars. I'm very into Princess Leia."

The answer sent shivers up and down Leah's spine. If she didn't know any better, she'd think that Lancel♡t was intentionally flirting with her, but there was no way he remembered her name from the signing the day before. She managed a brief word of thanks before making her way back to her seat. Nessa was grinning despite the aura of Vincent she'd been diligently trying to project for the last hour.

"I knew it," Nessa said as Leah sank in her chair. Leah didn't bother to ask what it was Nessa knew. If Leah were to guess, she figured it was that Nessa was in no doubt of her crush on the lead singer. Her friend was watching Lancel♡t pretty closely.

Chapter Twenty-six

MEL DUCKED OUT OF THE doors to the back hall, trying to act as casual as possible while he did so. Generally, no one paid any attention as they assumed anyone they didn't recognize was probably a con staffer. He was in a bit of a rush to make his appointment with Leah, though, so Mel didn't really notice the Vincent cosplayer leaning against the wall until he nearly stumbled into them.

"In a hurry, Mel?" Vincent asked.

That stopped him cold. "Have we met?"

"I was Princess Farah earlier, but it's Nessa Fierro. Leah's friend," she reached up and pulled the hem of her red collar down enough that he could see her face. "That was quite the panel you guys put on."

Every fear that Mel had about being unmasked ignited at once, making Mel's vision take on a white tinge. His heart was beating in his ears, and his head suddenly felt weirdly heavy, like it wanted to slip off of his shoulders. *Don't pass out. Don't pass out. Don't pass out,* his brain told him. *Calm down. Let's find out what she wants, and then you can panic... Maybe there's still time and you can pretend she's off the mark.*

"I don't know..."

"What I'm talking about?" Nessa finished for him. "Come on, Mel. I've got an ear for voices. I could recognize Tress MacNeille at the age of seven, and she's got range."

Damn, his inner voice responded. Mel knew very well who Tress MacNeille was. He had a cat named for one of her characters. This hallway was all but deserted, since it was off of the main thoroughfare and didn't link into any of the rooms that held panels, demos, or autograph sessions. There wasn't even an outlet to try to coax a con goer or two into turning the hall into a charging station. She'd done him the courtesy of confronting him in private, at least.

"What do you want?" he asked. Emotion clogged his throat, making his words come out much more quietly than normal.

"Honestly, I just wanted to get this out in the open. I know who you are, and I'm not going to tell Leah or anyone else. I took an opportunity this morning to tease you, but I'll keep your secret. Call it Con Code or whatever you like, but it's not my place to rat you out. Still—I really think that you should tell Leah... At some point," Nessa said.

"So... You scared me half to death to tell me that you aren't out to scare me?" Mel asked. He was genuinely confused at this point. It didn't make any sense to him for her to seek him out like this only to let him know that he was off the hook.

"You were already scared," Nessa said. "I wanted to get this out of the way so that you didn't worry your way out of spending time with Leah. She's been hurt. She doesn't need that again."

A flash of understanding suddenly fired across Mel's mind. This wasn't a session where they were bargaining for his secret identity, despite the fact that Nessa had led with that particular token. This was, in fact, the "If you hurt my friend, I will make you pay," speech. He'd never actually been on the receiving end of one of these speeches before, and the fact that he was getting one for the first time in his thirties almost made him laugh. Judging from the look on Nessa's face, that would not be taken well.

"I don't want to hurt Leah. I don't know how much she told you about our first meeting, but I've seen her in pain. I definitely don't want to be the cause of it," Mel said.

"She was the D'weasel you mentioned, right? The one you wrote a song for?" Nessa asked, her voice low enough that it barely reached Mel's ears.

He didn't say anything but dipped his head ever so slightly.

"That's what I thought. This isn't really much of a secret, so I'm not breaking any friendship rules by telling you: Lancel♡t has always been her favorite band member," Nessa pushed away from the wall and started walking away.

Mel watched her go, his head and his heart swimming through a whole sea of mixed emotions. He didn't want to hurt Leah, but his Spark was still out there somewhere. Lancel♡t was Leah's favorite: he felt like he might start glowing with the knowledge. Leah didn't know his secret, but her friend undeniably did. What if it spilled out on some drunken night? It didn't really seem likely that someone that came off as controlled as Nessa did would slip like that, but it was possible. Anything was possible.

WHEN MEL MADE IT TO the front of the Expo Hall, Leah was pacing the floor, drawing the eyes of at least one of the security officers stationed there. Her red hair was in its usual, slightly-unkempt ponytail, which he found completely adorable. Mel hadn't been able to make out the details of what she'd been wearing when she'd been standing next to the mic at the panel, and he hadn't been paying much attention that morning. Now, he could see a bloody handprint symbol that he was pretty familiar with on the back of her hoodie. He'd been playing The Elder Scrolls games for as long as he could remember. Here was yet another tidbit about this woman that made his smile twelve parsecs wide.

Leah's face lit up when she saw Mel approaching. With Nessa's cautioning remarks fresh in his head, Mel didn't think he should go in for the hug that he so desperately wanted to give her. It was a trial, but he kept his hands shoved in the pockets of his jacket, attempting to project "not in a hugging mood" vibes.

It apparently worked, because Leah didn't rush toward him and throw her arms around his neck or his waist. "Hey! I wasn't entirely sure you were going to make it," she said, the words bursting from her mouth like they were poorly restrained dogs and she'd let go of their leashes all at once. "Nessa couldn't come. She said she had a thing to take care of, and then she was going to her booth, so we might see her anyway, if we go over there, but not if we want to play something, and I kinda want to play something. But what do you want to do? We're hanging out, right?"

"Were you waiting long?" Mel couldn't quite keep the chuckle out of his voice.

"Maybe just long enough to kinda over rehearse what I was gonna say," Leah's face scrunched up in embarrassment. "Sorry about that."

"No worries. So, I gather that Nessa's not coming because she's going to her booth?" he asked.

"Yes," Leah said.

"And you want to play demos?" He was grinning at her, but he couldn't help it. In the overly large assassin guild hoodie, with her usual halo of fly-away hair, she was giving him an expression that reminded Mel strongly of Dot right before she demanded play time.

"Yes," Leah repeated.

"I think that's decided then," Mel said. "Let's go play some demos."

They held up their badges for the security guys and walked into a gamer's wet dream. Rows upon rows of set up consoles, VR pens, booths that held new and used games, game themed plush toys, t-shirts, and foam weaponry: it was all arranged so that no two booths were alike. Leah couldn't seem to decide which way to go first, so Mel tugged on her sleeve the way she had at the sandwich shop that morning. He guided her toward one of the VR booths, not really caring what the game was, only that it looked like it was something with two players.

Next, Leah caught sight of a GameDock8 exclusive and scrambled toward it, nearly colliding with someone that was running through the crowd in the other direction. Mel saved her by grabbing the back of her hoodie at the handprint. He was uncomfortably aware of her body heat with the near contact. So much of him wanted to pull her close, feel the heat of her against him, but he let go the moment she was out of danger. Her eyes met his in a questioning, almost playful moment, asking him if he dared go that extra step. He didn't. Not yet. Not until he was free of the question of whether his Spark was still out there. If he went down this road with Leah, he would have to let go of that possibility, and he wasn't quite ready for that dream to end.

Somehow, after the third booth, his hour of freedom was up. Telling Leah that he had to go was harder than it had been the first time. He asked if she still had his contact information.

"I think so," she pulled out her phone and went to the contacts page. "Maybe not... I don't seem to have a Mel in here, or even a Merlin," she gave him a bit of a sly glance, to show that she had remembered that little nugget.

"If you decide to call me Merlin, I don't think I'd mind so much," Mel said. It did have a certain ring to it when it came from Leah's mouth. Something in the way her tongue shaped the syllables sent pleasant little ripples through his gray matter. He pulled the phone from her grip and tapped on the icon for adding a contact, and punched his phone number in. "But here, I think we should be allowed to text and call each other from time to time, right?"

"Absolutely," Leah said. "I'll text you, so be sure to add me."

Mel nodded. He had every intention of adding her as soon as he got her message. Even so, he was aware that with her living in Houston, the odds of them crossing paths like this very often were slim.

Chapter Twenty-seven

WHEN LEAH GOT BACK from AXES, she didn't want to go back to sleeping on the trundle bed that she was borrowing from Nessa. She didn't want to continue pulling her clothes out of boxes and throwing them back in after they'd been washed. It was time for a new city, in a new state, and new furniture to go with it. Leah was ready to begin rebuilding her life now that her foundational self had been established. Nessa still had a ton of packing and preparation before she was ready for the next step.

"So, I had a thought, last night when I was brushing my teeth," Leah said.

She was on the couch, arranging a few surprises for one of her regulars that had just booked their third trip to Ireland through Leah's business. It was a free wine dinner at a castle that normally would cost someone an upcharge. The client had mentioned wanting to try one on their first trip, but she had been intimidated by the price. Since this was her third trip and Leah knew she still hadn't managed it, it seemed like a nice treat for someone that booked pretty regularly. The same woman had booked a few cruises and one trip to Portugal, but Ireland seemed to have that magic quality that kept her coming back. All of Leah's regulars had one or two places that she thought of as their "magic destinations." Once she recognized those, Leah always went just that little bit further to make the trip even more special. The "magic destinations" were what kept her in business.

"What thought?" Nessa asked. She was also working, though her work was currently bookkeeping. She had a second cousin or something that was an investment banker or financial advisor (Leah couldn't remember which), that handled Nessa's stock portfolio, but before Nessa moved, she had said something about personal assessment.

"What if I went ahead? I could go apartment hunting, find us a place, and start getting myself some furniture. You could come along once you're ready. We can split the cost of movers since I can't possibly get all of my stuff up there in one go," Leah said. It wasn't quite the breathless jumble that she had spewed at Mel (Merlin) that day in front of the Expo Hall, but it was close. She was unaware that the memory caused her mouth to quirk up on one side.

Nessa glanced up from her computer. There was no surprise in her features. If anything, Leah thought Nessa's expression was one that said Nessa had been thinking something similar but hadn't wanted to suggest it. "That actually occurred to me, too," Nessa said, confirming Leah's suspicions. "I just didn't want it to sound like I wanted you to get out of my hair or something."

Leah let out a huff that was part sigh, part laugh, "Nessa, if you had said exactly that, I wouldn't have blamed you. You've put up with me being in your sewing room for way longer than anyone else would've. Especially given that first month."

"It's not like you haven't given me rent money," Nessa said.

"It's not like you asked for it," Leah countered.

"Exactly."

"Anyway, so it wouldn't bother you if I went ahead and tried to find us a place?" Leah asked.

"No," Nessa said. "As long as you give me a digital tour and it meets with a few criteria."

They hadn't really talked about what they were going to be looking for in a new place, yet. Leah had just expected that she'd be hunting for something with roughly the same square footage, in a mostly decent neighborhood. "What criteria?"

"Neighborhood, two to three bedrooms. Preferably not on the first floor. I know there are burglars called second story men, but it'll still make me feel better. Plenty of closet space or with a nearby storage facility. I'd like both, but I'm not going to complain too much if I have to drive to a storage lot from time to time," Nessa said.

"Well, I will definitely keep you in the loop whenever I tour a place," Leah said. "Panoramics, recordings, websites. You'll get to look over anything I like."

A new thought occurred to Leah just after she'd made the promise to keep Nessa in the loop. "What if I find a house instead of an apartment?"

"In that case, staying off of the first floor would be a bit difficult, so I doubt I'd hold you to it," Nessa said. "One last requirement, though, and this is possibly the most important."

Leah lowered her laptop screen and took her hands away from her keyboard to show that she was paying very close attention to whatever caveat Nessa was about to impart.

"Anthony better be there to greet me when I arrive," Nessa made a I'm-super-serious-don't-mess-this-up face to really drive the point home. It made Leah laugh, which broke Nessa's ability to keep her eyes that wide. She crossed and uncrossed her eyes and massaged her cheeks, as though the face had felt unnatural and she was trying to make sure everything was back in place.

ELLEN OFFERED TO RIDE up to Indianapolis with Leah so that her sister wouldn't be driving the thousand miles all on her own. It wasn't that Ellen didn't think Leah could manage that long on her own, so much as she didn't want her big sister to have to be alone. Since their parents were also wanting Leah to stop by on her drive north, Leah agreed to pick Ellen up on her way through.

As she pulled her blue Chevy Cruze up the drive to her parents' house, Eomer shot out of the front door and greeted her by jumping in place until the car door gave him enough room to start anointing his non-furry sister with as many slobbery kisses as he could manage.

"Eomer! Eomer, you get back up here!" Daphne Walsh shouted from her front porch. Her voice hadn't reached the level that meant you-best-listen-to-me-or-hell-will-be-a-pleasant-alternative, also known as Mom voice, so he continued to try and climb into the car with Leah. His tail was wagging so hard, that it seemed to be dragging his butt along with it. "*Eomer!*"

And there it was. *Mom* was calling.

Eomer slunk back over to the patio, his tail drooping now, but still giving off a slight, hopeful wag every other step. He didn't go up the steps. Instead, he layed at the base of the porch where he rolled onto his back like he was hoping for a long-distance belly rub. Leah got out of her car and made her own way over to oblige him.

"Oh, sure. Greet the dog first!" Daphne grumbled. She came down the steps to hug her oldest daughter. It had only been a few weeks since Leah had been here for Christmas, but she knew that her mom was still adjusting to the idea that Leah was leaving the state. "I still don't know why you have to move so far from us."

"I need a fresh start, Mom. I'm not going to get that sticking close to home," Leah said.

"Well, there are plenty of places closer than Indianapolis that are still far away," Daphne argued.

"None of which have Anthony," Leah said.

"Why do you need Anthony if it's a fresh start?" Daphne made a face at her daughter that said very clearly that this logic was nonsensical at best, and it would take a natural twenty to change her mind.

"Because Anthony is the party healer and I wouldn't be here without him. My shapeshifting dragon of an ex-husband would have accomplished a total party wipe, and I'd still be waiting for a rez,"

Leah said. She'd not tried using this terminology before, but maybe she should have given the look her mother was now giving her.

Leah found herself wrapped in a new hug, one that was more of a warm blanket on a snowy day than a standard greeting. "My little adventurer is all grown up and slaying her own dragons. It's hard to see it from here, you know. Your father and I haven't hung up our capes yet, so it's still easy to think of you and Ellen as only starting out. Just promise to amble into your homestead from time to time."

With something between a laugh and a cough, Leah promised that she'd remember to come home from time to time and wrangled a promise out of her mom that her parents would come up to visit at some point once she and Nessa were established. Daphne took her daughter inside and plied her with homemade hot chocolate and freshly baked cinnamon buns. If Daphne had started her arguments with this, Leah may have had a much harder time resisting. Happily, though, it seemed that Leah had finally convinced her mother that this was a decision worth making. Eowyn slunk her way onto the couch, trying and failing to creep her way onto Leah's lap unnoticed. Eomer jumped up on the other side, sticking his nose into Eowyn's face. In her typical fashion, Eowyn rubbed her blonde striped cheek against Eomer's rich brown fur.

Gerald Walsh was out, but he was due back in time for dinner. Ellen was also not due until after she got off work. For a little while, Daphne sat in her favorite chair and watched the first episode of Stranger Things with her daughter, who was covered in a mountain of pets (really just the two, but they were excellent at changing into amorphous blobs of fur when the mood struck). After a bit, Daphne wandered into her kitchen to perform her edible alchemy that would morph things like flour and raw meat into dinner.

When Leah offered to help, her mom waved her off. Even though Leah also loved Stranger Things, she'd watched it recently enough not to really be in the mood to keep it going. She turned off the television and pulled her phone out of her pocket. The background had changed now. Though the pics of her and Alan still existed on her laptop hard drive in a folder that was buried in another folder that was labeled "Unused Icons," they were erased entirely from her phone. Now, her lock screen had an image of the Magical Space Skeleton Army in concert, and her main background was of some badass fan art she'd found of Lancel♡t riding a giant liveried quokka that she'd found on Tumblr. It was a good time for her to review some more lyrics from her favorite band's discography since she still had a few weeks to enter the contest.

IT HAD BEEN A LONG time since Leah had gone on her unplanned road trips with Alan, but she recognized the rolling plains of Oklahoma from those once happy times. It hurt, but not anything like the original Kali Ma feeling that had taken almost a month to release her. This was just a minor ache: a leftover, long forgotten in the fridge of life. Soon enough, after one of the most expensive toll booths Leah had ever encountered, she and Ellen had crossed the border into Missouri and the landscape changed. There were signs telling her to watch for falling rocks and religious billboards attempting to sandwich out the porn billboards which were attempting to crowd past the religious billboards.

"I wonder how much they spend trying to outdo each other like that," Ellen mused.

"It's almost like this whole state is split into two camps: the pious and the promiscuous," Leah agreed.

"They should probably form soccer teams and have it out on Tuesday nights," Ellen said.

"What makes you think they don't?" Leah asked.

"Because the billboards lead me to believe this is more of a tennis match," Ellen leaned forward and looked as far up as the seatbelt and windshield allowed her. "Looks like we're in for some rain. How soon do you need gas?"

Leah glanced down at her fuel gauge despite having been monitoring it closely for the last half hour. "We could definitely stop. I'm at about a quarter tank."

"Good, Ellen said. "I need to pee, and I just saw a sign for a few gas stations at the next exit."

As the car steered down the ramp and into the nearest station's lot, Ellen barely waited for it to make a complete stop, not even bothering to put her jacket back on before pelting toward the door. The blast of cold air that flooded into Leah's car was beyond anything that Leah had imagined. They hadn't seen any signs of frost or snow, so Leah hadn't really thought about how much colder it was going to be as they drove further and further north. She was shivering by the time she'd finished pumping the gas, and she could only imagine that Ellen would be even worse off after having to come back with her bare arms. In a show of sisterly compassion, Leah drove up to the side of the building and grabbed Ellen's jacket before heading in to use the facilities herself.

They decided to stop at the next Walmart or Target that they saw and invest in something a bit heavier than the thin hoodies that they'd been comfortable enough wearing in the more moderate Texas winter. Even as they came to this decision, the rains slammed down from the skies like a curtain of chainmail. These storms happened from time to time in Texas, but they were more the exception. The gas station attendant merrily observed, "Well, looks like a bit of rain. You girls be careful out there!"

Ellen, hugging what warmth she could into her jacket before they made a mad dash for the car, looked into Leah's eyes and said, "It's not too late to change your mind, you know?"

If Leah had been any less determined, she might have considered it. Between the cold and the rain, this trip seemed a lot more real than the nebulous idea that moving had been before. She was in a car that held her television and game systems, a few boxes of her more winter appropriate shirts and jeans, some towels, and an umbrella. She hadn't even looked into what the weather would be like on the way up. "Never give up, never surrender. Besides, you bought a plane ticket to get back home. I can't let you miss your plane."

Ellen nodded, as though it was the answer she had been expecting. Despite that, Leah was kind of glad that she had asked. It helped settle the question in her own head.

They stopped for a few hours of sleep just outside of Rolla, Missouri. The next morning, Ellen took the first shift. Navigating through St Louis, even with the help of a GPS app, was a bit of an emotional rollercoaster. When the Arch was dwindling in the rearview mirror and the Mississippi River was flowing beneath them, both sisters let out a mutual sigh of relief. Snow began dusting the landscape, and then it started to coat the world entirely. It was glittering over the fields like a sugary confectionery frosting, making both women very happy that they'd decided to buy gloves when they'd stopped for better winter wear. Traveling through Litchfield caused some appreciative mirth of varying degrees (more for Leah, who had visions of the undead sorcerer that secretly controlled the city, than Ellen), and then they finally reached Lafayette, Indiana close to five o'clock.

Anthony greeted Leah with his usual gigantic bear hug, and then gave Ellen an equally overwhelming greeting. Leah was kind of surprised that her sister not only allowed the hug but returned it. Her younger sibling wasn't generally much of a hugger when it came to non-family members.

"I can't believe you're actually here!" Anthony said, ushering them into his house. "I mean, we've been talking about your big move since before the holidays. I'm so excited that I'm going to get to have real game nights again!"

Anthony's house was smaller than Leah had imagined, but it had a coziness to it that seemed very fitting for the big man. Most of the furniture was made of dark woods, suede leathers, or dyed various shades of green. His walls were more of a honey color than the usual off white that people usually used as a neutral. The same TableTop print that Troy had had in his game room was hung over the fireplace mantel. In the exact same frame. Leah thought about Anthony's push for her to take all of Alan's toilet paper and decided not to ask.

There were bookcases just about anywhere Leah's eyes came to rest. One seemed to contain nothing but leather bound historical books and classical literature, while another held nothing but paperback editions of more modern histories. Yet another seemed to be dedicated to books on Asian history, and the one next to it only held books on ancient cultures.

"This is just my sitting room. Any time I have someone over for professional reasons, it pays to look like I'm not just a history professor but the biggest history buff on the planet. It saves a lot of arguments," Anthony told them. "Come on, I'll show you the rest of the house."

"Thank you, so much for letting me crash here as a home base," Leah said. "Is it okay if we unload before a grand tour, though? I kind of couldn't wait to bring my electronics."

"What you mean is you want to play your cowboy game before you bed down, and you can't do that if it's in the car," Ellen shook her head and flashed a smile at Anthony so that he would know it was just sisterly teasing.

"It's a valid point. I live in a college town. TVs and game systems are worth their weight in ramen and cheap beer," Anthony said. "We'll get your gear inside, and then I'll show you around."

Luckily, the contents of a Chevy Cruz only amounted to two trips for three people. They set the boxes and television in the corner of a guest room that had a double bed and a desk with a lamp. This room didn't have any bookshelves or wardrobe space, but the bed was piled with blankets. "I remember when I first moved up here, winters were the worst thing ever. Believe it or not, I now only have one extra blanket between my comforter and my sheet," Anthony said.

Leah looked her friend over, taking in his olive green sweater vest over a button-down pinstripe shirt and khaki pants. She knew he had the tweed jacket with the elbow pads. "No, I'd believe that about you. So far, everything I've seen of your house projects that 'I sell a drug called pedagogy, and it's not for the weak,'" Leah said.

Barking out a laugh, Anthony clapped her on the shoulder. "Oh, this is going to be fun! I've got to get that embroidered on a pillow for my office!"

"And we have," Ellen said, carrying in the two overnight bags on one shoulder only to toss them dramatically on the bed, "officially brought in everything."

"Onward! We march! To the kitchen!" Anthony raised one fist into the air as he led the sisters out of the room that Leah would live in until she found a new place to officially call home.

Chapter Twenty-eight

IT TOOK MEL A FEW WEEKS to stop checking his phone every five minutes to see if he'd somehow missed a text from Leah. He knew she likely had plenty of things going on in her own life that made him a low priority. Why would she text a near stranger in the Midwest about her day to day stuff? Why hadn't he texted her out of the blue to chat about something normal and safe, and not about what the Magical Space Skeleton Army was currently doing?

Of course, what they were currently doing was autographing the first five hundred CDs that had been preordered for their new album: Legacy of the Burrito Gods. Even though they had written their own songs and narrowed it down from those submitted to the group, all four of Mel's submissions had made the cut. He felt like a real musician again, with something real to contribute. Since the incident with Nessa at AXES, he'd felt a lot less concerned with the idea of being discovered. His worst fear had happened, and yet, the Magical Space Skeleton Army was still intact. Mel felt better than he had in years.

They'd been doing the autographs at Jessie's apartment, since Eevee was a lot more chill than Dot when it came to three people sitting on the floor with Sharpies and stacks of CDs. Dot had chewed through the plastic on one case, making Mel's personal copy worth absolutely nothing as a collectible. He was going to frame it anyway and give it to his parents. It would make a good piece for their D'weasel collection.

Jessie had given him the account information and told him that he could monitor his own stupid contest after she'd watched the first seven submissions. She wouldn't tell him what had been in the three videos that she had deleted, only handed him the ledger than she'd been writing notes in—it held contestant names, emails or addresses, and the word "DISQUALIFIED" written in all caps on three entries. It generally took a lot to get to Jessie, so Mel was pretty sure he didn't want to know.

Mel was just setting up his laptop to get started on submissions when he heard a knock on his door. He really wasn't sure what to expect, since the last random knock had been Betham, when Frankie had thrown him out for the night. Despite his lifetime of caution and well-developed habits of always checking the peephole before opening the door, something in him forgot to kick in his instincts for self-preservation. That was how he found himself looking into a pair of eyes that he'd never thought to see again, nor had he really wanted to ever see again.

Stephanie was standing outside his apartment, a hesitant smile, or possibly a grimace, just tugging at the corner of her mouth. Five years ago, her blonde hair had been kept shoulder length and seemed to glow like a halo of light around her ears. She'd been almost as naturally slim as he was, and her big blue eyes had struck him as guileless. Now, her hair was pulled back in a braid that hung down over one shoulder, and it seemed less luminous than it had in the past. While she wasn't super slim anymore (her hips had widened), she wasn't huge. She was wearing what he guessed was a fashionable coat, skinny jeans, and heeled boots. If he had just been passing her on the street for the first time, he'd have thought she looked like a mom.

For a moment that seemed determined not to pass, Mel just froze, letting the frigid winter air creep over his feet to lurk in the corners of his apartment. His brain didn't seem able to process the information it was being given. Stephanie. Here. Stephanie was here. Why? Why was *Stephanie* casting her long vanished shadow on his doorstep?

It wasn't until Dot meowed behind him, likely a query of her own as to why this person wasn't being invited in, or why wasn't Mel feeding her, that Mel felt time start up again.

"Why are you here?" Mel said. He was surprised at the lack of emotion in his own voice. It was a shock, but he didn't feel angry. He didn't feel much of anything other than confusion.

"I... God, Mel, I didn't know this would be this hard... I don't live in town anymore. I was here visiting a friend, and I... I wanted to apologize," Stephanie said.

"Apologize?" Mel repeated. There was something about this situation that made him feel like he had been called up to the blackboard to demonstrate a math problem that had been taught during his last sick day. It just didn't make sense, and yet someone was expecting him to know what to do. "Steph, it's been something like five years. Why are you here?"

"I was recently dumped by my boyfriend, my baby's daddy, and I realized how crappy it feels to come home to an empty place and find out that you're alone. It got me to thinking about how I did the same thing to you, and... Oh! Hello, little kitty!" Stephanie tried to move past Mel, into the apartment.

Dot, the friendliest cat in the world, seemed startled by the sudden attention and bolted down the hall into Mel's room. It was her safe zone whenever the dreaded vacuum made its presence known, and that was the only thing Mel had seen her run from prior to this encounter.

"So, would you like to go and, I don't know, talk over coffee? We could get caught up... reacquainted?" Stephanie tried again to edge her way past the door.

"I don't think so, Steph. Sorry to hear about your breakup, but you made it pretty clear how important I was to you back then," Mel said. "Have a good life."

"Wait!" Stephanie said. "You don't seem to get it! I'm here because I want you back, obviously. You wrote a song for me! Doesn't that mean something?"

"It did at the time," Mel wished he were enough of a dick to just close the door in her face, but it went against his grain to do that, even to someone like Stephanie. *How did I not see her for what she was back then?* he wondered. "Do you even remember what that song was called?"

There was a long silence while Stephanie blinked her big blue eyes in complete bewilderment. "It was... Vomit on Me, Baby?"

Mel shook his head. If this encounter had taken place the summer before, would he have felt the same way about it? He had no way of knowing, but now, it was clear to him that while he had been shattered by their breakup, Stephanie hadn't thought about him as anything other than a convenient back up plan. "Goodbye, Stephanie."

"Is it another woman? Did you find someone new to moon after? Is she willing to put up with your BS about a make-believe music career?" Stephanie's face had transformed from benignly hopeful to grotesque rage. If Mel had still been making his way through the Stephanie detox stage, the sudden flare of anger may have sparked more of a response from him. As it was, Mel didn't feel his own temper ignite to rage against hers. There wasn't even a sense of bitterness. His relationship with Stephanie was so firmly in the past that he felt it would be like getting mad at someone for letting the Eiffel Tower get built. It was old news, and it had already happened, so the only alternative left was to let it be.

"Quite frankly, Steph, it's none of your business. We were over a long time ago, and I've moved on. I suggest you do the same. Patch things up with your baby's father or find someone looking for a pre-made family. I want no part in it," Mel said.

"You fucking asshole! I don't know what I ever saw in you!" Stephanie walked a few steps away, and then found a small child's sock in her coat pocket. She flung it at Mel's door in a bout of flaccid fury. Mel watched as the sock fell short of its mark by several feet. Stephanie continued to stomp her way into the parking lot, despite the hazard of ice lurking beneath the snow.

Once he was certain that there was no possible way that she'd be turning around, he went into the corridor outside his apartment and scooped up the kid's sock to toss into his trash can. There was no reason to leave it for the maintenance crew to deal with whenever they got around to it.

The heater kicked into action with a rumble that sounded like the building itself was griping about how long the door had been derelict in its duties as a barrier to the cold. Mel shook his head, still trying to absorb the entire encounter.

Dot had crept back to the edge of the hallway and was bobbing her nose in the air, reassuring herself that all of the apartment smells were as they should be. Scooping the kitten into his arms produced a squeak of protest before the purring started. "Did that lady scare you?" Mel asked, rubbing Dot's belly with his extra hand. His cat was the picture of feline satisfaction up until Dot decided that she'd rather play than be cuddled.

Mel wrestled with her while she gently swiped at his hand, biting with mock ferocity before worming her way out of his grasp to launch herself onto the cat tower he'd gotten her as a late Christmas gift. It wasn't like she knew he'd been tardy with it, and even if she did, the dangling mice seemed to make it up to her. As he watched his cat frisk about her tower, he pulled out his phone and dialed Jessie's number. He knew this was the kind of encounter she'd want to hear about.

IN LESS THAN THIRTY minutes, Mel found himself hosting an unplanned viewing of the contestant videos on his big screen television. Betham and Jessie had shown up together, since Betham's car was currently getting a tune up, carrying bags of supplies for Mel to make food. Given that the not-quite-party was ostensibly to get his mind off of the Stephanie invasion, he pointed out that maybe they should be feeding him.

"Nonsense," Jessie said. "Cooking is a great way to boil out your issues, and you are by far the best cook in this little group. I make milk cry, and Betham's big talent is melting cheese onto stuff."

"I do make killer nachos, bro!" Betham said, his voice projected toward them from his position on the couch.

Jessie shook her head and rolled her eyes, not quite voicing her opinion on her brother's nachos.

Mel was investigating the assortment of ingredients that his friends had brought him, and he wasn't at all certain what they'd been anticipating. "What exactly am I going to make with five jars of tomato sauce, ham, potatoes, and eggs?"

"No idea," Jessie said. "We were just hoping something would go with what you already had in your magic pantry."

"It's not magic!" Mel protested. "It's just stocked!"

"Right. Because you actually buy stuff that's not just premade," Jessie said. "You plan for feeding people despite the fact that you never know when or if we'll come by. Tell me you don't just happen to have something planned out for us already."

Mel had, in fact, been figuring out a variation on a shepherd's pie, using the ham, eggs, and potatoes from the sack they'd brought in, plus an onion and a few things from his definitely-not-magic pantry. "Not... exactly planned out," he hedged.

"Uh huh," Jessie said, crossing her arms and giving him the most skeptical look in her arsonal. It was impressive.

"Fine. I have a plan. Now, get out of my kitchen unless you feel like helping," Mel opened the drawer that housed his potato peeler and Jessie seemed to evaporate and re-materialize just outside of the actual borders of the kitchen.

That didn't mean that she left him alone, of course. Leaning against the bar counter, Jessie watched as Mel peeled and washed the potatoes, put them on to boil, and moved on to chopping up the ham. "So, seriously, are you okay?"

"Honestly," Mel said, paying far more attention to the knife in his hands than the question. "I'm way more okay than I thought I'd be. At first, I thought I was just numb from shock, but now, I'm not sure that's it."

"What do you mean?" Jessie asked. "You seemed dazed when I talked to you just after."

"That's fair," Mel nodded, scooping the ham onto a frying pan and setting it on the burner. He wasn't ready to turn it on yet. It was a pre-cooked ham (most were), so it could wait until he'd gotten the onions and garlic into the mix. "I was shocked, don't get me wrong. It takes a lot of nerve to come back to an ex in the first place, but she was very much looking for me to jump right back in it with her, despite the fact she has a kid now. We never even discussed kids when we were living together."

"Are you fucking serious?" Jessie's eyes went wide with her own shock. "That's quite the pair of lady balls."

It took Mel a while to realize that he'd zoned into his cooking and he was in the middle of making a point of some sort. He dumped the chopped onion and garlic onto the pan with the ham chunks and turned on the burner. Once he retired from music, he could see himself opening up a diner or a bakery somewhere remote, or maybe just cooking more often for those that he cared about. "Anyway, like I was saying, I don't think I'm feeling okay because of shock numbing me out. It was like that day that you and Betham sat me down and told me to start looking again. I felt aware of something that I'd missed earlier. On that day, it was the fact that I'd closed myself off because of a bad experience. Today, I think I really realized that Stephanie was really, truly, never the person I thought she was. The Stephanie that I thought I knew, she never would've done what the Stephanie I saw today did. Granted, she burned the crap out of me, but that's not the same as showing up again and assuming that I'd drop everything just for another chance. Leah wouldn't do that."

Before Mel had a chance to stop talking, that last sentence tumbled out of his mouth, not consulting with his brain at all.

He hadn't meant to say anything about Leah, let alone compare her to his last serious girlfriend. Meeting Jessie's eyes, he could see that she was wearing her skeptical face again. "Uh huh," she said. "This is the same Leah who had the scary might-have-figured-us-out friend?"

Mel didn't respond, but he felt his cheeks growing red anyway. It was good that he didn't care for poker, because he did not have the face for it. Oddly enough, he was usually pretty decent at Werewolf, though. *A mystery for a later date*, he thought.

"If you want to call off the Spark search, you do know that we'll understand, right?" Jessie asked. "Because the more this woman comes up, the more I'm starting to think that whole Spark thing might just be a distraction."

"It's... not," Mel said. "It's still a question I need an answer to. I'm just... I feel like it might be the answer to a different question than the one I thought I was asking. If that makes any sense."

Of all the responses he'd anticipated, Jessie's laugh hadn't been one of them. "Mel, I think you may be one of the only people I know that can get stuck in a love triangle where the second party doesn't even have a face."

"Weren't very big into mIRC back in the day, were you?" Mel gave her a self-aware grin. No one could dance around in Spandex as often as he did without coming to terms with their own level of dork-iness.

Chapter Twenty-nine

LAFAYETTE, INDIANA was roughly an hour out from Indi-anapolis. Leah dropped her sister off at the airport with several hugs and instructions to give some away to their parents, as well as some tears and a plea to stay safe. Ellen promised she would text once she was back on the ground in DFW. Since it was a Monday, Anthony was being professional and doing his professor thing at a few class-rooms of students, which meant that Leah was on her own looking for apartments in a new city.

She'd done a bit of online research, cross-referencing apartments off of websites with a crime map of Indianapolis, and also marking off any complexes that fell beneath a three-star rating on Google. Even with excellent renting references from Nessa's uncle, Leah didn't anticipate finding anything in the four to five-star range. Not unless, by some abnormality of time and space, such a place also came in under budget. Leah couldn't see that happening, even on her most optimistic of days.

Anthony had told her she was welcome to stay in his guest room for as long as it took to find the right place, but Leah didn't want to take advantage of his hospitality any more than she'd wanted to continue sleeping on Nessa's trundle bed. *But, this is a new city*, Leah thought. *I should probably take advantage of being on my own to just feel its rhythm... Get a sense of where I am...*

Her phone was already stuck in its pop socket on the dash, so she asked it to take her to a game store. There were some options, so she chose one halfway across town and a route that would cross through Indy's downtown area. Leah figured that would give her a better feel for the city, which was what she was aiming for on this trip. Watching the city move through its pulses from behind her car window, Leah felt a pang of homesickness. It didn't surprise her, because she'd felt something very similar when she'd first moved down to Houston. The city in front of her wasn't the one that she'd grown accustomed to seeing on a daily basis. There were going to be some growing pains, some regrets (she and Nessa had shared a final burger at Escape from Philly Burger, where Ray had given them free departure shakes for being some of his first regulars). Ultimately, Leah felt pretty good about the vibe Indianapolis was giving her. She saw a game store nestled in the downtown area and decided to stop at that one, too.

As she walked into the store, a blast of heat compelled her to unzip her new coat. Someone greeted her and complemented her shirt, which had only been visible for about thirty seconds. It was one of her Lucas franchise shirts: heather gray, with the design in red, it had a half rebel/half Empire sigil and in classic logo font the top read "My maiden name is Jade." There was a line of Aurebesh on the bottom that didn't have a translation printed on the shirt, but Leah knew it said, "and I am a kriffing badass."

Leah soon found herself explaining that she was in the process of moving and this was her first time in the store, which led to an invitation to their open game nights and questions about what Leah preferred in a game. The staff really knew their stuff, but that wasn't that surprising when Leah remembered that this store was on the doorstep of one of the country's largest gaming conventions. It took all of the self-control she had not to walk out of the store with five new board games, and she was about to test her limits further by venturing onward, to the original shop she'd been aiming for.

She still walked out with a couple of expansions for Elder Sign that she'd managed to miss in raids on Houston's game stores.

A mile or two later, Leah's stomach reminded her that it was being neglected fiercely in this exploration of their new city. Even though it was a chain, and that was hardly exploratory, Leah was so excited to see a familiar build-a-burrito shop that she pulled in. The idea of leaving Tex-Mex behind had been one of the things she'd been dreading the most, so seeing signs of Chipotle and Qdoba in what was possibly her new neighborhood made things feel a bit more like home. There were a few people in line ahead of her, so when her phone released a "Yoshi!", she went ahead and checked the message.

Her heart fluttered in her chest as she saw the name on the screen: Merlin was texting her.

Unlocking her phone, she felt like she was moving in super slow motion. All sound bled away aside from that of her breathing; the rhythmic in and out from her lungs seemed more rapid than normal, and ridiculously loud. It was like wearing headphones that weren't playing anything. The text bubble expanded, and the world popped back into place. "How's life?" was all that it said.

Not sure what I was really expecting, Leah shook her head, embarrassed that she'd gotten that excited over a two-word text. She exited the window and shoved her phone back in her pocket, determined not to be one of *those* people when she got to the front of the line.

"Yoshi!" her pocket chirped.

Ignoring it took more effort this time. The mocha skinned woman in front of her was ordering for multiple people, though, so Leah dug the phone back out.

"You drive a blue Chevy Cruz with a TARDIS?"

Leah's breath was back in her ears. She and Mel had never talked about her car that she could remember. How could he possibly know that? "How could you possibly know that?" she texted.

"I saw you get out when you parked next to me," the response was fast enough that Leah wondered if he'd been typing it before she asked.

"What?" she sent, and before he had a chance to answer, she was typing out, "I thought you lived in Chicago."

As Leah waited for the screen to light up, the woman behind the counter cleared her throat. *Damn it*, Leah thought. *I ended up being that person.* She was caught between the impulse to run out to the front of the restaurant and check the car next to hers, and the desire to not completely irritate the person that would ultimately be responsible for her burrito's construction. "I... I'm sorry. I've got to... My uncle might have... combusted," she sputtered, edging her way back out of the line. The woman cocked an eyebrow at this, but seemed much less annoyed, so Leah counted that a victory and bolted for the door.

It opened just before she reached it, and she only narrowly avoided colliding with the man holding it. She jumped backward, recognizing it as the man she'd been rushing out to meet.

"Mel! What are you doing here?"

He looked every bit as surprised as she felt, "What am I doing here? I live in Indianapolis. What are you doing here?"

"You live here," Leah couldn't believe the odds. Of the entire Midwest, she'd accidently picked the same city that Mel lived in. He'd never clarified what part of the Midwest he was from, and for some reason, she'd assumed Chicago. "Shit. I mean, that's good, but I didn't know, you know?"

Mel's expression was one of utter bafflement, and Leah couldn't blame him in the least.

"I'm sorry. It's awesome to see you, really. I was just really not expecting this today," Leah said. "Or, any day...? You never said, and I got it into my head at some point that you were from Chicago, and then, well, I'm apartment hunting."

Leah waited for her words to sink in, pulling at the cuffs of her coat sleeves the way she did when she was nervous. When she'd first gotten the text about her car from Mel, she'd been alarmed that he might have been a creepy stalker person, even though she hadn't the slightest idea how he would have found her before any of her address changes or driver's license updates. Now, she was worried that he'd think she was the creepy stalker person, moving to his city after all of two meetings. It hadn't been on purpose, but she really, really didn't want to scare him off from whatever this was between them. He'd told her he liked her on their first meeting, and she'd discovered she liked him during their afternoon in San Antonio. Whether that fondness was romantic or friendship, she wasn't entirely certain, but she'd really hate to ruin it with this chance encounter.

He was still holding the door open, much to the consternation of the people behind the burrito counter. One of them shouted, "Hey! If no one's coming in, how about you shut the door!"

Shaking himself out of whatever spell had him tranced, Mel seemed to remember that he hadn't spoken since asking why Leah was present. "You... decided to move to Indianapolis?"

"I had to get out of Houston," Leah explained. "Everywhere I went, I kept running into shades of my past, or Alan himself. I needed a new start, and I'd never been to Indiana before, so it seemed as good a place as any."

Nodding, Mel still seemed a little shell-shocked, but he had the beginnings of a grin. "It's okay, Leah. I get it. You can breathe."

Taking him at his word, Leah let out a long sighing breath that became mist as it puffed out of her lungs. That was when she remembered that she hadn't refastened her coat since exiting the game store. "Is it always this cold up here?" she asked, struggling with her zipper.

"Not always, but this is pretty typical for winter," Mel said. They both looked up to see the mocha skinned woman approaching the door. Mel hurried to open it again, allowing the woman to step out. Now that Leah could see her more clearly, she realized that the woman had the right combination of self-possession and striking beauty to be a model. A lump of concern rose in Leah's throat when she caught on that this woman wasn't a stranger to Mel.

The could-be model immediately looked at Mel with a very puzzled expression. "Mel? I thought you were waiting in the car?"

"Jessie, this is Leah, from Houston. Leah, this is Jessie Dallas, one of my best friends," Mel said by way of introduction. When the woman took no offense, Leah felt the lump of momentary concern loosen.

Jessie shoved the bags in her hands over to Mel and gave Leah a firm, slightly aggressive handshake. It didn't seem like a stay-away-from-my-man sort of aggression, just a declaration of self. If Leah had to guess, Jessie was used to establishing herself as an alpha in business arenas. "Good to finally have a face to put with the name," Jessie said. "Mel's mentioned you a few times."

"Oh..." Leah glanced toward Mel, wondering just how much he'd told his friends about her.

"We'd best get back before my brother eats your cat food," Jessie told Mel.

"Right," Mel said. He took one step away, and then hesitated. "If you'd like to get together sometime, just call or text. I'm... I'll find some time for you."

Leah nodded, not entirely sure how to take that last part. On the one hand, she had arrived in his city entirely unannounced, so it wasn't like he'd necessarily be free to hang out, but the other part of her wondered what exactly it was that Mel did. Somehow, it seemed like it never really came up when they were together.

With her thoughts focused on the unexpected encounter, Leah reentered the restaurant and made her way back up to the counter. The employee that greeted her was the same woman that she'd run out on before. "How's your uncle?" she asked.

It took Leah a second to remember what the woman was talking about, but once she did, she couldn't help answering, "False alarm, but my aunt's on standby with a fire extinguisher."

Chapter Thirty

LEAH'S APARTMENT HUNTING in Indianapolis, the thought wouldn't leave Mel's head. He was driving more or less on autopilot, and it took Jessie's voice a couple of tries to break through the sparkly haze that seemed to have coated the world in the last few minutes.

"...ticket stub," Jessie said.

"Uh huh," Mel tried.

Jessie scowled at Mel. "You haven't heard a word I've said since we got in the car, have you?"

Mel considered contradicting her but telling her that he'd heard two words versus none didn't seem like an argument worth making. "Sorry. I was pretty zoned out."

"She's the one that we saw in San Antonio; the one with the Star Fandom of choice question, right?" Jessie asked.

"Yes," Mel said. He couldn't help glancing in his rearview mirror to see if Leah's car was behind them. That would change his view of the encounter in a hurry. It wasn't that he didn't believe Leah when she told him that her choosing his town had been an accident, but if he caught her following him home there would be some serious room for doubt. Mel was uncomfortable with this line of reasoning because he really wanted to continue to like Leah.

"Are you sure that she doesn't know who you—and by extension—who we are?" Jessie asked. Her tone was that don't-play-with-me-right-now that only came out when she was ready to get angry. "Seriously, Mel, if you told her your secret identity, now's the time to let me know. Also, did you know she was going to be in town?"

Sensing the dangerous mood that was currently seeping right through his air filters like the smell of a paper mill, Mel pulled over so he could look Jessie in the eye as he told her, "I did not tell her about our secret, but she had that friend that may have shared her suspicions. I don't think so, though. Leah's a D'weasel, and she didn't act like she thought I was anyone other than Mel."

"So what is she doing here?" Jessie demanded.

Handing Jessie his phone with the text exchange open, he told her, "She's trying to get a fresh start. Her ex-husband lives in Houston. Apparently, it's been hard to get away while they live in the same city, so she chose a place she'd never been."

"...and she thought you were from Chicago," Jessie said, letting out a long breath. "Just one big, weird coincidence."

"Seems like," Mel said. He turned on his blinker to get back onto the road. "You didn't seem that concerned when we were talking to her."

"It wasn't until we were in the car that it occurred to me to be concerned," Jessie shrugged. "I think I'm catching some of your paranoia."

"Maybe it's the fact that Stephanie showed up at my door earlier this week, and it's making your protective instincts kick in," Mel suggested.

"Also possible," Jessie said.

As quiet retook the car, Mel's bouncy cheer slowly reasserted itself. Things seemed a bit less shiny than they had before he and Jessie stopped for their talk. A thin shadow of guilt lingered in the corners of his vision because he hadn't mentioned that Nessa had a bit more than suspicions to share with her friend.

"LAUNCH CONCERT!" BETHAM greeted Mel and Jessie upon their return with the bags of burritos. "Supremely epic idea, no?"

"What's this, now?" Mel set their food down on the table and began moving his laptop out of the way. This sent some sort of feline psychic signal to Dot that she absolutely needed to be a part of the process. She was much less helpful than she thought was. Mel gave up on trying to work around the cat and plucked her off of the floor for a belly rub.

"We do a one-night show for the launch of our album! It's coming out late Feb, right? So what if we do a concert on the night of the release? D'weasels will love it, bro!"

Jessie dug into the bag, procuring napkins, a plastic container of hot sauce, and a foil wrapper of what looked like street-style tacos. She arranged the items around her chair and then went to pilfer the fridge for something to drink. "How old is this coffee thing?"

Mel probed the dusty corners of his brain for the answer, "Thanksgiving?"

"Sell by date is still good," Jessie said. "I'm gonna chance it."

"Dudes! Come on! Launch concert!"

When Jessie came back out of the kitchen, she looked concerned. "If we do a launch concert, we're going to have to find a venue outside of Indy. We did our New Year's Eve show in town, and people are going to start guessing that we live here."

Both Mel and Betham just stared at Jessie in mute disbelief. It had always been Mel's place in the group to voice cautions about probable discovery. Generally, Jessie was extremely cavalier and really gung-ho about things that would give the band more publicity. Anything to make the D'weasels happier, short of a swimsuit calendar. *Actually, I may have to suggest a calendar*, Mel thought. *No swimsuits though, unless they're over our costumes.*

That was when Mel realized that Jessie still wasn't sure that Leah hadn't figured them out. Mel was not at all used to this role in the band, but if Jessie was going to be the cautious one, someone had to come up with the alternatives that she normally provided, "Well,

Chicago is close enough for us to travel to in a day, or Michigan? Possibly Ohio? I don't think we've ever played Cincinnati."

Betham whipped his head from staring at Jessie to starting at Mel. "Dude, did you two body swap on me? Because I'm gonna be really real with you right now, and tell you that, Jess, you'll always be my sis," with these words, Betham grabbed Mel's hand and squeezed it with brotherly affection.

Mel retracted his hand from Betham's grip and rolled his eyes, "We didn't body swap, goob. We ran into Leah."

"Princess Leia? The Wars/Trek girl from San Anton?" Betham asked without skipping a beat.

This time, Mel and Jessie stared. "How did you figure that out?"

"Because when Mel told her at the panel that he was very into Princess Leia, I knew he didn't mean the late-great Carrie Fisher, because that night that I spent on his couch, he told me that his sci-fi crush was Kaylee from Firefly. Since the divorcee lady that he liked was named Leah, and the girl asking the question was giving off some mega Kaylee vibes, I did a web search for travel agents in Houston and cross-ref'd with recent divorces ala public rec'. Bingo-bongo, viola! Her professional website has an announcement that she's relocating, and her friend Nessa, professional cosplayer whose specs were on the AXES program, has a tweet saying that her roommate was unprepared for Midwest winter. Just a bit of mental calc, bro," Betham said.

For a long time, words were replaced with blinking as Mel and Jessie tried to absorb this onslaught of deduction. "You got all of that from my saying I was into Princess Leia?" Mel said after one of the longest silences of his friendship with the ever enigmatic Betham.

"Yeah, bro," Betham said, grinning as he decided that it was time to retrieve his burrito from the table. "Made sense to me that I check into the lady my man was diggin'."

Jessie opened her mouth to say something, closed it, and then tried again. "How many of my romantic entanglements have you cyberstalked?" she finally asked.

"Only the ones you told me about, chica," Betham said, taking a big bite of his burrito.

After processing that for a little while, Jessie finally shook her head. "Alright. So who all's up for a show in Cincinnati in February?"

Chapter Thirty-one

TWO DAYS AFTER THE random encounter with Mel, Leah was touring yet another of the apartments on her list of prospects when she realized that she wasn't paying any attention to whether this place met her criteria. Her mind was completely absorbed by the question of whether she liked Mel enough to give up on her Lancel♡t crush. That moment of pure electricity, back during the August concert had been amazing, but as hard as she tried, it was really hard to envision a relationship with a guy that was nothing but a mask in her head. Growing up in the household that she had, Leah had grown up with plenty of superhero crushes, and the original Tobey Maguire Spider-Man movie, with its iconic kiss (despite the interviews that revealed how very unromantic that scene had been to film), had featured heavily in quite a few of Leah's teenage daydreams. Even so, with Mel being that much more accessible, the idea of managing to find and convince Lancel♡t that she was more than just another groupie seemed more far-fetched than ever.

This is ridiculous, Leah thought as she thanked the apartment manager and headed back toward her car. *If I could just turn off that section of my head, I totally would right now. I want to find a place so Nessa can move up here and tell me just how ridiculous this is.*

Except that Nessa was even less reasonable about this stuff than Leah's brain was currently inclined to be.

Leah pulled out her phone and sent Nessa a text, anyway. *Can't concentrate on apartment stuff. Keep thinking about Lancel♡t and Mel.*

Before she even had time to turn off the screen, Nessa's response showed up in the text window. *Does that mean you're ready to move on?*

Sitting in the parking lot of a strange city, soon to be her strange city, Leah considered the question. She'd admitted to herself that she had a crush on Lancel♡t, and she liked Mel as something more than friendship really allowed. She was scared of trying to pursue either of them, but it was that nervous anticipatory feeling of a first date, not the fear of putting herself back on the road after a car crash. The memory of what she had with Alan could still cause her a bit of ache, but it was like the ache in her toe that she'd broken in middle school. Once in a while, if there was a storm coming in, there was a dull pain that warned her about a change in weather. It wasn't something that she even noticed unless something caused her to think about it.

Yes. I think so, Leah sent.

An image loading icon appeared, and Leah watched as the number of bytes rapidly ticked upward. When the pic finally appeared, Leah's jaw dropped. She'd heard the phrase, seen it in cartoons, and even some movies; but this was the first time in her adult life that she recalled physically being aware that her jaw's muscles had been functioning normally at one moment and completely gave up the next. The pic Nessa had sent her was one of those once-in-a-lifetime shots that caught Leah in crystal clear profile, touching hands with Lancel♡t in as clear a profile as was possible with his helmet on. Both of them had the same expression, as though they'd felt the heartbeat of the universe in an instant. Leah was astonished, angry, hurt, and confused all at once. Why had her friend kept this from her for five, going on six, months?

Because I was married on the night that she took this, her reasonable side reminded her. *You weren't ready to see it, and now, she's letting you see something that you already knew. This is just proof. Sharable proof.*

"Oh my god," Leah said aloud. That was it. She'd told Nessa she was ready to move on, so Nessa had given her a way to do just that. Nessa said before that she believed that the Magical Space Skeleton Army was looking for Leah, and she had sat on the very thing that she believed they were looking for, just to protect Leah until Leah decided she was ready.

Good luck, Nessa texted.

Any thoughts of continuing the apartment search today disappeared like a looted corpse from Leah's mental itinerary. She had to talk to someone, in person, and that could only be Anthony, currently. The first person that popped into her head was actually Mel, because as a fellow D'weasel, she felt he might understand; however, Leah was not so dim as to think calling a guy about another guy was in any way permissible, especially since she still had very conflicted feelings about both. She would head back to Lafayette, talk to Anthony, and get his take on things. With any luck, she'd have some scope on things by the end of the conversation.

"I'm never going to find an apartment at this rate," she told her steering wheel.

It seemed disinclined to respond.

AS LEAH POWERED DOWN her forward thrusters and locked the docking clamps (put the Cruze into park), the Magical Space Skeleton Army were conspicuously silent. Leah kept her radio off on the hour plus drive back to Anthony's house, hoping the quiet would lead to some sort of profound realization. The only thing that she'd really realized though, was that she couldn't make a decision. She liked Mel, but they'd never *actually* touched so she had no idea if there was any chemistry there. With Lancel♡t, the only thing she was certain of at all was chemistry. Well, chemistry and creativity. He made her laugh. So did Mel.

Leah unlocked the door with the spare key that Anthony had given her. "Anthony?" she called. "Are you here?"

There was no answer, but Leah wasn't going to be dissuaded lightly. She checked the kitchen and the laundry room, looked in the garage, and even peeked behind the shower curtains (though she was kind of grasping at straws at that point). Glancing at the clock in her room, Leah sighed and finally settled in to wait until Anthony got back. It was only one o'clock in the afternoon, and Anthony wouldn't be home until after four. Leah couldn't concentrate enough to try and work, though she did check her emails. Instead, she picked up a controller and powered on one of her consoles. She had enough games loaded that it didn't much matter which console it was, so long as there was some sort of undead/corrupted monstrosity to put down. Games usually helped her clear her head, and that was what she wanted.

Dark Souls, Leah thought as the title came up. *Perfect.*

BY THE TIME ANTHONY came in, Leah was engrossed with fighting something grotesquely gorgeous and nearly forgot that she'd come home in a hurry to talk to him. "Anthony! I needed to talk about something," she said, not taking her eyes off the screen. She was out of flasks and there hadn't been anyone available online to help her with this boss, so odds were good that she was about to lose a hefty number of souls. She'd missed the last campfire because she'd been distracted. *Perhaps Dark Souls was a bit ambitious for my state of mind*, Leah thought as she narrowly dodged an attack that would've meant her end.

"Should I come back?" Anthony asked, glancing at her screen.

"No, this should be over soon... Hopefully... I can..." Leah's words trailed off as she ducked around behind the sordid thing. She thought she had it as her character slipped through the narrow gap in the creature's defense. She hit the button for her backstab move, but then the thing suddenly hopped over her attack and was facing her again. Death screen. Leah hung her head with the loss, but it was not a forever defeat, only the loss of an afternoon. She'd come back and achieve victory in due time.

"Ouch," Anthony commiserated.

"Anthony, do you remember that guy I told you about? The one that I talked to at Escape from Philly Burger the day of my divorce?"

"The one that you ran into at AXES and around here only two days ago? You may have mentioned him," Anthony said. His grin took any possible bite out of his words. "Why do you ask?"

"Okay, so you know about Mel. Did I tell you about the Magical Space Skeleton Army concert and the whole connection with Lancel♡t thing?" Leah asked.

"Again, it may have come up previously. Are you going somewhere with this?"

Leah pulled out her phone and showed Anthony the picture that Nessa had just sent her. As Anthony's eyebrows shot up, Leah began talking about the way she felt about both guys and how she was afraid of pursuing one would be the end of something with the other. "There's something about it all that has me wigged the fuck out," Leah said. "I don't know how or why, but what if I were to pursue one of them and the other found out? As soon as one of them comes to the fore, the other is by necessity a backup, and I don't want anyone to be a backup. I just want... both."

"Leah, hun, you're not playing Pokemon. You can't really collect them all, you know?" Anthony said, chuckling as he did so.

"I know!" Leah said with more force than she anticipated. "Sorry... I mean, I know. It's horrible of me to even think something like that, right? I've tried to make up my mind, and it's like there's this rock that just won't budge."

Anthony still had Leah's phone in his hand, and he was studying the pic of Leah and Lancel♡t as though it would yield some sort of solution if he just stared hard enough. "I don't suppose you have any pictures of this Mel guy that we could weigh against this?"

"No," Leah said. "I can show you the texts that Mel and I have exchanged, not that they amount to much. Most of our interactions have been face to face."

Taking her phone, Leah's thumb slipped as she was trying to switch between conversations and instead of the back button she hit the menu button. A large number of open windows sprawled out before her. It had been forever and a half since she'd gone through and wiped the slate clean. Instead of hitting the clear all, Leah found herself scrolling through the list, trying to remember things like when she'd last opened her language learning app that hadn't been an accident. She had an open tab for her note-taking app. *When do I ever use my notes app?* Leah thought. She tapped the page.

For the second time in less than twelve hours, Leah felt her jaw go slack.

"What? What did you find?" Anthony asked. He looked over her shoulder and read, "Lancel♡t@magicalspaceskeletonarmy.com? So you looked up how to send Lancel♡t fan mail? Is this shocking?"

"I... didn't look that up," Leah said, remembering that first meeting with Mel much clearer than she had in months.

"Waroh heala!" Mel had said.

Leah had been confused enough to stop and wait for an explanation. Mel or Merlin, whatever he decided to go by, had been nothing but charming. He had allowed Leah to dump her metaphorical purse all over his plate, so a nonsensical sentence or two could be overlooked. "What?"

She was rewarded by his smile as he told her that he was going to be in San Antonio in January, and if she was going to be there or in the Indianapolis area for Gygax Con, he'd love to hear from her.

Opening her notes app, Leah had handed Merlin her phone. She figured she'd either save or delete the page at a later point in time when she was ready to think about something other than her failed marriage. Merlin had been positively glowing as he handed it back to her, even though she was careful not to look at the screen and give him any more hope than she thought necessary. After all, there was a good chance that she would never cross paths with this man again.

"Mel gave me that email address to get in contact with him. I forgot all about it," Leah said. Stunned didn't even begin to cover the emotion that was sizzling through her circuits.

Anthony returned his gaze to the open notes app on the phone, and said, "Well, I suppose that's one way to clear up your earlier issue. What are you going to do now?"

Staring at the email address, Leah considered her options. She had Mel's phone number, so she could just text him, but after the build-a-burrito incident, that didn't seem like a very good way to explain things. *"Hey, you remember how it looked when I just happened to be moving into your neighborhood? Well, here's proof that I know your big secret, too!"* That seemed like the best way to find out what a restraining order looked like with her name on it. If she sent the picture to the email, there would likely be similar issues. What if Mel didn't remember giving her his Lancel♡t email address?

What if the whole thing was a joke? Leah thought. It was certainly possible, but she thought she knew Mel better than that. Besides, it just seemed to fit. Every time the Magical Space Skeleton Army came up, he'd just been tense, or busy, or evasive. Thoughts just seemed to race into her head like a training montage in a sports movie. Merlin, Arthurian wizard, Lancel♡t, Arthurian knight, working at AX-ES, not con staff, Nessa bowing out before they were due to hang out with Mel, Nessa's expression when she heard Mel speak, when she heard Lancel♡t speak. Leah was back on her contact list and calling Nessa before she'd made the conscious decision to dial.

"Leah," Nessa said, her tone calm and collected, like nothing major had happened at all.

"Nessa! You knew?" Leah asked, not sure whether she was yelling or hissing. It kind of came out of her throat as both.

"Knew what?" Nessa's tone hadn't changed. She seemed completely unflappable. Leah usually appreciated that quality in Nessa, but for once, Leah just wanted someone to freak out with her for a little bit.

"You knew about Mel!" Leah said. "You knew that he was..."

Leah stopped herself. She couldn't just go around broadcasting Mel's secret to all her friends and family. It would be different if he'd given her permission, but he didn't even know that Leah knew.

Nessa saved Leah from having to finish the sentence, "If you are referring to a certain job that a mutual acquaintance of ours happens to perform in front of an audience, then yes. I knew."

"Why didn't you tell me?" Leah tried to keep her voice from betraying any one of the cocktail of emotions that she was currently feeling. Betrayal, anger, elation, understanding, fear, hope, anxiety; they were all in there to varying degrees.

"Con code," Nessa said. "Not my secret to give. Did he tell you?"

"No," Leah said.

The other end of the line was quiet. For a moment, Leah thought the line might have disconnected. She actually pulled it away from her ear to check that screen still showed seconds of call time ticking by. "Nessa?" she asked. "Still there?"

"Yeah," Nessa said. "Sorry. I was just... surprised."

"What do I do?" Leah asked. "I can't just tell him that I know."

Anthony tapped Leah's shoulder and gestured to her phone, "Put her on speaker. I think the three of us all need to brainstorm. Besides, this is way more entertaining than grading papers."

"Are you sure?" Leah asked. "I don't want to get in the way if you need to work."

"Please," Anthony waved away her concern and gestured to her phone again, "Whoever heard of a professor that works? I'll get a bad reputation if I give their papers back less than a week after they got turned in. Let's figure out a way to land you a celebrity boyfriend."

Chapter Thirty-two

MEL WAS READY FOR THE contest to be over. The deadline wasn't until March, but he was really tired of seeing the same video over and over and over. Video submissions tended to fall into three categories: Notice me, Senpai, Needless Nudity, and the least observed Actual Contestant. D'weasels came in all shapes and sizes, and that was rarely more obvious than when yet another unsolicited dick and his penis would wave at the camera (sometimes literally). The ones that were in the Notice me, Senpai category were generally pretty shrill, not bothering to mention anything required by the contest but unloading a ton of unwanted information about their life, family, dog, cat, sick relatives, dead relatives, wedding proposal requests, or special birthday shout out hopes for the Magical Space Skeleton Army to randomly fulfill. Actual Contestants said their name within the first few seconds, and oddly, they seemed to be the only group with that pattern.

"Hi! As you can see, I'm naked!" yet another of the Needless Nude started. Mel stopped the video, wrote down the username and wrote DISQUALIFIED in bold letters before deleting the video. *I don't understand*, Mel let out a sigh and went in search of Dot. Maybe having a cat with him would make things easier to deal with.

Clicking on the next video, he saw a young woman, maybe early twenties with brilliant blue hair. "Hi, I'm Cat Higgins, and my contact info is on this card," she held up an index card with her phone number and address. It took the camera a second to focus on the letters, obviously an auto adjust. Cat seemed familiar enough with her equipment to give it the time needed. *I think I've seen her ASMR videos, actually*, Mel thought, appreciating the professionalism. "My lyric submission is, 'Why are you a weasel anyway?' from *Dweeb Weasels from Space*."

That one seemed really popular, having almost twenty submissions. If it were a poll instead of a contest, Mel would already be working on lyrics.

He moved Cat's video to the Saved Submissions folder and clicked the next video. Dot put her paws on his chest and started trying to rub against his face. His kitten was determined to take her job of distraction seriously and so when Mel heard a familiar voice coming from his screen, he wasn't ready for it. "My name is Leah Walsh, but one of you may remember it as Koziol. I realize that this isn't strictly the personal information you had in mind when making the requirements for this video, but then again, it might be. See, I've got a pic that my friend Nessa took," and here Leah held her phone up so that it was visible in the camera. Mel saw his profile, the jaw tight with concealed emotion, and Leah's profile, her look one of utter, beguiling astonishment, with their hands touching in a sea of people. The lightning bolt feeling tinged on the edge of Mel's awareness. Leah. It was *Leah*. Leah was his Spark. So many times, so many near touches, so many opportunities; how had he missed it?

But she was speaking again, "See, I didn't know this picture existed until a few days ago, and when I found out, I remembered a lot of things that happened right around that time. I met a guy; one of the cutest and sweetest guys it's ever been my privilege to meet. He listened to me talk about, well, he knows what we talked about... and he put an email address on my phone. One that I think we both forgot about," Leah held up her phone again, this time showing a note-taking app that only said: Lancel♡t@magicalspaceskeleton-army.com.

This time the shiver that ran through him was not entirely pleasant. All this time, Leah had been walking around with his secret in her pocket. What if it had been someone else that he'd made that mistake with? But it wasn't. It was Leah. He couldn't get over it. He couldn't look away.

"I've run into that guy a few times since, and I couldn't stop thinking about that moment in the Houston concert either. Every time I've been blue in the last two or three years, Lancel♡t has been the voice in my head, offering me comfort and comedy. Then Mel showed up and offered me friendship and understanding at a time that I really needed a friend. I think something in me knew that they were linked, because I could never choose a favorite. The first time we touched, I felt the world melt. The first time we met, I wasn't free to like you yet. I'm free now. If this all means something to you, let me know. If this all just scared the pants off you and you never want to see me again, that's fair, too. I guess you'll find a way to let me know which it is."

She reached forward as though to stop the camera, and then paused, "Oh, and my favorite lyric is, 'Feel free to freshen my fortress,' from *Space Dictator: Looking to Hire*."

Mel had forgotten all about the contest. It took him a few tries to find his pen and jot down Leah's entry information. Everything in the world had gone kind of sparkly again, as it had outside of the burrito place.

Leah was his Spark.

Leah.

Leah.

He jumped up from his seat, startling Dot into escaping to her tower. Within moments, he had phoned both Betham and Jessie. As much as he yearned to call Leah right away, he had to consult with his band. As well as having a video confession from a fan with knowledge of his secret that he should probably tell them about, he had to let them know that the contest idea had worked better than he could've possibly anticipated. Mel also had the beginnings of an idea on how to send Leah his response.

Chapter Thirty-three

IN ORDER TO KEEP HER mind off of her contest submission and whether Mel had seen it or not, Leah had tackled the problem of finding her new apartment that she would share with Nessa. After several tours, and a lot of handshakes, she managed to find a place that was in budget, had decent closet space, was on the second floor, and while there weren't storage facilities next door, there was a storage place only a few blocks away. Nessa was given a virtual tour of the model apartment, took her own look at the information on the website, and gave her blessing.

The application was available online, which meant that Leah and Nessa were both able to sign the lease. Anthony rode down with Leah on the day she was going to pick up keys.

"Just an observation, but don't people usually take their stuff when they move into a new place?" Anthony asked.

"If it's all the same to you, I think I want to buy a bed before I start shifting my stuff out of your house," Leah said.

"Oh, I see. You're just using me for my mattresses. Well, fine. Maybe I'll just start using you for your game collection," Anthony crossed his arms, though there was nothing serious about his tone.

"I thought that was a given," Leah flashed a smile in Anthony's direction.

There was an unspoken layer of tension below the veneer of play for both of them, though. It had been a few weeks since Leah had recorded and sent her video to the Magical Space Skeleton Army. No one wanted to be the person to suggest that maybe Mel had been scared away by the revelation, but the longer it took for a response to come, the more it felt like that may have been the case.

Pulling into the "Future Residents" parking spaces, Leah jumped out of the car and went into the office. She emerged only a few minutes later with two gate fobs and the keys jingling in her pocket. As soon as she was back in the car, she gave the fobs to Anthony so he could stick them on his sun visor. They got to test them out at the gate.

As apartment complexes went, this one was pretty. There were trees everywhere, and they had the feel of old growth as opposed to being purely decorative. Leah parked in the one assigned spot that she and Nessa would share once Nessa made it up. Although Leah hadn't really discussed it with Nessa, Leah was intending to give Nessa the space as often as possible. It only seemed fair after the way Nessa had taken Leah in during the split with Alan.

The buildings themselves were cream boards and soft red brick, with dark gray roof tiles. Not really anything special, but Leah found it homey. She couldn't help remembering the apartments she'd lived in before she and Alan had bought the house. Those had been painted a sunny, buttery yellow, which she had initially loved but had grown to dislike as it seemed more and more relentlessly cheerful. This more neutral palette seemed much safer.

Leah unlocked the door and ushered Anthony into a wide common space. The kitchen was divided from the space with a breakfast bar, and the bedrooms were down a hall that opened near the mouth of the kitchen. Between her income and Nessa's, they'd been able to qualify for the optional breakfast nook area that was on the opposite side of the kitchen. The same soft red brick from the outside was lining the fireplace in the corner of the living room. Leah was already looking forward to Nessa's big overstuffed chair being set up close enough to the fireplace to curl up with cocoa while watching the snow drift through the big window.

"So... It looks like an empty apartment," Anthony observed.

"Yes," Leah agreed.

"Big empty apartment," Anthony said.

"Yes," Leah agreed.

"I think you need some... stuff." Anthony wandered through the kitchen, opening drawers and cabinets as he went. "No one ever leaves enough weird shit for people to find when they move into an apartment. Houses, with all the attics and basements, you can leave all kinds of things. Apartments, with the professional cleaning crews, you're never going to get creepy doll altars or a life-sized cardboard cutout of Jessica Rabbit or anything fun."

"There are times when I question your idea of fun," Leah said.

"All I'm saying is, if you want to face melt some Nazis with the Ark of the Covenant, don't leave it in an apartment that they're about to rent," Anthony said, opening the pantry. "Cleaning crew would toss that shit right out."

Leah was chuckling at her friend's absurdity when her phone alerted her that she'd gotten a text.

It was from Mel.

This is it. He saw the video, Leah thought. It was a strangely lucid thought for the turmoil that the rest of her was currently experiencing. She felt like her heart had struggled its way into her esophagus and then morphed into a blender that was stuck on puree. "It's Mel," she said.

Anthony was at her side in less time than it took her to blink. He had his phone out and up to his ear, and Leah barely registered that he was rapidly filling Nessa in on the state of things. There wasn't much to tell, yet. It was a text, and an unopened one at that. Leah's universe teetered on a crossroads that didn't mean much to the world as a whole, but one that could easily shape her future. She opened the text.

It was a QR code.

Leah blinked.

It was still a QR code.

A second text appeared while she stared at the screen: this one was a link announcing that the Magical Space Skeleton Army was doing a one-night concert on February thirteenth, in Cincinnati, to celebrate the launch of their album.

Finally, Mel sent two words: *Please come.*

"Nessa, we are so buying tickets to this show," Anthony said. "Now, we gotta go. It's time to find this lady a bed. Leah's gotta have time to air out her new mattress before concert night."

BY THE NINTH OF FEBRUARY, Leah's mattress had lost that just-opened smell and her new sheets and blankets, while still newish, smelled of familiar laundry detergents and fabric softeners. Nessa had arrived with the moving truck less than two weeks ago, and things were still finding their places. One box was full of toilet paper. Leah had opened it and given Nessa a questioning look.

"I thought maybe it could become a tradition," Nessa said. "Whenever we move, there's a box of toilet paper."

"Is this pilfered toilet paper?" Leah asked.

"Not unless they give you receipts for pilfering," Nessa said.

"I get them from the IRS," Leah shrugged.

"Then, yes. That toilet paper was pilfered. We have a fresh load of pilfered paper," Nessa shook her head and went back to figuring out which of her costume chests were going to stay in the apartment and which were going out to her new storage facility.

Carrying the box into the hallway bathroom, Leah stopped at the doorway to her bedroom and looked at the pile of empty boxes that she'd unloaded into her closet and the small chest of drawers at the foot of her queen-sized bed. She was officially in her own place, with everything she owned under one roof. Nessa was her roommate, not by necessity but choice, and Anthony had already invaded their place twice for game nights. Life had reached a benign equilibrium. For the first time since she and Alan had signed the divorce papers, Leah really felt like she was home. There was a nervous fluttering in her chest whenever she thought about the impending concert, but no matter how that turned out, she knew it would be okay. She was going to be okay. It was a good feeling.

"ARE YOU SURE YOU'RE going to be okay?" Nessa asked. "I can pull over if you need me to."

Leah nodded. Her nerves had reached a breaking point as they reached the outer suburbs of Cincinnati, and she'd started to turn a bit green. "I'll be fine. I just wish I knew what the hell Mel was planning. I had nightmares all night about him having them dress me in a silver bikini and blue face paint, just to have the whole audience laugh at me while an edited version of my video played, which somehow made it look like I was admitting to having a golf shoe fetish."

"A golf shoe fetish?" Anthony repeated. "How oddly specific. Did you mention golf in that video?"

"Not the point," Leah said, feeling her stomach shift again. *I will not throw up. I will not throw up. I will not throw up...* she tried repeating it over and over to herself like a mantra. It wasn't helping.

Nessa turned on her car's stereo system. Leah must have left one of her CDs in (she'd bought the physical albums as well as downloading the mp3s to her phone), as the first thing to start playing was "Then She Puked on Me."

Oddly, that helped a lot. Leah's stomach stopped flipping and she remembered that she was going to a concert for her favorite group; whatever did or didn't happen with Mel, Lancel♡t would still be out there, making people happy. Her nerves transferred their energy into excitement. She still didn't know what the QR code was for, exactly, but when she'd called the venue, they'd told her to present it at the roll call ticket counter.

Even though they arrived three hours early, there was already a line halfway down the block for those that already had their tickets. Anthony and Nessa wished Leah luck and went to go stand in line.

"Wait," Leah said. "What if this is the joke? I get up there and they tell me that it just says, 'Get lost, loser,' or something?"

"I don't think he'd do something like that," Nessa said. "You're going to have to trust him."

Leah took a deep breath and walked up to the booth.

"Yes, ma'am, how can I help you?" a very smiley guy asked.

"I have this QR code," Leah said, offering her phone. She'd taken a screenshot and blanked out Mel's name and number, just to be safe. She didn't want to be the leak that ruined his privacy.

"Okay, ma'am, I have a security guard that's coming through the door on my left. He's going to screen you and then bring you through to our inner office. Here's your phone, and a print off of your pass clearance. Give that to them when they take your picture. And congratulations!"

With a brief, "Thanks," Leah took the phone and the printout and then jogged over to where the security guard was beckoning her. There was a metal detector that she had to walk through, followed by a wand that they ran over her shoes and pockets. At the office, they took her printout, instructed her to stand on a square and took her picture. A plastic all-access backstage pass with her photo was hung on a lanyard and then given to her while a phone call was made.

They told her to wait on the bench outside, and someone would be by to get her shortly. Despite the level of flustered anticipation that Leah was experiencing, there was a part of her that felt the entire process reminded her of being sent to the principal's office.

A blonde woman in a well-worn Dio shirt wearing a headset came right up to Leah, and said, "Hi, you must be Leah."

Scrambling to her feet, Leah confirmed that she was Leah.

"My name's Francesca, but if you expect me to respond, you'd best call me Frankie," Frankie offered Leah her hand. "We're going to set you up with a special booth for the show. You here alone, or did you have anyone that you wanted up there with you?"

"I... I have two friends outside," Leah said. She pulled up a pic on her phone because she felt Frankie was probably going to ask, "They're names are Nessa and Anthony."

Frankie gestured to the nearest security guard and had Leah show him the picture, too. Within a matter of minutes, Leah was flanked by Nessa and Anthony.

"Before I lead you up to your booth, I have a non-disclosure agreement, pretty standard gag, for all three of you to sign on anything you hear or see while in your booth or behind the scenes. No photography of the band while they are rehearsing or out of costume. No recording of any kind. If you find any of these terms unacceptable, you may turn in your passes and return to the line," Frankie said. An assistant materialized next to her with a clipboard of forms and a pen. No one opted to return to the line.

As Frankie led them through the maze of backstage halls, Leah craned her neck, watching for a glimpse of the man she'd come to see. When Frankie opened a door that revealed a staircase, Leah started to realize that it was unlikely that she was going to see Mel before the show. "There are drinks and snacks available," Frankie said as they reached a balcony box that looked down on the stage and the open floor that would soon be filled with D'weasels. "The phone is linked to the bar if you'd like to place any special requests. I've got to go help with sound tests, but I'll be back to check on you after."

When she was gone, the three friends looked at each other and then went to investigate the available snacks. What else was there to do with two hours until the show? Leah picked up an oatmeal raisin cookie and tore it into bite size chunks while she gazed down at the stage and tried to think of something other than what to say when she finally did see Mel.

Chapter Thirty-four

"SHE'S HERE. ALL SET up," Frankie told Mel. She shot a wink at Betham, who was only partially Frimmydukes at this stage and shut the door behind her.

Mel began pacing the floor of the dressing room, more nervous now that he knew Leah had shown up than when he'd been worrying that she might not. "What the hell am I doing? I should've just called her. 'Hey, you know my deepest secret? Cool, I don't have to hide who I am for half of our relationship. Let's see a movie.' Instead, I'm doing... whatever this is," Mel ranted.

"This was your plan," Jessie reminded him. "If you'll recall, Betham and I told you to go for option A."

"Yes, but you two also told me that I needed to make an effort in my next relationship. This is me, making an effort."

"Dude, chill," Betham said. His Frimmydukes vest was halfway on, and his mask was sitting on a nearby table. He was going out to help with soundchecks as soon as he was fully Frimmy'd, but Mel appreciated that Betham didn't seem to be in any bigger hurry than normal. "Sit on the Stool of Destiny and take a mental journey."

Allowing himself to be pulled toward the stool, Mel perched on its wooden top and closed his eyes. "Okay, mental journey."

"First road," Betham said. "You don't do the song, we go on as before. Leah thinks the whole box thing was mega cool, and the two of you date anyway. Things may or may not last, but you regret the unsung song. Second road, you do the song, and it doesn't mesh. Things don't work out, but you did your best. Third road, we do the song, and roll a nat 20."

"Two of your roads include the song," Mel said, opening his eyes.

"It's a great song, bro," Betham pulled on the rest of his vest and snapped on his mask. "I'll see you two on stage."

Jessie watched as her brother departed and shook her head. "If he weren't blood, I'd swear that Frimmydukes was actually the real personality and Betham was the alien he portrays. He's not wrong, though. It is a great song."

"I sense a 'but,'" Mel said.

Turning away to apply her Lady Bug makeup, Jessie shrugged, "Not exactly a 'but.' I just want you to be careful. This woman was divorced only last year. Maybe it wasn't her fault, and the guy was a total prick. Maybe they just fell out of love. Maybe it was fate that she dropped into your path just as things were falling apart. I've dated divorcees before. They tend to be prickly and have a lot of triggers that don't come up in your average hookup."

"That's not a 'but?'" Mel asked.

"No," Jessie said. "That's just a caution. I saw the video. I saw the way you looked at her, then and at the burrito place. Keeping the two of you apart, or trying to, would just be mean. I try not to be mean to my friends like that."

Mel climbed off of the stool and stood behind Jessie, watching as she applied red to her cheeks in quick, sure strokes. He could see worry in her eyes if he looked hard enough. There was a bit of pain there, too, though she had it buried deep. "You were serious about someone once. A divorcee?"

"I told you a long time ago," Jessie said, "I wasn't built for commitment. Had he asked it of me, I would've tried. Luckily, he was smarter than I was at the time."

Offering Jessie a comforting shoulder squeeze, Mel turned around so that she could regain her composure. It was rare that Jessie shared anything truly personal about her romances, though the stories that she found entertaining or dumb would come up from time to time. Uncertain of what to say, Mel let the moment pass. He figured sometimes, friendship was just about being present. There was nothing he could say that would fix the past, and it had only come up out of concern for what he may face in the future. The only thing left to him was donning his gear and becoming Lancel♡t.

For years, Frimmydukes and Lady Bug had been tweaking and evolving, while Lancel♡t had worn the same helmet and tunic. Part of what tonight was going to bring was a new look for the Knight of Rock.

He'd asked for Jessie to help him figure out a completely new costume from the ground up. His silver body suit was replaced with a black one, to help the new pieces really pop under the stage lights. Over his chest was a heart, as there had been on his old tunic, but this one was much larger and encircled by a yellow crown. Mel strapped on his pauldrons, which were red with yellow trim. A red utility kilt covered his lower half, since the tunic had covered certain areas for the first half of his career and pants didn't seem very Lancel♡t. The final touch was the helmet. Since the silver had been removed from the rest of his outfit, the old one just didn't look right anymore. His new headpiece had the view panel that he'd popped out of a Master Chief Halloween helmet affixed to the front of a Greco-Roman helmet with a red plume. Mel knew he'd probably catch some flack for the helmet not being medieval anymore, but he wasn't supposed to be the real Lancel♡t of legend. He was supposed to be a goofy-ass alien that picked the name once he got to Earth. The only piece of the costume he left alone was the red sneakers (which were replaced every time he wore out a pair anyway).

The new helmet impaired his vision less than the average pair of sunglasses. He was a new Mel, so he felt it was time to be a new Lancel♡t, one with a clearer vision of what lay ahead.

D'WEASELS PACKED THE Cincinnati venue, cheering until their lungs must have been completely void of air. The reception to Lancel♡t's new look was overwhelming. Mel thought that his entrance may have gotten as much applause as Lady Bug's for once. As much as he appreciated the roar of acceptance, his eyes lingered on the box above the crowd where a redheaded woman was grinning and cheering. Like she could feel his gaze on her, she mouthed an exaggerated, "I love it," and made a heart with her hands over her own chest.

In that moment, Mel knew that the song he wrote during the period between seeing Leah's video and this show would be played. Betham and Jessie had given him the space to do it, but they had a backup song ready to go in case he chickened out. His days of taking the easy option were over, though. Leah was worth the effort. She'd been worth every effort he'd spent to find her, comfort her, and be with her. If she didn't want to be with him after this, then she'd still be worth it. She had been his muse in his darkest hour, and she'd been his Spark all along. This was the way he'd always dreamt he would feel about someone.

He went through the first set, singing each word as though Leah was the only person in his audience. Not one note fell flat, not one beat edged past him. When it came time for the song, he still felt a moment of hesitation, but he plunged ahead. "This next song isn't actually part of the new album," he said. "It's a little experimental, but I'd like to share it with you anyway. Would you like to hear it?"

The audience gave an enthusiastic affirmative. Mel didn't look up at Leah this time. He didn't want to risk losing his nerve now. He gave his guitar strings a quick stroke, and then leaned into the microphone, "This song is called *Take My Hand*." Then he launched into the song.

All in one moment,
I went to another place.

All in one touch,
I didn't see your face.
It only took a spark to set a fire.
It only took a smile to make the feeling grow.
I told you I liked you the first time that I met you,
But even then, I didn't really know.
It's been my challenge,
My own epic quest.
Putting my heart on the line,
I've got to get something off my chest.
Let's take on the world together.
Come on and take my hand.
Come on a love rollercoaster with me.
Come see what I've got planned.
We'll invade the halls of Valhalla,
And paint the corpses with mead.
We'll hop in my spaceship
And push it past lightspeed.
Just you and me versus the galaxy.
We'll kill them with our class.
We'll touch down on Planet Jenkins,
And invite them to kiss our ass.
I got invitations to our war party engraved
And packed super ultra-bazookas for two.
I just need to know if you're in or out
Because it's not an invasion without you.
Come join forces with me.
We'll take on the galaxy.
Come join forces with me...
We'll rule the galaxy.

As Mel let the final notes drift away, he looked up at the box that Leah had been in. She wasn't there.

Chapter Thirty-five

AFTER THE FIRST TWO verses of the song, Leah got up. She now understood the feeling which had driven Mel off the stage during the concert in Houston. "I've got to get down there. I've got to get down there!"

"Okay! Okay..." Nessa jumped up and got to the door before Anthony could tear his eyes off the stage. "I guess we're going to test just how All-Access these passes really are."

"I'll stay put," Anthony said. "As much as I want to see how this pans out, I've got a feeling I'll just slow you two down."

Within two steps down the hidden stairwell, it became obvious that there was a security guard at the bottom, likely to make sure that the VIPs stayed put as much as to see that they weren't disturbed. Nessa held up a hand to tell Leah to hang back. As Nessa descended the stairs, she put a little extra sway in her hips and went up to the guard. "Hi!" Nessa's voice was bright and friendly. "I don't suppose you could escort a girl to the bathrooms? These places are always such a labyrinth!"

Even with training, Nessa was hard to ignore when she wanted to be. The guard turned his back to the stairs long enough for Leah to get down them and walk off in a direction that he wasn't looking. After a few yards, Leah wasn't sure she was heading the right way to get to the stage, but she kept moving. The moment that she turned back, she was sure someone would notice that she didn't belong back here.

When she came to another corridor, it was a relief to see that some helpful person in the past had decided to put up arrows pointing out the direction that the stage was in, as well as arrows pointing back the way she had come labelled "Office," and "Private Balcony."

The song, *her* song, was pumping through the corridors even this far behind the scenes. Leah wasn't sure why Mel had included Valhalla in his confession of desire, but it still worked for her. She didn't care what Mel wanted to do together, so much as she cared that he'd written her a song. Leah longed to see him, to pull off the mask and draw him into her arms. She wanted his embrace, to finally know what that felt like. He wanted her, wanted to be with her, wanted to be a part of her life.

Leah wanted that, too.

All at once, the hallway she was in spilled out into the backstage area. Another security guard asked to see her identification, and she held up the pass like she would at a convention dealer's room. "Are you sure you're supposed to be here, ma'am?" the guard looked skeptical. "It's supposed to be crew only during the show."

Shit, Leah's tongue refused to work as she tried to find something, anything, to tell this last hurdle between her and Mel. They were so close! She could actually see his backside as he leaned into his microphone. "I... I need..."

"She's with me," Frankie said, taking Leah by the arm and escorting her into the wings. "You stay here, alright. Audience can't see us. That's part of the deal with dating these guys."

"You..." Leah looked harder at Frankie and flashed briefly on that night at Pancake Hut all those months ago. "You were at Pancake Hut, right? In Houston?"

"Yep, and since you're back here, I assume we're going to see more of each other. I'm dating the guy that plays Frimmydukes," Frankie said. "I'm also the tour manager."

Frankie looked out across the stage and grinned at Frimmydukes, a much softer look than Leah had thought the woman capable of only moments before. "It's not exactly easy, you know, dating a star.

Even one of these guys. They're pretty down to earth, as amnesiac aliens go. Good people." Frankie looked Leah up and down, as Lancel♡t belted out a line about bazookas for two. "I've got a feeling you're good people, too. Lancel♡t doesn't fall easy."

Unsure of what to say, Leah just gave the older woman a smile and tried to swallow the knot of nerves that was building up as Mel invited her to join him in ruling the galaxy. It was hard to stay put when his head tilted up and she knew, she *knew*, he was looking for her.

Lady Bug, sensing that Lancel♡t wasn't fully attentive to the moment, announced that she was going to retire to her chambers and required her attendants to join her for a brief respite. The warm up band would play a song or two and then the Magical Space Skeleton Army would march (or rock) on.

Frimmydukes had to tap Lancel♡t on the shoulder in order to get Mel to put down his guitar and leave the stage. Leah was practically vibrating on her toes, wanting to run out to meet him. The moment he caught sight of her, he began jogging. As soon as he made it out of sight of any curious D'weasels, Mel had Leah in his arms. Fizzy warmth spread through her entire body as they made contact, erasing the worries that Leah had been harboring about that first spark being a one time thing.

A portion of her brain registered that Mel was carrying her while they embraced to a spot that possessed at least the seeming of privacy. The moment he was free to do so, Mel yanked off his helmet and placed it beside them on a metal folding chair. He didn't speak, just gazed into Leah's eyes. She met his gaze with her own, tilting her head to answer the unspoken question. As their lips met, they both felt a fervid blaze that put their first lightning bolt moment to shame.

Epilogue

LEAH SAT ON MEL'S COUCH, Dot happily curled in her lap as Leah dealt with a few last minute emails to her clients. She'd had to arrange a trade off with another agent for the next three months, because the Magical Space Skeleton Army was about to tour Europe. Mel had warned her that connections could be patchy, especially when they stayed in the castle in Scotland. *I'm going to stay in a castle in Scotland!* Leah's inner squee was loud enough that she was surprised Dot didn't hear it.

Nessa had agreed to cat sit, since Izzy had finally moved out of Frankie and Betham's house. Anthony had complained that three months was far too long to leave their characters in peril, but since Jessie had pointed out that Betham would have plenty of real world inspiration for new dungeons after the trip, Anthony had allowed himself to be soothed.

The concert in Cincinnati had been several months ago, but things had flowed together so naturally since that it was hard to remember a time when Mel hadn't been a part of her life. He'd brought Leah over to meet Dot the day after the concert and seemed very happy that Dot came to greet Leah like an old friend. The members of the band, mainly Jessie, had been a little slower to warm to the notion that Leah came as a package deal with Nessa, Anthony, and her family down in Texas. (Just Gerald, Daphne and Ellen. The extended family thought that Mel ran a sound effects studio or something. Leah wasn't really sure what her father had told them.) It had been Anthony's hugs that won her over, as far as Leah knew. That or the Lady Bug scepter that Gerald Walsh had presented her with. Leah hadn't even known her dad was a fellow D'weasel until that unexpected interaction, when her parents had come up to "see the new apartment," after they found out that their daughter was dating again.

It wasn't like Leah had gotten on the phone and announced whom she was dating, either. That had been Mel. He'd told Leah that if they were going to be serious, he wanted to be able to be himself when the inevitable family holidays started happening. There had been a bit more to it than Mel grabbing the phone and saying, "Hi, I'm Lancel♡t from the Magical Space Skeleton Army, and I'd like to date your daughter." Waivers, non-disclosures, and some other agreements had gone between the Magical Space Skeleton Army's lawyer and Ellen before the big reveal. Still, there was more paperwork to date Mel than there had been to divorce Alan.

Leah didn't think much about Alan these days. When he did cross her mind, it was fleeting. She'd heard from someone that he and Brooke Bailey had deleted each other's photos from their social sites. Troy had tried to call her at that point, but Leah had let the call go to voicemail. Maybe someday, she wouldn't remember the accusations he'd hurled at her, but she wasn't there yet.

Right now, she was happy. She was dating a funny, creative, caring man that adored her, and she loved him. Leah felt something was just *right* about the world. This was what it was like to be in love, again.

Acknowledgements

FIRST, I'D LIKE TO extend my thanks to my wonderful husband, Terence. He's always my first audience. He's my biggest supporter and my inspiration. Despite the late nights and frayed nerves that finishing a book usually bring to the fore, he's always ready with a hug and a few comforting words. Thank you, my love. You are my everything.

Next, I'd like to extend many heartfelt thanks to my parents. Dad, Mom, Stephen, I love you and I wouldn't have gotten here without you.

A huge thank you to my beta readers. You guys are seriously the best. Katja, Wendy and Alexis all get a special shout out. My books shine so much brighter because of your attentions. Love you all.

Another big thank you to brosedesignz! I love my coverart so much, and I've got many more books in me. I hope to work together more in the future.

I'd like to thank all the musicians and artists out there that strive to bring what joy they can to this world. Things have been rough recently in a lot of ways, and I appreciate the light you bring to the darkness. A more personal thanks to Weird Al, Ninja Sex Party, TWRP, Oingo Boingo, Tenacious D, Galavant, Cybertronic Spree, Rachel Bloom, Bad Lip Reading, Garfunkel and Oates, StarBomb, Team Unicorn and Felicia Day for being on my playlist while I was writing this book.

Thank you to all of my readers. If you're holding this book right now, in any form, please know that I appreciate you so much. You make my dreams possible.

And a thank you to Wil Wheaton... For protecting the rest of us from a lot of cursed dice and for being freaking adorable. It's my book, so why not?

To find out more about Christina Dickinson and her upcoming works, please visit her website:
christinadickinsonwrites.com